Promise

Cassie Gregg

Copyright © 2016 by Cassie Gregg

This book or any portion thereof may not be reproduced or used in any manner whatsoever without the express written permission of the publisher except for the use of brief quotations in a book review.

Printed in the United States of America

First Printing, 2016

ISBN: 978-1-5356-0435-2

Dedication

Without the love and support of my family and friends, none of this would have been possible. For teaching me to always chase my dreams, no matter how crazy, thank you Maj and Papa Bear. I love you to the moon and back and more than there are stars in the sky.

For the support, hours, and hard work you put in to help me along the journey of writing this book, I couldn't have done it without you Greg. You're the best friend, sounding board and editor a girl could hope for.

I want to thank all the authors out there, who inspired me to take up writing and sparked an imagination in me, I thank you from the bottom of my heart. You instilled romanticism in me that I am forever grateful for. You've inspired me to create a fantasy and search for it in reality.

Contents

Prologue 1
Chapter 1 33
Chapter 2 48
Chapter 3 65
Chapter 4 77
Chapter 5 83
Chapter 6 90
Chapter 7 96
Chapter 8 106
Chapter 9 118
Chapter 10 133
Chapter 11 142
Chapter 12 151
Chapter 13 161
Chapter 14 174
Chapter 15 179
Chapter 16 186

Chapter 17	200
Chapter 18	214
Chapter 19	225
Chapter 20	231
Chapter 21	243
Chapter 22	260
Chapter 23	269
Chapter 24	283
Chapter 25	295
Chapter 26	306
Chapter 27	310
Chapter 28	312
Chapter 29	313
Chapter 30	319
Epilogue	321

It started off unlike any other childhood friendship: with mud, tears, and a pinky-swear *promise*.

Prologue

Summer 1989

THE SUMMER BEFORE I STARTED school, my father moved us from our home in Lloyd Harbor, New York, to his family's old estate on Wilmington Island, Georgia. He'd opened another branch of his business in Savannah and turned it into his new headquarters, which saved him the travel back and forth to New York City. He and my mom had decided they wanted to raise Madeline and me in the South, just as they had been. When my grandmother Montgomery passed away, Daddy saw it as the perfect opportunity to relocate.

I started school that fall at the local elementary school and Madeline at the middle school. I stuck out like a sore thumb. I didn't talk like the other kids, and everyone in class already knew one another from Sunday school. Both my parents were from the South originally, but Maddie and I had adopted the Northern accent instead of theirs. I was shy and didn't make many friends and stuck mostly to myself. One day after school as I waited for my sister to walk home, a group of older boys began picking on me. They pulled my pigtails and mocked my Northern accent.

Cassie Gregg

When I told them to stop, they just laughed and taunted me more. I started to run home so they wouldn't see me cry, but they chased after me.

I was fast, but my school dress made it hard to run away. When they caught me, they pushed me down into a puddle of mud and ran away laughing. I sat there in the mud and cried. When I looked up, I saw that one of the boys had stayed behind. I recognized him from school. He was one of the popular boys, a year ahead of me; he always seemed to have friends around him at lunch and at recess. Older, younger, teachers and students alike all flocked to him. I'd heard someone say it was because of who his father was, but I didn't really care. He played with the bullies, and I didn't like him. He stood with his hands in his pockets, looking down at me. I was about to start yelling at him, but he spoke first. He said he was sorry that they'd ruined my dress because it was really pretty. He came closer to help me up, and when he saw all my tears, his face seemed to crumble before my eyes. I asked him why he was being so nice to me, and he said it was because everyone deserved to have a friend to protect them. I asked him if we were friends now, and he pulled me up to my feet, looked me right in the eye, held out his hand, and said yes. Then, to my surprise, he made me a promise to always be my friend and never let another person make me cry ever again. I thought it had sounded nice, but I had to make sure that he'd meant it, so I made him pinky swear. The moment he locked his pinky with mine, there was nothing that could separate us.

His name was Ethan Stone, and he had the bluest eyes I had ever seen. I remember everyone always talked about my eyes because they were smoke gray with streaks of blue, just like my mother's, but his were a clear, sky blue that flickered and changed with his emotions. I remember when I looked up into his eyes as I sat in the mud, crying, that I wondered how it was possible to see a person's very soul in their eyes. But in his, I knew it was true. He had a way of masking his expressions from the world, but if you looked into the endless blue depths of his eyes, you could see every emotion he felt. It was those eyes that held such hope, promise, and sincerity that ultimately made me forgive and trust him. That and it looked like he would start crying himself if I didn't stop. I knew in that moment that someone with those eyes would never hurt me.

He walked me home from school that day, and every day after. When I walked into the kitchen covered in mud with tear-stained cheeks, my mother abandoned her company and scooped me into her arms. As fate would have it, Ethan's mother had come by that day to discuss a ladies' luncheon for a charity she sponsored. I hadn't known that the Stones lived in the house next to ours until my mother told me so that day. The women stood in the kitchen, shocked at the state of my clothing, having abandoned their strategy meeting. When Mrs. Stone noticed Ethan stood behind me, she scolded him, "Ethan Grayson Stone, you better explain yourself."

I remember the lost look in his eyes as he looked up at his mother's stern face. I squirmed from my mother's arms and walked over to his side and put my hand in his. I looked up at Mrs. Stone and told her that Ethan saved me from the mean, older boys and that he was my friend and "if he got in trouble, then I'd have to get in trouble too." I could see the amusement in both our mothers' faces as I stood there holding Ethan's hand, defending him.

Without waiting for an answer, I turned to him and asked, "Your middle name is Grayson?" His shoulders slumped more, and he nodded his head.

I liked the name, but he didn't seem to. I pulled my hand from his and asked my mother if Ethan and I could take our cookies to the fort. He perked up at the mention of the fort, and my mother smiled in recognition of what I was doing. As I pulled him through the back door, our mothers' laughter followed after us. Cookies in hand, we headed for the new fort my father had built for me. It would become our place, for just the two of us.

We spent our childhood running through the fields and weeping willows, playing tag and imaginary games. The tree house that my father had built for me stood strong in an old oak, secluded at the back of the property behind the stables and barn. It was conveniently tucked near the border of the Stones' property and ours. We couldn't be separated with a stick of dynamite, thick as thieves, everyone said. Ethan and I walked to and from school together every day. When we got home we'd grab a snack from our housekeeper, Patty, and a handful of my mother's cookies. Hands full of food, we'd run for the fort. We'd do our homework and talk about our day and every other mundane thing that popped into our heads. We camped in that fort and talked about our dreams.

We loved to play in the stables and brush the horses my father had gotten for my mother, my sister, and me. As we got older, we'd spend hours at the lake behind Ethan's home, cooling off from the hot Savannah heat. From the moment we'd decided to become friends, Ethan and I were inseparable. When I got the chicken pox, Ethan got the chicken pox. When Ethan learned to ride his bike, I learned to ride my bike. When I learned how to swim, so did Ethan. Where one went, the other followed.

Everyone had always called me Charlie, short for Charlotte. My mom was the only one who'd called me that; not even my teachers called me Charlotte. Daddy had always wanted a boy, and when I came along after Madeline, he was the one who'd started the nickname. Much to my mother's chagrin, it stuck. Ethan, however, was the one who started a new nickname shortly after we became friends. One day while we were playing tag in the stables, he called me Lee, and from then on, that was all he ever called me. I loved that he called me something unique. He'd always known how to make me feel special. It was the afternoon that I'd learned his middle name that I started calling him Gray. It started off as a joke to annoy him, but soon he grew accustomed to me calling him that. I was the only one he allowed to call him by his middle name (or close to it). He said the name made him sound stuffy and old, but I'd always liked it.

After their introduction, Mom joined many of the same charity boards and coalitions as Mrs. Stone. As result of our and our mother's friendship, our father's inevitably became friends too. They joined one another on many business ventures and became a veritable powerhouse in Savannah. Everyone in Savannah knew that the Stones and the Montgomerys went together like shrimp and grits. The authentic friendship between our two families was as sincere as they came. Ethan was the youngest child of his family, as I was for mine. His older sister Jessica was a few years younger than Madeline, but they got along just fine. Never like Ethan and me, though. Over time, my love for Ethan became that of genuine friendship, and I couldn't imagine my life without him in it.

Promise

One thing that our friendship had brought us was a guaranteed confidante in one another. We told each other everything, from what we'd had for lunch to what we dreamed for our futures. There were no secrets between us. He told me of his dreams to play baseball, and I told him that I didn't want to follow in Daddy's footsteps like Maddie wanted to, but instead I had a dream of owning my own bakery. He told me that I'd have all of it one day. He believed in me, just as I believed in him.

Ethan went to high school a year ahead of me, and by Christmas, things had already begun to change between us. Girls noticed Ethan with increasing interest, and it seemed even the older girls loved Ethan. Through it all, though, he always made time for me, even if it wasn't as much as before. We fell into our own group of friends at school, he with the popular jocks and cheerleaders and me with the regular people. My friends were more into school and books than sporting events and fashion trends. Ethan was a star jock with multiple varsity letters. I joined many different school clubs. But through all the changes, we never lost one another. Even though they'd known us forever, no one understood how we were still almost inseparable after so many years. No matter what was going on, as long as I had Ethan, I knew that everything would be okay.

Cassie Gregg

Then the summer before ninth grade came, and my life changed forever. It was the last day of school, and it was a perfect summer's day. The high school had gotten out early, and Ethan had skipped last period to get ice cream with a freshman girl he liked, so I'd run home to see what Mom and Patty had baked for our last day of school. I remember hoping she hadn't finished so that I could help them make whatever they were baking. As I sprinted up the porch stairs, I knew instantly that something was wrong. The house didn't hold the sweet aroma of baked sugar, and where there was usually music or my mother's singing, there was only silence. As I came through the foyer, I saw my parents were sitting in the living room: my mother in her favorite chair, my father behind her, resting his hands on her shoulders. My sister was sitting on the couch across from them, her head hung low. As I entered the room, my mother looked up, and for the first time that I could remember, there were tears in her eyes.

"Charlotte, honey, come sit down with your sister. We need to talk with you."

I remember the panic at the thought that I'd done something wrong, but I couldn't remember what it was I'd done. I sat gingerly next to Maddie, but never in my wildest dreams could I have expected what came next.

That was the day I learned that a single word could instill both fear and hate: cancer. Such a simple word, but with it came incomparable pain. That summer was the first in eight years that I didn't spend every day with Ethan. For a while, my parents excused themselves from all social obligations while Mom went through treatment. They'd decided to avoid making a public announcement, to keep things relatively calm for Mother and in hope that she would go into remission and no one would be the wiser. But when Mom stopped responding to treatment and there was nothing more they could do for her, we had to tell everyone.

Ethan and the Stones were shocked by the news but became infinitely supportive. They even took Maddie and me in to shield us from when Mom had a bad day... or week. Daddy took a leave of absence from work to be at her bedside, but the disease hadn't just worn down Mom's body; it had worn on Daddy too. Mom had been the light of his eye. Even at a young age, I knew that my parents were still madly in love with one another. I grew up reading fairytale love stories and watching the real-life fairytale play out in our house.

I watched the way they held hands and looked at one another. They stole kisses when they thought we weren't looking, and their laughter was always genuine and plentiful. The way my father would call my mother "Elizabeth" when he was frustrated, and she retorted with "Jackson" every time. I saw the way he smiled at her and his eyes brightened when he called her Lizzy. It was the most endearing sound I'd ever heard. He'd always talked about how much he loved his girls, but I knew that there was no one in the world who would or could take my mother's place in my father's heart ever again. She was his forever, as he'd always said. I'd always hoped to one day have the kind of love that they shared. The forever kind.

When school came around in August, we were told she had only weeks left, and I couldn't bear to leave her side for fear that she'd leave us while I was at school. Daddy had let me stay home from school and had hired a private tutor so that I wouldn't fall behind. I knew Mom wouldn't have wanted me to miss out on school; she knew how much I loved it. I spent a few hours every morning in our library with Mrs. Abernathy. She was a kind, patient retired teacher who awarded me the time to escape the pain of my mother's illness.

At night, Ethan and I snuck out and met at the fort, where we lay side by side and looked at the stars. Our parents knew, but they let us have the time away together anyway. Ethan would tell me about what was happening at school and how he was doing with his different sports teams. I'd tell him about my lessons and how Mom was doing. We even talked about how one day I wanted a forever love like my parents had. Sometimes I'd silently cry the tears I held in from everyone else, and he'd hold

Promise

my hand while he promised that he was there and wasn't going anywhere.

It had been another one of those ordinary days that turned out to be a life-changing one. I had planned to bake Mom's favorite muffins and bring her breakfast in bed. I'd woken up extra early and baked a batch to perfection with Patty's supervision. When I carried the breakfast tray into her room, the first thing I noticed was Daddy on his knees at her bedside, weeping into his hands clasped tightly around hers. It was then that I knew—she was gone.

The funeral service and reception were a frenzy of faces and voices. Prayers and well wishes were all given, and it all seemed to be blended into one teary-eyed blur. Daddy ran on autopilot for a while but quickly found solace in his work. He would spend hours at the office or traveling. Patty took over the day-to-day care, stepping in and stepping up in a parental role. She was a godsend to our family. On the rare occasion Daddy was home, he spent his time locked away in his study, working.

Madeline started disappearing for days on end and getting into trouble at school. Daddy was never around to really punish her. That had always been Mom's job anyway, so Patty did her best to keep thing in line, but sometimes that seemed to just make things worse. It was the toughest time our family had ever been through. I couldn't stand to be called Charlotte anymore, for the pain that laced through my heart at the memory of my mother. She'd always taken pride in the fact she was named after both of her grandmothers, so she was over the moon when she had two daughters to pass the names along to us as well. Madeline was given Marie, my mother's middle name, and I was given Elizabeth Grace, my mother's first name. Mom had always loved to call us by our full names, especially when she was scolding us. She made them sound so elegant, the way they rolled off her tongue in her proper, Southern enunciation. It would never sound the same again.

Ethan had been there for me as one of the only constants in my life. Not once did he let me go to sleep alone. If I'd start to cry, he'd build us a fort in my room and stay with me all night until I fell asleep. He never complained, never told me to get over it and stop crying. He never fed me the line about proper Southern women not letting anyone see them cry. He'd just sit there while he talked to me about baseball or lie down next to me and silently hold my hand. Our parents never said anything about it, but I knew we couldn't keep it up for much longer. When Maddie went away to school across the country in California, things started to settle back down again, just in time for me to start high school.

By my junior year, everything seemed to go back to normal, our new normal. Ethan had a new girlfriend

Promise

every week, and it'd been my job as his best friend to be an endless supply of advice and cover stories. I'd missed a lot in my year away from everyone, but Ethan never changed. He hadn't looked at me like the girl who lost her mom to cancer. He'd looked at me like he always had, as his best friend. We were both busy with our own things at school, but we always made time for one another. He was busy being the star athlete and all-around socializer. He was graduating soon and had a lot of decisions to make about where he'd go to school. I was busy with student body president, DECA, and running as cross-country captain. What free time I did have, I spent with the horses and playing the piano. Ethan always teased me about all my extracurriculars and made it his mission to get me to relax.

That usually came in the form of a party at the lake on his property. There would be a big bonfire when the sun went down, music, and laughter. When Ethan first learned to play, he'd bring his guitar to the fort and play whatever new song he learned or wanted to learn. I'd in turn learn the lyrics and we'd put on our own little concerts, just the two of us up in that old fort.

With a few beers and the moon high in the sky, Ethan would grab his guitar and coax me to sing along. I'd always try to decline, but he never let me. After a relentless bout of nagging, I'd finally sit down and sing along to the song he was playing. It would be quiet at first while I sang, until others would join in. Those nights we spent out by the lake with our friends and classmates made for great memories.

After everyone cleared out, we'd climb up into that old fort and talk into the quiet hours of morning. He'd talk about how his family expected him to be the fourth generation of Stone men to join the family law firm, but what he really wanted to be was an architect. He didn't want to be a lawyer, but instead he wanted to create beautiful structures. The way his eyes lit up when he talked about it melted my heart. I knew that it was his dream, but I also knew that he'd never follow through on it. He'd never want to disappoint his family, even at the cost of his own dreams, and it saddened me to no end. He had always encouraged and supported me to follow my dreams, but as much as I told him to do the same, he wouldn't. So in the sanctuary of our fort, he'd share his dreams and draw all his ideas in a sketchpad I'd gotten him for Christmas. When it came time to apply for college, we both had our many options, but as fate would have it, even a year apart, we ended up together again.

Ethan had offers to play baseball at almost every division-one school in the country and pressure from his father to go to Harvard. I'd gotten cross-country offers from a few of my schools, but more academic scholarships than others. I'd narrowed it down to four schools. My father pushed his alma mater, Harvard, but I knew that I'd end up at my own place. It shocked me that Ethan went against his father and accepted an offer to play baseball at Yale, but he had compromised with his father that if he got to choose where he went for undergrad, he'd go to Harvard for law school. I gave Ethan an architecture book for graduation, and the smile on his face was one that I'd remember for the rest of my life.

It seemed like fate that while Ethan had been recruited by Yale, I was too. When my acceptance letter came from Yale, I called Ethan immediately and squealed like a little girl. He laughed and I swore him to secrecy that I had ever made that noise. It ended up that I declined my scholarship for cross-country so that I could focus on my studies.

In our first semester together at Yale, I watched as Ethan carried on his player ways, aided by the fact he was the Bulldog's star pitcher, and continued the path to join his father's law firm. Being the somewhat introverted bookworm that I was, I threw myself into my studies, as well as joining the running club. No one had understood my decision to decline a scholarship, except for Ethan. He knew that as much as I loved to run, my dream of owning my own bakery meant so much more to me. So spring of my freshman year, I'd declared a double major in business and economics with a minor in communication, while Ethan continued with the pre-law program.

September of my sophomore year, another (not so) ordinary day changed our lives and the lives of millions.

My college boyfriend, Gavin, had gotten a call from his mother crying hysterically about not being able to get ahold of his father. We'd had no idea what she was talking about, but then the campus around us fell into chaos. Students and faculty frantically used their phones, and everyone ran to the nearest television to watch the news. September 11, 2001, would forever live in my mind.

A few weeks after the World Trade Center fell, Ethan showed up at my apartment in the middle of the night.

"Lee, I need to tell you something." He looked so troubled and scared. I hadn't seen him look like that in years, not since Mom had been sick and he was trying to figure out how to make it better for me.

"Whatever it is, Gray, you know you can tell me," I reassured him. He looked questioningly at me, unsure if he should say what he'd woken me up to say.

"Did you want to build a fort?" I joked in hope that it would wipe the tortured look off his face with a little injected levity.

"We're not little kids anymore, Charlie. A fort's not going make this any easier," he snapped at me.

Promise

"Gray, what's going on? Please just tell me what's wrong. You're scaring me," I pleaded with him, understanding the severity when he called me Charlie.

"I enlisted."

Time seemed to stand still in that moment. There was yet another single word that impacted my life.

"Gray, I don't—" I paused, trying to absorb what he'd just told me. "I don't know what to say," I confessed.

"Tell me I made the right choice. Tell me I'm not crazy for doing this." He stopped his pacing and turned to me, his eyes pleading.

"Ethan," I implored and reached for his hands. "Of course you made the right choice. You could never make a wrong choice if it is in your heart. And if this is, the right choice would be to follow what's in your heart, that can never lead you wrong." I paused, hoping that what I said would appease him, but the anxiety on his face hadn't lessened.

I continued on, "I know you, Ethan. I know you better than anyone else in this world, and I know that you wouldn't be you if you didn't try to help. You're the boy that picked a little girl up out of the mud and pinky swore to not let another person make her cry ever again, because you couldn't stand the sight of her tears. You're the boy who pinky swore never to let that same little girl go to sleep alone, scared from her nightmares, because you wanted to protect her from them. You're the boy who pinky swore never to leave. You're the...man who is going to pinky swear that you'll return home safe and sound." By the end of my speech tears had pooled in my eyes, but I refused to let them fall. I had to be strong for Ethan, like he'd always been strong for me.

"I can't tell you what this means to me, Charlie. I was so scared to tell you, that you'd be mad at me, that you'd hate me," he finished on a whisper.

"I could never hate you, Gray! Why would you even think that?" I exclaimed, flabbergasted that he could have ever thought that.

"Because I'm leaving you."

"It's not the same, Gray, and you know it!" I interrupted.

"Fine, but I'm giving up on all of my plans. I'm halfway done here, as are you, and we're both so close to reaching our goals. I'm walking away from all that. I'm giving it all up."

I'd never heard Ethan doubt himself. He'd always been the cool, confident one. I knew I needed to make him see that what he'd done was the furthest thing from giving up. That what he was doing was amazing.

"But, Gray, don't you see? You're walking away from this goal, but you're walking toward a new one. You're not giving up, not even close. You're just doing something new, something admirable and honorable. You're putting aside your dreams to serve your country, and I could not be more proud of you." I hugged him to me tightly. "Everything is going to be okay, Ethan."

"Promise?" he asked hopefully.

"Pinky swear," I assured him with a full smile as I hooked my pinky with his.

Ethan left for basic at the end of that October, and it would be our first Thanksgiving and Christmas without him. His absence was felt by all of us that holiday season. We kept in touch with letters and e-mail as best we could, but it wasn't the same. Just when I thought I couldn't handle not seeing my best friend any longer, we got word that he'd been granted leave and was going to be coming home. Two weeks before Ethan's long-awaited return, his platoon received orders that they'd been called up for deployment. It would be a year and a half before he would have another chance to return home.

Life seemed to keep moving forward, though; one week turned to one month, one month became six. But with every day that passed, I missed him more and more. The longer he was away, the stronger my feelings for him seemed to grow. I spent more time with his mother, Amelia, and his sister Jess while he was away. We'd formed our own little support group of sorts. I'd make frequent trips home to visit them, and we talked almost daily on the phone. I sent them baked goods and checked on how they were doing, just as they had done for our family when my mother passed. I diligently watched the newscasts for the listed casualties overseas. I'd hold my breath while I watched the names come on the screen of the evening news, and only when I didn't read his name was I able to breathe again. Then there was the suffocating panic every time I got a call from Amelia or Jess, afraid they were calling to tell me something had happened to Ethan.

Another crushing blow came when he called home to tell his parents that he'd extended his tour, just one month before we expected him home. He'd be overseas for another two years, and he wouldn't be home anytime soon.

Even so, life went on. There were a couple guys I dated, but they had come and gone. My mind (and heart) seemed to only be able to focus on school and Ethan. E-mails and letters were my only means of communication to my best friend, and we talked as often as we could about anything and everything. He told me about what it was like over there, and I told him what I'd been doing at Yale. No matter how many letters I wrote or e-mails I sent, it never felt like enough.

It was on my twenty-first birthday that I realized I didn't just love Ethan, but I was in love with him. To not have him there to celebrate yet another holiday seemed to make the small longing in my heart grow to an indomitable size. It was on that day that I went out and did the first impulsive thing I'd ever done. I got a tattoo.

When the guy at the tattoo shop asked what I wanted, I told him a simple infinity sign on my left pinky. He was intrigued about why I wanted that specific tattoo, and when I told him about Ethan and our penchant for pinky swearing, he was genuinely delighted to do the tattoo for me. He made it the perfect size for me to cover it with a ring so that no one would see it. I didn't want everyone I knew to ask me about it, because the moment I told them the story, they'd assume that it was because I was in love with Ethan. And while that might be true, I didn't want it to be broadcasted. I didn't want Ethan to know, because I knew that we'd never stand a chance. I wasn't his type, and he'd never see me as anything more than his best friend. And if keeping my tattoo a secret kept Ethan in my life, then that was what I was going to do.

Ethan continued his heroism overseas, and I continued in pursuit of my dreams stateside. I stayed at Yale to get my MBA and focused on my goal, which helped to keep my mind off of Ethan, for the most part. It felt like every time Ethan sent an e-mail or letter, he was telling me he wouldn't be coming home. I'd started to accept and expect the fact that I wouldn't see my best friend for years to come.

Cassie Gregg

In December of 2005, I graduated from Yale with my MBA, and Ethan surprised me when he called and congratulated me. I cherished that call more than anything, because the first time I graduated, he'd been on a mission and didn't (or couldn't) make contact until a week after the ceremony. The second time around, he'd been there, on the phone to hear them call my name. Unfortunately, the connection was poor, and he had to go almost immediately when I got on the phone with him. He did tell me, just when I was about to say good-bye, the best news I'd heard in years. He would finally be coming home. He said that after his tour ended, he would be done for good and coming home.

A week after graduation, I moved back home to Savannah and used a portion of the money my paternal grandparents had left me to purchase an old bakery in the heart of downtown. It was the perfect location to build my dream. I began renovations the day after I signed the lease. The space was perfect and was large enough to convert the front section into an eat-in café with a deli and bakery counter. There was room outside for an outdoor-seating patio, and the corner lot made it a great place to sit with a cup of coffee and watch the city whirl by. The large, professional kitchen in the back was an amazing asset, and with a few upgrades and a little TLC, it was my ultimate gourmet-kitchen dream. The renovations at the café were completed in six months, and Montgomery's Cafe officially opened for business in June of 2006.

After I purchased the café, I started to look for a place in Savannah so that I didn't have to commute in from the island every day. Since I wouldn't let Daddy pay for anything involving the café, I accepted his graduation gift of a beautiful three-story house on Forsyth Park in the south historic district of Savannah. Because my father does nothing by degrees, the house had five bedrooms and five bathrooms with a single-car garage and street parking space. It was a well-kept antebellum house with a newly renovated interior that had an expansive wrap around porch leading to a fenced-in backyard with a small pond as well as a second-story deck.

The house had vaulted ceilings and an open floor plan on the main level and original hardwood floors throughout, with tons of windows to let in natural light. Long, straight wooden staircases that added grandeur to the house separated the three floors. In the back of the main level sat a gourmet kitchen that was the envy of any chef. The master suite on the second level opened out onto a balcony that extended the entire length of the house and overlooked the backyard through French doors. A large bay window, on the third floor that I'd converted into an office, overlooked the picturesque street and nearby park.

The house sat on a corner lot with unimaginable curb appeal that drew you to stand and stare at its beauty. A large oak stood regally in the front yard, casting shade over the paver walkway leading to the large front door. Placed on a gorgeous tree-lined street just down from Forsyth Park, which offered the perfect place for my daily runs, it was only several blocks from the café.

The café had been open for a couple months, and business could not have been better. I'd hired a couple more staff members to combat the influx and constant flow of customers, but never had I imagined that Monty's (as the locals had come to call it) would be so successful. I had feared for the ability of my small business to break into the already well-established businesses in the area, but I'd managed to bring in not only tourists but also locals. My dream had finally become reality.

It had been a particularly hectic day, and while I was busy restocking the prewrapped baked-goods shelf, I heard the bell over the door chime. Without looking up, I called out, "Be right with you!"

The room seemed to go quiet all at once, and I knew something was going on. I looked over my shoulder toward the counter, where my co-baker, Megan, and manager, Louis, stared open mouthed at whoever had just walked through the door.

"Lee?"

Promise

Everything inside me went still. I slowly turned around and saw a man, dressed in military fatigues, filling the entire doorway. He seemed to command attention and space with both his physical presence and...something else. He'd grown so much, changed even more, that I wasn't sure I believed it was really him. Where once there had been an athletic, lean boy, now stood a war-hardened, muscular man. His legs, chest, and arms were bulky with well-defined muscles that strained against his fitted uniform. Chiseled features were highlighted by the contrast of his sun-tanned skin and black military-cropped hair.

Before me stood a man, no longer the boy I once knew, staring right at me. My gaze traveled over his face, still unsure I was really seeing him, until my eyes met the expressive blue pools of his. He'd always had the most beautiful blue eyes.

Reality set in, and I bolted into action. I dropped the box of baked goods I'd been holding and ran for him. A smile, entirely Ethan's, spread across his face as he dropped his pack and opened his arms to catch me.

"Ethan!" I exclaimed as I launched myself into his arms. He caught me with ease and spun me around, laughing as I cried and laughed into his neck, thanking God over and over that He'd brought Ethan home safely. The patrons and staff around us stood and clapped at the spectacle of a man returning home from war.

"You're here. You're really here," I whispered reverently into his ear as he set me down and tightened his arms around me.

"I pinky swore, Lee," he said, and I could feel his smile on my neck. I touched the ring on my pinky and sent up another thankful prayer. I pulled his face between my hands and searched it.

"You're not allowed to leave ever again," I said through my tears.

"Hey now. None of that! This is supposed to be a happy occasion! I just fulfilled one promise. Don't make me break my lifelong promise by making you cry," he admonished softly.

"It's okay, really. They're happy tears. I'm just so glad you're home and safe." I clutched his head tighter between my hands and looked into his eyes, searching for confirmation that he was okay.

"I'm so glad you're home, Gray."

"I'm glad to be home, Charlie. God! I missed you," he answered. Then he lifted his head to look around the café and smiled mischievously down at me. "So does an old war veteran get to have a famous Montgomery brownie on the house or what?" he laughed, dodging the elbow he knew I had targeted for his ribs.

"I just so happen to have a policy about that," I said as I pointed to the sign above the register that said, "Military eat free!" Beside the sign was one of my favorite pictures of Ethan and me from our first semester together at Yale. It was a fall day, with leaves changing, and our friends had gathered in the quad to enjoy a sunny afternoon. My roommate Cassie had snapped the picture just as I hopped onto Ethan's back, broad smiles aimed right at the camera. It always brought me such pride to tell everyone about Ethan when they asked about the sign.

"Have a seat, and I'll bring you out a plate."

"Man, it's good to be home." He said to me as I retreated behind the counter to get him food.

As I returned from the kitchen with Ethan's plate, I looked up to find him seated at a small table where several patrons stood around him. They were all smiling at him; a few shook his hand, and others passed along their gratitude and praise for his bravery. I could see that Ethan's charm hadn't lessened in his absence, and his winning smile was warm and gracious to all who approached him. I smiled to myself and proceeded to his table with a plate of the house special and a plate of sugary sweets in my hands. With Ethan back and my business thriving, all had started to feel right in the world again.

Over the next few months, life seemed to swing back into an old balance again. His first weeks back, Ethan seemed to just float around, unsure of what he wanted to do. When I asked him what his plan was, he said he wasn't sure what he wanted to do anymore. I asked him about going back to school and then on to law school, but he said he couldn't stand the idea of it. So when I mentioned going back to school for architecture, he denied me at first. But after a week of my hounding and not-so-subtle hints, he admitted that he really did want to follow his dream.

I couldn't have been more proud of him when he registered at the college to earn a degree in architecture and business. When he graduated, I had all his hidden drawings and sketches from the fort bound into a book to serve as a reminder for him to always follow his dreams. He hugged me so tightly when he opened it that I feared he broke a rib, but his pure joy and happiness made it all worth it. A month after graduation, he started a small architecture company that specialized in corporate buildings and structures. He took on a partner to take care of the business end of the company so that he could focus on the creation part. He'd hired one of his old platoon buddies, Dan Lewis.

After only six months, his company Stone Creations, grew exponentially and had expanded into a diversified architecture firm that designed and built corporate, residential and recreational buildings nationwide. After a year, he started an international division dedicated to mission and charity work created specifically to build schools, hospitals, and homes in third-world and developing countries. He'd assimilated into a new life and thrived.

Coincidently, Ethan found a house in the same neighborhood as me and moved in soon after he returned home. When a new listing posted shortly after Ethan returned, it seemed too much like fate for him not to take it. While I opted to make my place my own, Ethan, surprisingly, made little changes to his house, except to turn his basement level into a full gym that he used daily. It was great to have my best friend so close again. We'd always lived close to one another, even while we were at Yale. We were able to resurrect old habits and traditions with his proximity that had long since been forgotten. In the mornings before work, we'd meet up at the park and run the trails. He'd often bring Reese, his beautiful Rottweiler, to run alongside us, well, between us, while we ran.

We'd used to run together at Yale, and even in the cooler climate of Connecticut his shirt never lasted long, if he even showed up in one at all, and it continued to surprise me that in the Savannah heat, he never took his shirt off once. He'd wear his Marines shirt from boot camp or his old sleeveless Yale shirt, but he never took it off. The first time I saw his tattoo, it shocked me. I never would have imagined him getting one, but it seemed to fit him perfectly now. I constantly thought about showing him my little tattoo hidden beneath my pinky ring, but my courage always wavered, and I never did.

Ethan tended to gravitate to my place rather than his own, saying that my place was bigger and more comfortable. I never really understood why he said that since his place was actually larger, but I did agree on mine being more comfortable. Over time I'd turned my house into a home, while his place felt like a barely lived-in bachelor pad, even after two years. I'd offered to help him decorate and make it homier, but he always seemed to come up with an excuse not to. It was surprising to me that a creative architect would live in such a plain house, but he claimed he was too busy with the firm to take on a personal project, so I let it go.

Even though I'd loved having Ethan home, my feelings hadn't changed since my birthday revelation. I had to find a new balance between us, so he wouldn't know how I felt. I knew we could never cross that line. He'd never see me as more than his best friend, another sister even. So I did what any sane, lovesick woman would do: I tucked away my feelings and secretly pined. Every day seemed to get a little better, and when the opportunity to open my heart to someone new came along, I met Ben.

The shop had been open for a couple years, and I came across many people and faces, but the day Ben came into Monty's, I took notice and remembered him. He was

Promise

strikingly handsome, well mannered, genuinely kind, and funny. He was opposite in coloring to Ethan, with his sandy-blond hair, hazel eyes, and light complexion. He came regularly to get coffee and the muffin du jour. Finally, after two weeks of flirty smiles and witty banter, he ask me to dinner. It started as a few dates here and there, nothing serious. Between his schedule and mine, we didn't have a lot of free time to see one another, and we agreed to take things slow and see where it went. It didn't take long before it did, in fact, turn into more.

After a month and a half of dating, I knew I loved him, but it was a new feeling, one I had never felt with anyone before. I'd had a few boyfriends in the past, but never had I felt the same way about them as I had with Ethan. It took some getting used to when the parade of women in and out of his life started, but I had Ben, and the best thing for both of us was to move forward. Even though I loved Ben, deep down I knew it wasn't the same kind of love I had for Ethan, but it was new and exciting, and I didn't want it to end.

Ben was accomplished, driven, intelligent, funny, kind, and wildly handsome. I had always seen myself as rather plain, not one of the gorgeous socialites he'd dated in the past. I didn't put much weight into appearances and social status. It was a novel stance in comparison to the other women of my standing. I knew I was pretty for the fact that I resembled my mother, who was entirely beautiful, but I'd never seen myself as the type of girl who'd turn heads or stop traffic, not like the women Ethan always had around him.

I was the nerdy bookworm who was always nice and befriended everyone. I was the girl who came home from work with flour in her hair, smelling of cookies and chocolate, and loved running her own small café. I was the woman who spent her Thursday afternoons cooking meals for the local shelter. Ben, however, was being groomed to take over his family's hotel business, a veritable empire that was way beyond my understanding. An Ivy League grad himself, he'd graduated top of his class at Princeton, with a degree in business economics. He had talent, brains, charm, and more money than Croesus, but he never threw his wealth or status around—another thing I loved about him.

After six months of dating, I decided it was time for him to meet the rest of the family. The perfect opportunity was at the wedding in May of Jessica, Ethan's sister and my best friend.

Chapter 1

CHARLIE

Present Day, May 2008

I WALKED UNDER THE SPANISH moss-covered oaks that lined the street and stopped outside my gate to pull the mail from my mailbox. As I walked through the gate and down the walkway to the front porch stairs, I dialed Daddy's number to remind him to bring Mom's pearl necklace for me to wear this weekend to meet Ben's parents. I listened as the other end continually rang until my father's prerecorded message picked up. I thought about calling the house and leaving a message with Patty, but after checking my watch, I noticed the time and realized he'd probably already left for the wedding, so I decided to forgo any kind of message.

I was running late, as usual, but if I moved quickly, I'd make it there on time. Being that I was a bridesmaid, I was supposed to have been there hours before the ceremony, getting ready with Jess, but I'd gotten a call last night from one of my bakers to tell me they'd caught what was going around and, unfortunately, I would be down three kitchen staff this weekend, so I'd gone in to cover the work they were doing for Jessica's wedding. Jess said she understood and that it was fine as long as I was there before the ceremony started. I had two hours to get ready, pack, and get to the church before I'd officially be late. I'd only meant to work a few hours that morning before opening, but, per usual, I lost track of time in the kitchen and was now hustling to get ready.

I slid the mail into my purse as I reached the top of the stairs. I found myself slightly out of breath from the brisk walk from the bakery and pulled the keys from my pocket. I was too busy going through a mental checklist of what I needed to pack for this weekend to analyze why I was at all winded. I had to pack for the weekend with Ben and his family, get cleaned up, and get ready for the wedding. I still couldn't believe one of my best friends was getting married today, but I couldn't be happier. I'd known the day I introduced them that they were perfect for each other, but I'd never imagined they'd move so fast.

Ethan still lived in the same neighborhood as me, so when I put the key into my door, it didn't surprise me that Ethan emerged from the sidewalk behind me in jeans and a T-shirt, carrying a garment bag with his tux. He gave me a knowing look, shook his head, and followed me into the house. I hurried into the house and made a dash for my

Promise

bedroom. Ethan grabbed a beer from the fridge and wandered upstairs to my bedroom after me. I was throwing things on my bed to pack while simultaneously pulling my things out for the wedding, spinning around my room like the Tasmanian Devil. I saw Ethan standing in my bedroom doorway, the beer dangling from his fingers, his features pulled into a pensive look.

"Tough day?" I asked, nodding toward the beer he'd grabbed.

"Tough week. I'll be glad when this project is done," he sighed as he took a long pull from the already half-empty bottle. I was one of the few people in Ethan's life who understood his decision to start an architecture firm. The day he registered for classes, his mother called me to talk him out of it, but I was so proud of him I told Amelia that I couldn't possibly do that. When I'd asked Ethan about it later, he'd said that his parents still had hopes that he'd come work for his father and one day take over the practice. They didn't understand why he chose to be an architect instead of a lawyer, but I understood that it was something he needed to do because it was his dream.

I never knew what had finally convinced him to follow his dreams, but I assumed it had something to do with what he went through overseas. He still got a haunted look in his eyes every now and then, but he refused to talk about it. When I asked him about his deployments, he

35

changed the subject or gave a bland answer about fighting for our country but never told me any details, so I stood by him and did what I could to be there for him.

"How's Dan?" I asked thinking about his newly married partner. He'd met Dan his first day of boot camp, and they'd been friends ever since. I liked Dan, and the fact that he still watched Ethan's back made me like him even more. I trusted him to look out for Ethan, which, in my eyes, made him family.

"He's good. Loving married life. I guess he and Deb are thinking about kids soon," he said while scrunching up his face like he'd tasted something sour.

"Are you ever going to settle down, Gray?" I laughed as I held up another dress to decide if I wanted to pack it or not.

"You know I will one day—when I find that special girl worth settling down for," he answered before he took another sip of beer.

"And what might this special girl be like?" I asked, genuinely curious about what he considered important enough to settle down for. We hadn't talked about this in a long time, and, now that I had Ben, I felt like I had to make sure he'd find someone. Lord knows every girl I saw him with ended the same way.

Promise

"Oh, you know, the elusive 'one,'" he said, using air quotes. I gave him my best disapproving look, and he let out a deep sigh.

"I don't know, Lee. She'd make me happy. We'd be happy to just be together. She'd be interested in me, not my family name or money, not looking for some kind of advantage from me. She'd be my best friend." He paused, looking over at me, then cleared his throat.

"Second best friend," he corrected with a smirk and then added, "She'd be someone I can just be me with, laugh with, talk with. Someone I don't have to change for. Someone whom I could support and would support me in return. She would love me as unconditionally as I loved her. She'd be the love of my life, my forever." He trailed off, looking out the French doors at the serene landscape below. I'd never heard him refer to anyone the way my father had talked about my mother. All the times I'd talked about wanting to find my forever, not once did he ever say he wanted the same—until now.

"Well, she's out there, Gray. I know it." I smiled over at him in hope that it would lighten the dark mood he seemed to have fallen into. He was quiet for a little while before he spoke again.

"I suppose you're right," he finally answered, looking over at me.

I couldn't read the emotion that passed across his face, but I couldn't help but feel like I'd missed something. Shrugging it off, I decided now was as good a time as any to bring up Ben. "So, speaking of forever…"

Ethan's head snapped up to look at me, his eyes narrowing. I quickly continued on. He was acting so strange today.

"So, I'm bringing Ben with me to the wedding." He appraised me as I put the last of my clothing into my suitcase and pulled out my toiletry bag.

"Yeah," he said slowly, looking intently at me, but seemed to think better of what he was about to add. "I figured you would. Why are you telling me? It's Jess's wedding, not mine," he replied. At that I moved into my bathroom to gather my toiletries and makeup.

Taking notice of everything I'd piled into my suitcase, Ethan interrupted my mental checklist. "I know you're a girl and all, Lee, but do you really need so much for one night? And since when do you need so much stuff to go out anyway? What happened to your simplicity motto?"

"I'm going away for the weekend, with Ben. That's why I brought it up," I tossed back at him. He straightened and took a step into my room.

"I thought you said it was nothing serious?" he asked, his voice dangerously low.

Promise

"When did I ever say that to you? And what does it matter that he is or not?" I countered.

"It matters to me," he seethed.

"Jesus, Gray! Since when do you have a problem with Ben? I thought you liked him? And you don't see me getting angry about how you conduct your 'relationships,'" I quipped.

"That's because I'm not getting serious about some chick I barely know."

"G, I've been dating Ben for six months. It's not like I'm just hopping into bed with a complete stranger."

"You better not be," he said under his breath, but not low enough.

"Excuse me?" I spun around quickly and faced him.

"I didn't work this hard for you to just throw it all away on the first guy to stick around."

"What did you just say? What the hell are you talking about, Ethan?" I yelled, angered and confused by his words.

"Nothing. I'm just saying you shouldn't sleep with just anyone," he said calmly.

"Hypocrite much?" I asked, getting frustrated with his attitude.

"We're different people, Charlie. You know it's different."

"Yeah, I do. Which is why I brought it up. I wanted your advice for this weekend. I think this might be *the* weekend, you know?" I hinted, feeling the blush creep up my neck and coloring my face.

"For God's sake, Charlie, you can't even say *sex*, and you think you're ready?"

"You're not my father, Gray. I'm asking you as my friend what you think I should do."

"I can't tell you that, Charlie. Nobody can. If you think you're ready, then do what you think is right."

"What I think is right? What are you talking about, Gray?"

"All I'm saying is that you have to do what's right for you and only you. You always told me that you wanted to wait until it was with someone you loved—"

"That's why I'm asking, Gray," I interrupted quietly. Ethan went so still I wasn't sure he was even breathing. "Gray? Say something."

Instead he just shook his head.

"We used to be able to talk about anything."

"This isn't just anything, Charlie," he said uncomfortably.

"I know, but as my best friend, I thought you'd at least be happy for me."

"I am happy for you, if this is what you really want."

Promise

"Why are you saying it like that? Of course this is what I want, he makes me happy...and I love him." From the corner of my eye, I saw him flinch.

"Fine," was all he said.

"Fine," I mirrored. Silence descended as I finished pulling the last of my things for the wedding out.

Clearing his throat once more, Ethan spoke up. "So what's the big deal with this weekend?"

"He's taking me to his family place up in Charleston. His father's business partner is hosting some huge benefit for charity they have every year. I guess his whole family is going to be there and a bunch of other important people."

"Sounds exciting," he said sarcastically.

Might as well get the rest out, quick like a Band-Aid.

"He's talked about getting married, Gray. This weekend is his chance to introduce to me to his whole family." A pained expression covered his face.

"Really, Charlie? You want to marry this guy?"

"I've already told you he's not just some guy, Ethan. He makes me happy, and he's a great guy. I'd think you'd be happy for me."

He let out a big sigh and ran his hand through his hair. "I am happy for you. I just don't know what you're so worried about."

"I'm just worried about making a good impression."

"Why? You have nothing to worry about, Charlie. You've been around these kinds of people your whole life. What's the difference now?"

"The difference is that Ben and his family are like Southern royalty. Plus there's the whole sex thing."

"Just be yourself, Charlie, and they'll love you. As for the sex thing, as you said it, there are no expectations. There never should be, and if there are, you shouldn't do it. You know your heart and your head. Just follow them and they won't lead you wrong."

I smiled at him as I placed my hand on his arm.

"Thanks, G. You always know what to say to calm me down. You're the best." I reached up and kissed his cheek. He smiled shyly over at me but looked away as an unknown emotion crossed his face. I wanted to say something, but I didn't know what. After another beat I asked, "Is everything okay, Ethan? You seem, I dunno, off."

"It's..." He paused. "I'm fine. It's just work," he stated, but I could tell it was forced. He didn't want me to know the real reason he was upset. We'd never kept anything from one another before, and I couldn't understand why all of a sudden we were.

"You know you can talk to me about anything."

"I know, but it's nothing, really. Don't worry about me."

Promise

"Easier said than done," I said lightly. "How about when I get back after this weekend, we have a movie night? Just you and me, like old times. We haven't hung out just the two of us in while," I offered.

"That actually sounds really good to me, Lee. Just let me know when you get back in town, I'll grab takeout." Then he turned on his heel and headed out of my room. Before he got too far, he turned. "Do you have everything you need? We're already running late, and I have to pick up my date still," he said, looking down at his watch.

"Is there going to be enough room for all of us in the car?" I quipped, thinking about what leggy, busty model he'd be bringing as his date. I didn't know where that came from, but it didn't feel very good.

"Lee—" he began but was interrupted by my cellphone ringing. Looking at the caller ID, I saw Ben's name and the picture the two of us had taken at the symphony last winter.

"Hey, babe!" I answered brightly. From the corner of my eye, I saw Ethan still and looking back at me. That same unknown emotion flashed in his eyes, what looked an awful lot like jealousy and hurt, but he looked away before I could determine if it really was. I snapped my fingers to get his attention and held up my finger to signal him to wait. On the phone Ben told me he was on his way to pick me up.

"I'll see you in twenty," I told him hurriedly as I zipped up my suitcase and double-checked that I had everything I needed for the wedding. As I hung up the phone, the ridiculous smile on my face was too much to cover, and when I looked up, Ethan was scowling at me.

"What's wrong?"

"Nothing. Why didn't you tell me Ben was taking you?"

"I'm sorry. I thought we were meeting there, but he called this morning and said he'd pick me up. I guess I forgot to mention it."

"You *guess* you forgot to mention it?"

"Look, Gray, I'm sorry I forgot to say something. If you were bringing a date, why did you offer to take me anyway? It would have been less of a hassle," I asked, hurt that he was getting angry with me.

"You're not a hassle, Charlie. For God's sake, that's not what I'm saying." He took a deep breath to calm himself. "Just forget it. I've got to pick up my date." I didn't know what to say to him. He was acting so strange.

"Okay."

"I'll see you at the church." And with that, he abruptly turned and left my room. I watched him walk down the hallway, puzzled by his behavior. When I heard the sound of the front door open and then shut, loudly, I turned my curling iron on and set out to put on my makeup.

Promise

Half an hour later, I walked down the stairs, ready to meet Ben at the curb out front. As I exited the porch, I looked up to see his gorgeous face and tall frame leaning against the gate, waiting for me at the end of the sidewalk. He looked so handsome in his suit I still had no clue how I'd managed to make him mine. As I approached, he looked me up and down, a beautiful smile playing across his face. Taking the bag from my hand, he set it down and brought me into his solid body for a hug as he whispered in my ear, "You look absolutely breathtaking."

I smiled as I turned my head into his neck and inhaled his expensive cologne. We pulled apart, and he looked into my eyes like he wanted to say something, but instead he kissed me. Gently at first, but it quickly turned passionate as he held me to him like I was about to slip through his fingers. We pulled apart, breathless, looking into each other's eyes.

"Hi," I said.

"Hi back." He smiled. I gave him one last chaste kiss on his lips.

"Okay! We have to get going, I'm already late! Thank you so much for giving me more time to get ready!" I laughed as he reached to put my bag in the trunk. He opened my door, and I slid into the plush leather seat of his luxury sports car. Rounding the front, he hopped into the driver's side, started the car, and just as quickly, we pulled into traffic. Ben reached over and laced our fingers together and placed a soft kiss on the back of my hand as we pulled to a stop at a red light. I sat back and enjoyed the smooth ride to the church, my hand tucked gently in his as jazz music played softly through the car.

We approached the church, and I started to get more and more excited for Jess. But with that excitement came the nervousness of Ben and Ethan being around one another. The few times they'd crossed paths they were civil with one another, but I could tell there was tension between them. I didn't know where it came from, but it was there. And after Ethan's behavior earlier, I was worried about how he'd act around Ben if left alone for too long. I was also worried about him meeting the rest of the family. He'd met Daddy a few times, but tonight would be the first time they'd spent any amount of time together other than a dinner or two.

Since Mom had died, Daddy'd had hawk eyes on me with everything I've done. He'd given up being overbearing with Maddie back when she was in college. He got the message loud and clear when she moved across the country to go to Stanford. I, however, was Daddy's little girl, and he felt the need to always keep an eye on me. Except when I was with Ethan. He trusted him implicitly to protect me. I hoped he would feel that way about Ben one day too. Ben seemed to sense a change and squeezed my hand gently, pulling my attention back inside the car.

I smiled back at him as he said, as if reading my mind, "Everything is going to be okay." I looked over at him, and he added, "Just relax. I promise to be on my best behavior." He winked at me, and my smile grew genuine.

"I know you will. I'm not worried about that. I'm not worried about them liking you—they're going to love you. It's more about this weekend with your parents, and I want everything to go smooth for Jessica today. There are a lot of expectations that I feel like need to be met, and I'm just worried I won't live up to them or something bad will happen and—" I was practically out of breath from my rant before Ben interrupted me, smiling.

"Babe," he cajoled, "everything is going to be just fine. And if it isn't, we'll work it out, whatever it is. If you can't stand it anymore at my parents' place, we'll go somewhere else, just the two of us. How does that sound?" he asked, and I nodded with a smile.

He leaned over and kissed my lips. Short but sweet; all my fears melted away, and I finally felt ready to get out of the car. We made it to the front of the line of cars and pulled up to the valet stand at the church. I stepped out of the car and waited for Ben as he handed the keys to the valet. We ascended the steps hand in hand, and for the first time in almost an hour, I finally felt like myself again.

Chapter 2

I GRUDGINGLY LEFT BEN BY himself in one of the pews after he assured me again that he would be fine. He sent me on my way with a smile and a kiss on my cheek. I made my way down the hall to the room reserved for the bridal party and gently knocked before I entered. I walked into the room and found Jessica standing in front of a floor-length mirror as her mother attached the veil to her gorgeously styled hair.

"Jess, you look amazing!" I said in awe of my longtime friend.

"Thank God you're here!" Jessica squealed as she turned from the mirror and hugged me. She'd always had a flare for the dramatic, but in that moment I felt completely blessed to have been given the chance to befriend both Stone children. Granted, my friendship with Ethan was something else, but Jess and I had grown closer and closer in the years that Ethan was overseas. I don't think I would have made it through if it weren't for her.

"Sorry I'm late. I got caught up at the cafe," I offered in apology.

Promise

"It's okay, Charlie. I know how it goes." She smiled back.

"But there is nothing more important right now than you." I smiled at her. "So tell me why you look like you're about to cage fight," I whispered conspiratorially to her, noticing the tension around her eyes.

"Mom has been in rare form today. I think she's more nervous about today than I am." She rolled her eyes in the direction of her mother, who was fussing over the other bridesmaids' dresses. It was easy to see where Jess had learned to be dramatic, just look to Mrs. Stone. At least she came by it honestly.

"You know how she gets. Don't pay her any mind. Today is your day, and I couldn't be happier for you and Grant," I reassured her gently. "Are you ready to go? It's got to be almost time?"

"I am most definitely ready. I'm not nervous, just excited and anxious to get this over with so Grant and I can start our life together," she answered confidently.

"Your lives have already started together, Jess. You're just starting a new chapter, a beautiful, new chapter." Looking over my shoulder, I added, "I'll go get everyone moving." I smiled brightly up at her as I handed her the beautifully constructed bouquet of yellow and white roses. "Oh!" I added. "Philippe was loading the truck when I left this afternoon. Everything looks fantastic and, if I do say so myself, very tasty!"

"I can't thank you enough for doing that, Char. I know it was a lot of work with the large guest list, but I really do appreciate it!"

"Anything for you, honey. You know that. All right, let's go get you married!"

* * *

I stood in the processional line at the entrance to the sanctuary, patiently waiting for the music to begin. When the music started and the doors opened, the slow choreographed march of the men and women before me began. The two ushers, college buddies of Grant, walked the mothers down the aisle to their seats in the front pews. Then the five bridesmaids in front of me all stepped up and took the arm of their respective groomsman, waiting on the other side of the entrance. As the girl in front of me stepped up to the aisle, I turned to find Ethan staring at me.

My eyes met his, and he mouthed, "I'm sorry," to me over Kevin's head. I smiled brightly to let him know that it was all right, and when I stepped up to the door at my queue to take Ethan's arm, I got my first glance of him and just stared.

Promise

"You look beautiful, Charlie," he whispered so only I could hear him. He was still looking at me, but there was an intensity in his eyes I'd never seen before, and it was making me incredibly nervous. He'd never looked at me like that, and his gaze was positively unwavering. My eyes were caught in the deep blue pools of his, and I couldn't look away as the feeling of restless butterflies scattered in my stomach. I'd only ever felt it back when we were in college. I thought I'd felt it when I met Ben for the first time, but compared to what I felt now, there was no way it was the same.

I'd just been contemplating marriage with Ben, and now I was trapped in a heated stare down with Ethan. At the thought of Ben, my gaze swept out into the church in search of him. I caught sight of him as he sat between both of Jessica's grandparents. He looked absolutely adorable sitting there politely watching the procession; my heart melted at the sight of him. Realizing I still hadn't said anything, I shook my head to clear my errant thoughts.

"Thanks," I said lamely. "You look very handsome as always," I added cheerfully as I ran my fingers over his lapel. Heat radiated from his strong chest and traveled up my arm and spread into my chest. The feel of him below my hand mesmerized me. I looked up at him and found myself trapped in his steady gaze once again. Realization dawned, and I removed my hand from his chest and slid it gently into the crook of his elbow, where he tucked it safely under his hand. My skin tingled where his hand lay gently over mine, and I tried to clear my wayward thoughts, but the longer he touched me, the more nervous I became.

For the first time I was noticing how unbelievably beautiful he was. He moved with the quiet grace of a dancer, his movements fluid and gentle. It shocked me that a man with his size and muscular build could look so graceful. In appearance alone, he was intimidating in stature, but his quiet strength and confidence comforted me. The tuxedo he wore wrapped around his powerful physique, accentuating his broad shoulders and chest, tapering down to his narrow hips. His chiseled jaw drew my attention as the thought of what it would feel like to press my lips to his skin flashed unbidden into my mind. His smooth, full lips parted slightly as I subconsciously gasped at the sight of him so close. I didn't know if he knew what I was thinking, but I had a feeling he did. I had a feeling he was thinking it too.

My breath stuttered past my lips at the thought of what it would feel like to have him reciprocate those thoughts. I'd always known he was good looking, but I'd thought myself immune to him all these years. I knew women found him attractive—he went through enough of them for me to know that—but never had I ever, in our entire friendship, felt that kind of attraction to him. Maybe it wasn't attraction I was feeling but residual frustration from our argument earlier. Something still felt unsettled with him.

I finally forced my eyes to look away from him and prayed he couldn't tell what I had been thinking. The slight blush on my cheeks was, hopefully, masked by the makeup I'd put on for the occasion. As we took our places next to the altar, I looked back out into the sea of faces for Ben. When I saw him, however, he wasn't looking at me; instead he was zeroed in on Ethan. I followed his hardened gaze and was met with the sea-blue orbs of Ethan's eyes as he stared back at me. My breath caught in my throat at the intensity I found there. I closed my eyes and turned away to face down the aisle. I let out the long breath I'd been holding as the wedding march began and Jessica came into view. She was beaming at Grant, who had an equally exuberant smile on his face. There was so much love between them that it was hard not to feel it.

I chanced another glance at Ethan, who smiled warmly at his sister's approach. His entire face transformed when he smiled, and I couldn't take my eyes off him. He was breathtaking when he let his guard down. When his eyes flicked to mine, his smile grew to a face-splitting grin that caused mine to do the same, and with that, my best friend was back. My mind raced as it tried to figure out what had passed between us earlier. I felt it and now I knew he felt it too, but it had never felt like that before, and I didn't know what to do because I wanted to feel it again.

By the time my mind cleared, Jess was asking for Grant's ring, and I handed it over quickly. They said, "I do," and the preacher pronounced them husband and wife. Grant swept Jess into his arms and dipped her in a dramatic gesture before they sealed their vows with a kiss. When he righted her, both of them laughing, they were introduced as Mr. and Mrs. Grant Foster.

Jessica beamed at Grant as they took each other arm in arm and made their way back down the aisle as the church erupted in cheers and applause. I needed to get to Ben and away from the confusing feelings the man across the aisle from me was evoking. I needed the familiarity of his arms and the reassurance of his words. We just had to get through the reception and then we'd be off for the weekend, where a little distance from Ethan might help to sort out some things.

I caught up to Ben outside the church to let him know that I'd meet him after we finished taking pictures. He said he'd pull the car around and wait while he made calls for work. As I turned to go, he grabbed my hand and brought me into his arms and kissed me thoroughly. I stepped away, and we were both breathless. I looked up into his

Promise

eyes and felt all the indecision I'd had about the weekend melt away. I smiled sweetly and gave him one last, quick parting kiss before meeting back up with the wedding party. As I reached the group, Jess looked over and started laughing. She walked up to me and wordlessly handed me her lipstick as she fought her grin. I felt my cheeks flush with embarrassment at the realization that Ben had taken off all of my lipstick. I smiled gratefully as I reapplied and looked up to see Ethan scowling at me from the cluster of groomsmen. I didn't know why he looked so grim, but I had a feeling it was my doing.

An hour later, we arrived back at the front of the church to send the newlyweds off to the reception. True to his word, Ben greeted me with a soft kiss as he brought me to his side. I felt myself relax into him as he walked me to his waiting car. We chatted about the service and my friendship with Jessica as we navigated through the city toward the Regency.

We arrived at the reception, and the time had come to introduce Ben to the rest of my family. Daddy was the first to approach us.

"I'm glad to see you got the pearls. You look as beautiful as your mother did when she wore them." He smiled warmly as he hugged me into his chest.

"Thank you for remembering. I know she'd want to be here for Jess's big day." Feeling Ben stand patiently behind us, I reached for his arm and pulled him back beside me.

"Daddy, you remember Ben."

"How could I forget? Good to see you again, Ben."

"Good to see you too, sir."

Daddy still liked to play the tough-guy routine, but then he and Ben talked about business, which somehow turned into a boisterous discussion about golf, and before I knew it, they'd set up a tee time at Daddy's club.

My sister joined us and went right in for a hug that Ben graciously returned. When she released him she came at me with her arms held out. She wrapped me in a tight hug that had my ribs almost aching.

"Maddie, honey, can you ease up? I can't breathe, and you just saw me last month," I rasped.

"I know. It's just these damn pregnancy hormones. They make me all weepy and motherly," she said and laughed. She was in her second trimester and had the cutest baby bump I'd ever seen.

"That's precious cargo you're squashing there. I don't want my niece or nephew to come out with a lumpy head," I laughed.

"Niece."

"What?"

Promise

"Niece. Your niece will have a lumpy head," she laughed.

"You're having a girl! When did you find out? I thought you had to wait a few more weeks!" I exclaimed.

"They can check at four months, and when Max and I went to the doctor's this week, they told us." She smiled warmly as she smoothed her hand over her small belly.

"Oh, Maddie! I'm so happy for y'all! She is going to be the most spoiled little girl this side of the Mississippi." I beamed and hugged her tightly to me once more. We both stood there, watery laughter spilling from our chests.

Maddie had softened from her former self who'd fled to the other side of the country. She'd swear it was the pregnancy, but honestly I thought it had happened when she'd met Max. She let go of the past and the hurt. Max was a professor and one of the smartest men I'd ever met. He doted on Maddie, and she adored him. He had light-brown hair worn slightly long and hazel eyes that shined when he talked about Maddie or physics. He had high cheekbones and full lips set in a handsome face. His olive complexion held a bronze tone year-round. He resembled a man who'd just walked off a runway, not a college physics professor.

When Max took a job at UGA, he and Maddie moved back to Georgia, and it didn't take long for her and Daddy to reconcile. Their relationship had found its way back to where it had been before Mom got sick, and I was glad for it. I still attributed most of the changes to Max. He brought the old Maddie out, and it made Daddy and me so happy.

Smiling down at his wife, Max stepped in beside Maddie as he placed one arm around her shoulders and extended his other to shake Ben's hand.

"Maxwell Greene." He said kindly and extended his hand in greeting to Ben. "It seems the ladies have forgotten their manners."

"Hey now! This is exciting stuff here," I protested.

"It's all right, babe." Ben laughed and then turned to shake Max's hand. "Ben Wentworth."

Again, somehow, the men managed to steer the conversation to golf while Maddie and I caught up on all things baby. A while later, Mr. and Mrs. Stone joined us at our table to say hello.

"Mr. and Mrs. Stone, I'd like you to meet my boyfriend, Benjamin Wentworth. Ben, this is Henry and Amelia Stone, Jessica and Ethan's parents," I introduced.

He stood and offered his hand first to Amelia, then Henry. "Pleasure to make your acquaintance, ma'am, sir."

"The pleasure is all ours, Benjamin." Amelia smiled up at him, but as she looked over at me, her smile slipped slightly, and I'd swear I saw a tiny bit of sadness had filtered into her eyes.

Promise

"Please, call me Ben," he corrected warmly. It didn't take long before Ben had enchanted everyone at the table. He fit in with all of them effortlessly, and it felt like they'd known him for years. I wondered why I had been so nervous about him meeting them all. We were all cut from the same cloth, and he was a genuinely, wonderful man.

* * *

While the hors d'oeuvres were served, Jessica and Grant arrived to a raucous applause and cheers. As soon as they walked into the ballroom, they began greeting their guests. After they'd made their rounds to the other guests, they made their way, hand in hand, over to our table. We all stood to congratulate the happy couple, and even Ben stood up to hug Jessica and shake Grant's hand.

While the men grouped together in conversation about the stock market, Maddie shared the exciting news with all the women at the table as we began plotting and planning for the pink bundle of joy due in the fall.

Jessica turned to me and smiled brightly. "He's really great, Charlie. I'm really glad you two found each other," she whispered conspiratorially.

"Me too. It almost doesn't seem real sometimes," I said in return.

Smiling over at her husband, Jess added, "I know," and turned back to me. "Have you seen Ethan?" Jessica asked, looking around the large ballroom for her brother.

"Sorry, no. I haven't seen him since the church," I answered as we both scanned the room for him.

I felt Ben tense beside me as his grip on my waist tightened. I looked up at him, and his face was hardened to stone. I was about to ask him what was wrong when my eyes caught Ethan walking through the door. He was trying to fix his tie as a leggy redhead clung to his arm, attempting to fix her inappropriately short dress.

"Jess," I said, nodding my head over her shoulder to where Ethan had walked in with his date. She turned and took in the scene, scoffing at the behavior of her brother. Mrs. Stone lowered her eyes as Mr. Stone shook his head at his son. I knew that they let him live his life how he wanted to, but I also knew that they had expectations of him and that he disappointed them with some of his choices.

While I supported most of his decisions to go against them, I couldn't support the choices he made when it came to women. Ethan had a habit of dating "unscrupulous women," as Amelia would say, but my reaction to this woman was out of character. I wasn't sure what it was, but I had a feeling it had to do with jealousy, though I had to admit that it even shocked me that he'd behave in such a way at his own sister's wedding. Something was seriously going on with him these days, and it saddened me that I didn't know what it was.

"Don't worry. I'm sure she has a great personality her stylist picked out for her," I remarked snidely. The men chuckled quietly, but the women made sounds of disgust in their throats. I could tell Mrs. Stone was further dismayed by her son's behavior. I caught her eye and smiled apologetically, but she just waved me off with a smile and winked in Ben's direction. I had her approval. She'd been like a mother to Maddie and me since Mom passed, and she was one of the most important woman in my life. I wanted her to support my relationship with Ben, even if she wasn't blood related.

Half-jokingly, I whispered to Ben, "I bet this one's a model, and her name is Cherry." He chuckled, as did I, but stopped abruptly when someone behind us cleared her throat. I cringed as I turned to Ethan and his date standing there.

"My name is Rebecca, thank you very much," she said petulantly and looked at Ethan to jump to her rescue, but he was focused on a silent conversation with his father. I covered another laugh with a cough as I thought to myself how delusional she was.

Jessica looked upset, most likely because of the girl Ethan brought to her wedding. She didn't try to conceal her displeasure as she stood there staring daggers at the woman. To put an end to the awkward silence I extended my hand to Rebecca. "I'm Charlie," I offered with a forced, polite smile, "and this is my boyfriend, Ben."

She stared down at my hand with disgust but quickly turned her attention to Ben, who had stepped closer beside me and offered his hand to her. Rebecca's eyes glinted as she took him in. I could see the dollar signs and lust in her eyes as she stared openly him.

"Pleasure to meet you," she purred as she slid her hand into Ben's. Ethan again seemed indifferent to her, even the obvious perusal of another man.

"Hey, G," I said softly, hoping to bring him some ease. He just looked up at me, and something in his eyes made my voice catch in my throat. He looked like a wounded animal caught in a trap. I felt as trapped in his eyes as he must have felt, because I don't know how long we stood there looking at one another, but it left me feeling sad when Rebecca cleared her throat angrily. When I looked over at her, she glared back at me, her eyes cold and angry. Ben looked confused, and I knew he wanted to ask what was going on between us, but I prayed he didn't. Even I didn't know what was going on between Ethan and me.

I didn't know why Ethan was making this so difficult. I wished he'd just tell me what was going on with him. He looked Ben up and down, shook his hand, and gave an excuse about needing something to drink. As he moved away, he pulled Rebecca by the arm away from our group. She looked back at me with a cold, appraising gaze that chilled me to the bone. She must have felt the tension that pulsed between us and clearly felt threatened. When they reached the bar, I could see the two of them arguing and knew that something was definitely going on.

After they left, Ben pulled me aside to ask what I'd been hoping he hadn't noticed.

"What's going on with you and Ethan?"

"Nothing is going on. You know this, Ben. We're just friends."

"That's what you keep telling me, but it doesn't look like that to me."

"Ben, honestly, nothing is going on between us. We're just having one of those weird best-friend moments."

"If you say so," he said, unconvinced.

"I do say so, and I thought you trusted me."

"I do trust you, Charlie, but it's just hard for me to believe that nothing has ever happened between you two."

"Well, nothing has and nothing ever will. He's my best friend—that's all. Will you please let it go? You have nothing to worry about."

"I believe you, Charlie, I do, and I'm sorry I brought it up again," he said with a sigh.

Cassie Gregg

"It's all right, just as long as you promise not to let your imagination run away with you again. I'm happy about who I'm with," I said cheekily to him as I moved closer into his body.

"Good, because I'm happy with you too." He smiled back as he wrapped his arms around me and gave me a playful kiss on the lips.

Again I found myself praying that I was telling Ben the truth and that he really didn't have anything to worry about when it came to Ethan, but after today I really wasn't so sure anymore.

Chapter 3

A LITTLE WHILE LATER, WE took our seats for dinner and enjoyed easy conversation, laughter, and delicious food. When I looked up from my slice of cake and caught Ethan's eyes across the table, he was looking at me with that indescribable expression again. I gave him a questioning brow in the direction of Rebecca. He shook his head but returned the same brow to Ben. Preoccupied with our silent conversation, I hadn't realized that the table had gone quiet, awaiting my response to a question I'd been asked.

"I'm sorry. What did you say?" I turned, blushing from embarrassment.

"I was just wondering how the café is doing, dear. This cake is delicious, so I know that if your other stuff is half as good as this you must be doing well. I haven't heard from you in a while, and with Henry and me so busy traveling, we haven't had a chance to stop by in a while," Mrs. Stone said with a smile.

"Thank you, Amelia. I was so excited when Jess asked me to make her and Grant's wedding cake. The café has been really great, actually! I'm in the middle of negotiations to buy the space next door and expand the seating area and bakery," I answered, unable to keep the excitement from my voice. It was a new idea, but it was one that left me feeling giddy at the thought of it becoming a reality. Having a whole area for special-order cakes would free up the congestion that was in the café now.

"And you know that y'all are welcome to stop by anytime! Even if you can't make it during hours, you know where I live. I'd be more than happy to whip you and Mr. Stone up a batch of blueberry muffins for the road." I smiled at her, knowing she and Henry loved my blueberry muffins.

"Always such a sweet girl." She smiled in return.

"It's really just all that sugar," I retorted with a chuckle.

The table joined in on our laughter as everyone enjoyed their slice of cake, one of my recent masterpieces. Rebecca was silent the entire time Mrs. Stone questioned me about the café and instead picked at her cake like it was diseased. I couldn't help but laugh at the scolding look Ethan gave her. When I finished my slice of cake, I could feel Ethan's eyes on me, and it ramped up my nerves again.

Deciding to go with the oldest trick in the book, I excused myself to the restroom to avoid looking back at him. I hadn't been able to get a read on him at all today, and

Promise

that was what bothered me the most. I had always been able to take one look at him and know what he was feeling or thinking—had been that way since we were kids, just as he could do the same to me. But ever since he'd gotten back from overseas, it had gotten harder to get a true read on him. There were times when he was unguarded and I didn't have to guess what he was feeling, but there seemed to be more and more times lately that I'd look at him and not have a single clue what he was feeling. I was both sad and unnerved by the new development.

I stepped from the stall to wash my hands and stared at my reflection. Ethan was my best friend. I should have been able to just ask him what was going on. We'd always been able to talk to one another. The longer I looked at my reflection, the clearer the answer became. I wasn't sure I wanted to know his answer if I asked, because I was afraid of what he'd say. I was afraid that he'd confirm what the little voice inside told me every time I entertained the idea that Ethan would see me as more than a friend: that it would never happen. It was that fear that kept me from confronting him.

I was drying my hands when the door opened and the unmistakable clack of four-inch stilettos echoed into the cavernous bathroom. I looked over and saw Rebecca standing in front of the door, blocking my only way out. She stood with her arms crossed over her chest, hip stuck out as she stared directly at me, although it looked a lot more like she glared at me.

"Can I help you?" I asked dryly, hoping my indifferent tone would cover the anxiety I felt building inside me. Apparently those four words were all she needed to get going. She launched into a tirade of epic proportion. I was so stunned that I missed most of what she said. I only got bits and pieces, but none of it made any sense until she got to the end. She was telling me to stay away from Ethan now that she finally had him. I don't know why—maybe it was her dramatic demeanor or her sheer audacity—but I started to laugh. And it wasn't just a harmless chuckle; I felt myself give way to full-blown laughter.

That seemed to only enrage her more, as she stomped up to me, causing me to stumble into the wall behind me. She pointed her long, manicured nail in my face and said, "I've heard all about you, Charlotte. You're little Miss Goody-Two-shoes. All the boys fall for you, but then they leave you," she spat. She stepped closer to me, forcing me further back into the wall.

"You're just a silly girl who doesn't know how to handle a man. How long do you think you have left with Ben? A man like that won't stay around for long if you aren't giving him what he wants. And trust me, all men want the same thing. What does a little virgin like you know about satisfying a man anyway?"

Promise

By this point I was almost in tears, but I wouldn't let her see me cry; I wouldn't let her have the satisfaction. With more steel in my voice than I thought possible, I said, "I'm glad to hear that you and Ethan talk so much about me. Must mean he's bored with you if I'm all he can talk about. But I'll tell you this—not that it's any of your business, really—but you don't ever have to worry about Ethan and me. He's been my best friend since I was five years old and nothing more. If you're so worried about us, why don't you go ask him about it yourself? Let me guess—he's already told you that there's nothing going on between us, we're just friends, and your insecure tiny head didn't believe him. I dare you to go out there and make him choose between you and me. I can damn near guarantee that he will chose me, his best friend, over a slut like you."

I was seething. I couldn't stay there a second longer, and I could feel my confidence slipping away from me. I knew I had to get away from her.

"Stay away from me, Rebecca, and you can be damn sure that I'm going to stay away from you." On that I pushed past her to the bathroom door and pulled it open abruptly, but her next words paralyzed my steps.

"I think I figured it out: Ethan's infatuation with you—it's pity. He feels sorry for the motherless virgin who has no chance of ever landing a man." She smiled cruelly at me.

Pain like a white-hot iron struck through my heart, but I pushed it aside and looked over my shoulder at her and said, "This coming from the poster child for daddy issues." I wasn't proud of that last statement, but my insides had gone numb, except for the pulsing hurt of Ethan's betrayal.

I strode out of there as quickly as I could without running and headed for the nearest place I could to be alone. I slipped from the ballroom, and from the corner of my eye I saw Ben get up from the table, his face etched with concern as he watched me flee. I thought I heard him say Ethan's name, but I didn't stop—I couldn't. As soon as I cleared the ballroom, I ran down the empty hall of the hotel and pulled open the first door I came to, revealing an empty closet. I stepped inside and closed the door behind me. I slid to the floor and finally let the tears I'd been holding back fall freely. No sooner than the tears escaped did I hear a knock, while Ben called my name through the door.

"Charlie? Char, babe, open the door," he pleaded quietly as he continued to try the locked doorknob. Deciding to let him in before he caused a scene, I reached up and unlocked the door, scooting back as it slowly opened to reveal a very concerned, very confused Ben. Light from the hallway broke into the darkness of the small room as he bent down and sat on his heels. Noticing my tears in the light, he swiftly moved forward and lifted me easily into his lap.

"Charlie, what's wrong? What happened?" he asked again quietly. By now my tears had turned into sobs, as the realization of what had just happened sunk in. I couldn't seem to get any words out, only large, gulping sobs. He squeezed me to him tightly and stroked his hand over my head, over and over in a soothing rhythm.

"Baby, tell me what's wrong. Please, Charlie, you're scaring me," he pleaded, but my sobs continued making it hard for me to breathe. "Just breathe, Charlie. In and out. Nice and easy. There you go. Just breathe," he soothed as he continued to run his hands over my head. I leaned forward until my forehead was rested on his chin and I felt both of his strong arms wrap around me.

"He told her," I said quietly after I'd calmed down enough to speak. "She called me Charlotte." I trembled as a wave of fresh tears began to fall. "Then she talked about my mom." I sobbed heavily into my hands while he rocked gently and waited for me to continue. Finally, after a few minutes, I was able to start again. I lifted my head and searched for the right words to explain what had just happened.

"I need to tell you something," I said slowly.

"You can tell me anything, Charlie, you know that," he crooned softly as he cradled my head and wiped the tears from my cheeks.

"I want you to know that I didn't keep this from you to deceive you. It's just that, every time I had this talk with a guy, it changed things, and then not long after, he'd leave me, and things have been going so well with us, and I didn't want to lose you just yet. I guess it's just made me self-conscious, and I have this huge insecurity because of it, and only one person knows how I feel about this, and he just gave it as ammunition to his flavor of the week," I spat, anger replacing some of my sadness.

"It's all right, Charlie. Just tell me what it is; it won't change anything between us, or how I feel about you," he promised.

"I hope not. You mean so much to me, Ben, and I don't want to lose you," I said as fresh tears began to well in my eyes. I took a deep breath and released it with my confession. "I'm a virgin," I said meekly, lowering my head to look at my tangled hands. He sat there for a moment and just looked down at me before a smile slowly spread across his face. He tilted my head up with his finger and smiled sweetly,

"I know, Charlie, and I don't care," he stated simply.

"What do you mean you know?"

"I mean that I'm not stupid, and I could tell that you weren't ready. I mean, yes, I'm surprised that my suspicions are correct, but, babe, there's nothing wrong with that. And if I'm being honest, I'm relieved."

"Really?" I asked unsure.

"Absolutely, Charlie. I think I love you even more because of it. I've always been worried that there was something with Ethan in the past, and I believed you when you said there wasn't, but the way he looked at you—I couldn't let it go. But this once and for all settles it for me. I have nothing holding me back from you anymore," he answered confidently, leaning down to give me the softest, sweetest kiss I'd ever gotten. I reached my hands up to tangle my fingers in the short hair at the nape of his neck and moved closer into his body.

Our kiss deepened as he flattened my body to his. Finally pulling away, he rested his forehead to mine and looked deep into my eyes, cradling my face with his hands, and looked at me with the same expression he had earlier. Realization hit that he'd just told me he loved me, and I hadn't said anything. He loved me. Ben loved me! My heart felt like it had been filled with too much air and was about to burst.

"Because it means the woman I love will be all mine," he whispered.

"I love you too, Ben," I replied honestly, returning his heated look.

"I don't care how many men you've been with, Charlie. All I care about is that you're with me now. Let the past be the past. All I care about is your future, our future. We can take things slow. There's no rush for us. We have all the time in the world." He smiled down at me.

"How did I get so lucky?" I asked, sliding my arms around his waist.

"It was the muffins. I'd do anything for those muffins," he chuckled as I laughed and nodded into his chest.

"Was there something else bothering you? You said some things about your mom and your name," he said, with his lips pressed to the top of my head. I leaned back out of his embrace with a sigh as I thought about all that had just transpired in the bathroom.

"While I was in the bathroom, Rebecca cornered me, basically attacking me, saying how I had to stay away from Ethan and how she didn't know how I could get you when I wouldn't sleep with you and all this other stuff. And then she said Ethan was only my friend because he felt sorry for me because my mother died," I said somberly.

"Hey, hey!" he interrupted. "It's okay. I get it. She's a piece of work, but so what? Who cares what she says or thinks?"

Promise

"It's not that, Ben—well, it is, but she could only have known that stuff if Ethan told her. He told her my most private things, and about my mom. My best friend in the entire world just told his weekly fling the most personal thing about me, and she used it as a weapon to hurt me. She used my *mother* as a weapon. Sad thing is, I let it work!" I raised my voice.

"He broke my trust. He just broke my heart," I said sadly, looking down.

"Charlie, look at me, babe," he whispered, gently lifting my chin with his fingers. "Everything is going to be all right. Maybe Ethan thought he could trust her, or maybe he didn't realize what he was saying. He has had a lot to drink tonight. Either way, from now on I'm going to protect you. No matter what it is, I'll protect you."

"Thank you." I smiled shyly at him, even though inside I was beyond sad. Ethan had always been the one to protect me. Never could I have imagined that I would need protection from him.

"I don't know if I can go back out there and face him. I just want to go home," I added lamely.

"Don't let them ruin this for you, Char. Jess is your friend, and I know you want to be here for her, and you should. You don't have to face Ethan when we get back out there. We can avoid him easy enough. Come back with me. The music's started, and I would like nothing more than to dance with my beautiful girl." He smiled brightly. "Plus, I know your dad wanted a dance with you as well."

"You're right, but then can we go?" I asked hopefully.

"Of course, whatever you'd like." He smiled.

We exited the closet, and I told him I'd meet him at the table, realizing my makeup was wrecked. He nodded his head but said he'd wait outside the door for me. I smiled, rolled up onto my toes, and gave him a slow, meaningful kiss.

"You'd better get moving before I say forget it to the dancing and we just leave now." He winked cheekily at me. I smiled into his lips and gave him one last quick kiss before I headed into the bathroom.

Chapter 4

I EMERGED FROM THE BATHROOM, having fixed my makeup and done the best I could to cover up the puffiness of my eyes. They always seemed to glitter a special shade of gray after I cried that always gave me away. I knew that if any of my family looked too closely they'd be able to tell, but it was beyond my control at that point. I looked up to find Ben leaning against the wall right where I'd left him waiting. I smiled at him and took his proffered arm.

"Ready?" he asked.

"For anything." I smiled over at him.

We walked arm in arm back into the ballroom, where the music steadily played. I noticed Ethan stood by the bar with some of his old buddies, but he stopped talking when he looked over at me. He must have noticed my eyes, because his were a mixture of confusion and concern. He made to move toward me, but I shook my head no and steered Ben off our path, back to the table. I apologized to everyone for being away so long and kissed my father on the cheek and pulled him up to dance. Ben walked over and asked Amelia to dance, and I smiled at the gallantry he presented as he moved the two of them onto the dance floor. I couldn't believe Amelia got to dance with Ben before me, but the smile on her face as he charmed her was priceless. He really was an amazing man.

The band started up a new song, and my father pulled me close to him as we swayed and spun around the floor. We hadn't danced like this in a long time, and it brought back so many memories. He used to twirl me around the living room when I was a little girl, and we'd laugh and spin, and he'd release me only to pull Mom into his arms. It was just another way I saw their love for one another. He'd taught me to how to dance for my cotillion, where we danced to a few songs and then again at Maddie's wedding, but it had been years since we'd had a moment like that together.

"I like him, Charlie," he said, pulling me from my thoughts. I looked over his shoulder at Ben and nodded a smile.

"I can see he makes you happy, and that's all I can ask for. He seems like a good man."

"He is, Daddy. He really is," I said fondly.

An upbeat song began to play, and Jessica pulled me from Daddy's arms to join her, and the other bridesmaids circled together. It had been a long time since I'd let loose, and it was nice to just relax and have fun.

I had the feeling of being watched again and looked up to see that Ethan watched me intently. My good mood

Promise

soured instantly. Just looking at him, I felt the betrayal of what he'd done course through me. He must have seen the hurt in my eyes, because he was quickly on his feet and moved toward me. Rebecca, thankfully, intercepted and pulled him to the opposite side of the dance floor.

After a few more songs, I was in desperate need of a drink. I was waiting in the small line at the bar when I felt a large body come up behind me and place a warm hand on my arm. Thinking Ben had finally come to collect me for our dance, I leaned backwards and instantly went still when I realized it was not Ben behind me. I turned quickly and saw that it was Ethan, who stood there looking at me questioningly. I searched the room for Ben, and I saw that his back was to me as he talked with my father and Henry.

"What's wrong?" he asked, placing a hand on my shoulder. A harmless gesture, but it felt all wrong. I stepped out from under his hand, and it fell heavily at his side. Hurt and confusion swarmed into his eyes.

"Tell me what's wrong, Lee. Did something happen? Did Ben do something?" he asked as he spared an angry glance in Ben's direction.

"No, it's not Ben, Ethan. It's you. Leave me alone." I waved. "Go find your new toy to play with," I remarked sharply.

"Whoa! Hold on! What did I do? Char, I'm sorry. I don't know what you're talking about. Please just tell me what's going on."

"Stop!" I yelled. "Just stop, Ethan," I added, catching the attention of a few people around us, including my dad and Ben. I saw his face change instantly, pulling tight with tension and anger. Relief flooded me as I saw Ben make his approach.

"You really have no idea what you've done, do you, Ethan? And that just makes it so much worse. I don't want to talk to you. I'm just not able to right now. So please, leave me alone." I moved to step around him and saw that Ben was almost to me, worry marring his handsome face. As I was about to pass, Ethan grabbed my arm and spun me around.

"Stop! Charlie, why are you acting like this? What did I do? Just tell me what I did!" By now we'd caught the attention of more people. I smiled around at them reassuringly.

"Let go of me, Ethan. You're causing a scene," I said through my teeth as I began to pull from his grasp, but he instantly tightened his grip just as Ben arrived at my side.

"Let her go," Ben commanded in a voice I'd never heard him use before. I looked up at him, and he was as hard as stone, his heated gaze burned into Ethan's.

Promise

"She's asked you. Now I've asked you. Let her go now, Ethan. I won't ask again," he warned.

Maybe it was his tone or the look of panic on my face when he grabbed me, but Ethan released my arm and looked between Ben and me. I'd never seen Ethan back down from a fight before. Then again, I'd never seen him back down from anything. When he gave one last pleading look to me, I averted my eyes, and he turned and left. Ben enveloped me in his big arms, and I sunk into his warmth and pulled strength from him.

"You okay?" he whispered, his lips pressed into my hair. I nodded, pulling slightly away to whisper thank you into his lips before sealing mine onto his. Through our haze, I heard the soft tones of "Come Away with Me" floating around the room. Without a word Ben led me to the dance floor and pulled me tightly against him. I saw my father's worried gaze as he looked over at me, and I smiled reassuringly to him. When I saw him visibly relax and return to his conversation, I let myself get lost in the sway of our dance, lulled by the sultry voice of Nora Jones.

The longer we danced, the more a warm sense of peace washed over me, and it was something I hadn't felt in a long time. I could still feel this pit in my stomach, and I didn't know what it was, but deep down I knew something wasn't right. Ben tilted my chin up as he lowered his head and kissed me gently. The song came to an end, and I looked up into his flashing hazel eyes and gave him a knowing smile. He returned with a knowing smile of his own before he ushered me off the dance floor, his large hand comfortably at the small of my back.

He walked me over to Jessica to say one last congratulations and good-bye. After we made the complete rounds to all my family and friends, we made our way to the front doors to get Ben's car. Ethan was nowhere to be seen, but I tried to push him from my mind as Ben wrapped an arm around my shoulders to block out the crisp spring breeze.

Waiting at the curb for the valet to bring the car around, I felt my phone buzz from within my small clutch. Ben squeezed me into him a little tighter, and I resolved to check it later. Ben opened the car door for me, and I climbed in and settled in my seat. We were headed straight for the airport to catch our flight on one of the private planes that Ben's family owned to fly to his parent's place in Charleston. The next big step in our relationship was just hours away. Soon I would be meeting *the* Mr. and Mrs. Wentworth.

Chapter 5

I WOKE A SHORT TIME later, warm, bouncing rhythmically like I was floating. I opened my eyes to see a beautiful jaw above me as I was carried through a large ornate doorway. I realized that Ben was carrying me up a grand spiral flight of stairs. I tried to take in my surroundings, but it was too dark to tell where we were. I could tell it wasn't a hotel, but it most certainly looked to be as clean as one. It was nice, wherever it was. After a few minutes of staring at his gorgeous jaw, I shifted ever so slightly and pressed my lips to the tender spot just below the corner of his jaw. I felt, rather than heard, his groan as he tightened his hold around me.

As he finally settled me down, my feet barely touched the plush carpet before he walked me backward. I felt the bed at the back of my knees as he ran his hands down my body to the hem of my dress. In one swift move he had my dress unzipped as I pushed his jacket off his shoulders. His hands pressed with the perfect amount of pressure to my hip and back as I leaned forward and claimed his lips in a searing kiss. He returned my kiss with equal heat as I fumbled with the small buttons of his dress shirt. I could feel my hands tremble, and he did too, because he covered both of my hands with one of his and stilled my movements.

He tilted my chin up to look into my eyes. "This isn't what I had in mind for tonight. I know you're not ready yet, and I don't expect us to do this now that you've told me everything." He placed a gentle kiss on both my hands. "Why don't you go get ready for bed, and we'll lie down and relax? It's been a long day," he offered.

I sighed, a bit relieved but also a bit frustrated because I finally felt like I'd met someone worth sharing this part of myself with, and he was putting it off. I wasn't ready before, but now that I knew we loved each other, I felt a need for him I'd never had before.

In the bathroom, I washed my face of all the wedding makeup, moisturized, took down my hair from its tight up-do, and then brushed my teeth. Looking around the room, I realized I hadn't grabbed my pajamas or my bag from the car. Walking back into the bedroom in only my bra and panties, I noticed that Ben was nowhere to be seen. The door to the bedroom was slightly ajar, casting the room in a soft light that allowed me to see the room better for the first time. It was spacious, with a dark-wood king-size sleigh bed sitting in the middle of the room, flanked by matching nightstands. French doors and windows took up one wall leading to a balcony. A black Steinway grand piano sat in the corner facing the windows while two large reading chairs sat in the opposite corner.

Ben's dress shirt draped over the back of one of the chairs, so I walked over and picked it up. I held it to my nose and inhaled the rich smell of his expensive cologne. It was distinctly Ben, and I couldn't help but smile at the thought of him. Walking over to the window, I pulled back the drapes to reveal more floor-to-ceiling windows that illuminated the room with light from the full moon. Beyond the balcony, I saw a large expanse of grass with the outline of a large house in the distance.

I turned from the breathtaking view to finish getting ready for bed. I looked around the room for my bag but couldn't see it anywhere, so instead I slipped out of my bra and into Ben's shirt. I laughed at the absurdity of me trying to be sexy. I'd never tried like this before with a man, but I'd let that stupid woman get in my head. There was no way I could pull off the sexy look. Cute, yes, but not sexy. This was totally Ethan's area of expertise. He'd be the perfect person to ask for help, but then I remembered that I wasn't speaking to my best friend, and my mood darkened. The click of the bedroom door broke me from my pity party.

"Be out in a minute," I called out to Ben.

I straightened his dress shirt over my shoulders and felt it slide silkily down my body until it rested midthigh.

His sleeves engulfed my arms in all their fabric, so I rolled them up to just below my elbows. With one last glance in the mirror, I shook my head and left the bathroom.

I stepped out into the bedroom and stopped short when I took in the scene before me. Ben lounged on the bed in only his pajama bottoms. His smooth, muscular chest was on display for me as he rested his head back into his folded arms against the headboard.

"Sorry to leave you alone, but I went out and got the bags from the car and grabbed a few DVDs from the home theater," he said, still resting his head back.

He lowered his head to look and me and went completely still. He stared at me with an expression on his face I couldn't read. It seemed to just be my night for it.

"Ben?" My voice cracked with nerves. "What's wrong?" I asked, looking around the room to find the source of his catatonic state.

"You need to go change," he grunted huskily, and I froze. I knew I shouldn't have tried this look. I didn't know why I'd even bothered. I couldn't look sexy like other women, especially not to a man this gorgeous. Rebecca had been right. And that thought hurt more than anything Ben was about to say.

"Wh-what?" I stuttered, pulling at the hem of the shirt to try and cover more of myself while I looked down at my toes. He didn't like it. I'd finally felt ready to take the next step with a man and he wasn't interested.

"Babe..." he started as he rushed to stand and joined me at the bathroom entrance. I dropped my head further as I turned to go back into the bathroom.

"Babe, stop," he repeated.

I ignored him and tried to push past his large frame to retreat into the bathroom, but he was just too big for me to move.

"Char, wait."

I pulled away again, needing to get to the bathroom before he saw me cry...for the second time that night.

"Charlie, stop!" he practically yelled, causing me to stop instantly. He rounded on me as his hands firmly grasped both my arms. I still couldn't look him in the eye.

"What, Ben? I was going to change, just like you asked. I get it." I made another futile attempt to get past him and into the bathroom, but he blocked my path again with his large body. I sniffled and tried to catch the tears threatening to fall.

"Charlie, are you kidding me?" he seethed. I flinched back, unsure of what to do. "Charlie, look at me," he whispered as he tilted my head up with gentle fingers on my chin. "You are without a doubt the sexiest, most beautiful girl—woman—I have ever laid eyes on," he whispered reverently. I could hear the sincerity in his voice, and the ball of tension that had built in my chest slowly began to unwind.

"Babe, the only reason I said what I said, which I realize was completely moronic on my part"—he shook his head at himself—"was because at the sight of you just now, wearing my shirt and looking too damn sexy for your own good, I realized I wouldn't be able to keep my hands to myself the rest of the night, and I don't want to rush you. I want to keep my word to you, because I meant it. But, babe, if you come walking out of a room looking like that again, with no warning, I can't be held responsible for my actions to follow," he warned quietly but playfully.

A broad smile broke onto my face as I looked up at him and into his eyes. He really did want me. As if he'd read my mind, he said softly, "I love you, Charlie, all of you. Every single part of you is beautiful. Never, ever doubt that."

With that said, I jumped into his arms and sealed my lips to his in a passionate, heated kiss meant to convey all the emotions and love I felt for him. His arms tightened around me and lifted me as I wrapped my legs around his waist. The heat of his bare chest soaked through the thin material of the dress shirt and warmed me to my toes. He walked us back to the bed and gently laid me down and followed.

Promise

Masterfully, he pulled the covers back as I scooted into the middle of the bed to be closer to him. Once in the bed as well, he reached over and snugly pulled me to his chest, wrapping his long arms around me and secured me to him. I settled further into his warm body as he slid the covers up around us both.

"I love you, Ben," I said into the darkness.

"I love you too, Charlie," he whispered into my ear as he tightened his arms around me.

With my head on his chest and an arm draped across his stomach, I drifted off to sleep, lulled by the sound of his even breaths.

Chapter 6

I WOKE TO THE SOUND of birds as the bright morning sunlight beamed through the open curtains. I felt warm, really warm. I turned my head, only to be greeted by two beautiful hazel eyes staring back at me. I felt heat creep into my face that turned my cheeks a light shade of pink.

"Good morning, sleepyhead," he cooed as he snuggled closer into my neck.

"Good morning, handsome," I giggled as he tickled me with his morning scruff.

"Were you watching me sleep?" I asked, turning over on my side to face him.

"Only for a little while. You looked so peaceful I didn't have the heart to wake you. However, my mother called a little bit ago and said that brunch is almost ready and that we should head over to the main house soon. So..." He exhaled. "Up and at 'em! Time to meet everyone," he said as he patted my hip. I wasn't sure I'd heard him correctly.

"Everyone? I thought you said it was just your parents."

"It was, but my mother got a little carried away, like she does, and called my siblings and grandparents to come by this morning. They're all in town anyway for the gala, but they all wanted to meet you for themselves before the event."

I stopped in my tracks and turned on him. "What? Ben! I can't meet your whole family today—that's... that's...I don't know, insane!" I sat on the edge of the bed in a lump.

"Hey now, I just met your whole family last night, and it went just fine. You have nothing to worry about," he tried to reassure me.

"I know, but that's different! Your family owns like half the city, and they're like business geniuses! How could they approve of someone like me?" I heard the whine in my own voice and wondered why I ever thought this was a good idea. The Wentworths were world renowned for their corporate empire and real estate holdings.

On top of that, his grandmother was a Windsor, of *the* Windsors. That meant she came from old Southern money...a lot of it. My family was wealthy—I'm not naïve enough to think they weren't—but we were nowhere near Wentworth or Windsor wealth. Few people were. There was no way his family would look at me and find me adequate for their son, their heir. I couldn't believe what I'd gotten myself into.

"Charlie, you have nothing to worry about. You knew you were meeting my parents this weekend. What are a few more relatives? They're just people, like everyone else. The only difference being that we happen to have a lot of money and we have our name on a bunch of buildings. Besides that, you are a beautiful, intelligent woman with dual degrees and an MBA, all from an Ivy League. You've built a successful business from the ground up, and you continue to be successful in everything you do. You're active in multiple charities and sit on a board or two of your own. You cook meals for the local shelter every week and give generously to countless others. Your family runs in the same circles as mine; you grew up like I did. You have nothing to be ashamed of because you decided to become a baker instead of a mogul of your own or a housewife. No matter what path you chose or what upbringing you had, they'd still welcome you because you are the woman that I love."

"But..." I trailed off.

"Out of lame excuses?" he chuckled. "Just breathe, babe. It'll all be fine."

I took a deep breath and exhaled. "All right, all right, I'm calm. But I get dibs on first shower!" I laughed as I kissed his cheek and skipped quickly into the bathroom to take a shower.

Once I had showered, dried, clothed, and rechecked my appearance five hundred times, I waited for Ben to come out so we could get brunch over with. I didn't want to show up late and start off with a bad impression. I knew he'd said there was nothing to worry about, but this felt more like an interview than any introductions before. Since Ben and I had discussed marriage, this all seemed a lot more serious than a simple meet-the-parents. This was his family's chance to determine if I was good enough for their family, for their son. Needless to say, my nerves were frayed more than an old Christmas sweater.

After I'd thoroughly stressed myself out, Ben finally emerged, looking every bit the casual aristocrat that he was.

"You look great, babe," I said, admiring my view of him.

"Thanks, Char. You do too. You should wear dresses more often. You definitely have the legs for 'em," he commented as he appraised my legs again.

"Well, I'll keep that in mind for the future." I winked at him.

Shaking his head, he asked, "Ready?"

"As I'll ever be." I smiled at him.

I followed Ben downstairs and out to the car. We made the short drive up to the main house and parked the car next to the array of other luxury vehicles in the driveway, their drivers clustered together in conversation. Meeting me on the passenger side of the car, Ben reached over and laced his fingers through mine and locked our hands in a tight grip.

As we approached the beautiful glass door, Ben squeezed my hand to check that I was ready to go in. I smiled up at him, reassuring both of us, and took one last deep breath before he opened the large door. Instantly, the beauty of the house shocked me. Everything shined with the look of a brand-new home. It smelled of polish and cleaning solvent, and not a single object seemed out of place. A stunning woman approached us as we walked farther into the entryway.

"You must be Charlotte. It's so nice to finally meet you." She reached a slim hand out to me, her diamond bracelet sparkling in the morning sun.

I flinched at the sound of my full name but replied. "Hello, Mrs. Wentworth, it's nice to meet you as well. And please call me Charlie. Thank you for having me. You have a very beautiful home," I said with a pleasant smile, returning her delicate handshake.

It was easy to see that Ben took after his mother. Her blond hair and intelligent hazel eyes were a stunning combination. Her fair complexion was artfully made up, and there was only a hit to her age in the small creases around her eyes when she smiled. She was small in stature, with a petite frame that moved with an elegance only those born into generations of debutants could master. She was friendly, but the straight set of her back and shoulders personified class and status.

Ben stepped up to put an arm around my shoulders in a comforting gesture. "I told you, Mother, she prefers to be called Charlie," he lightly admonished, leaning forward to kiss his mother on the cheek in greeting.

"My apologies, Charlie, and please call me Sylvia—Mrs. Wentworth is my mother-in-law," she said with a wink. I nodded politely at the offer and began to relax just slightly as the introduction came to an end.

"Benjamin, honey, it's so good to see you. Thank you for agreeing to come up for a visit," she said smiling warmly at her son. "Rosa has everything ready for us. Come along now, and let's introduce this beautiful young lady to the rest of the family. They're all eager to meet her," she said dramatically with the flip of her perfectly styled hair. We followed Sylvia down a large hallway toward the distant sound of voices.

Chapter 7

Brunch had been a success, much like the wedding had been. His family was nothing like I'd expected them to be. His grandfather was my favorite of all. Reserved, but with a quiet humor that I enjoyed greatly, he struck me as an extremely intelligent and thoughtful man. Mrs. Wentworth was a funny lady, but I could still sense the deep Southern roots she came from.

Ben's father, Thomas Wentworth, was the toughest to impress. He was handsome, his brown hair with just a touch of gray at the temples. As much as Ben had his mother's coloring, his sharp, angular face and tall, broad-shouldered frame came from his father. Unlike his wife, his skin held a touch of sun from days spent doing business out on the links. And just as Ben had inherited his father's handsome good looks, he'd also inherited his charm. Thomas Wentworth was nothing if not charming, but it was easy to see that where Ben used his charm to flatter, Thomas used his charm as a tool in business. Still an active businessman, he had an imposing demeanor, and while he was polite and charming, it was easy to see that he had little time for idle chitchat, much like Ben's

Promise

older sister, Catherine, who was the female version of their father in every way.

Ben's younger sister, Alice, was as sweet as her name. While Catherine was the spitting image of her father and Ben was a complex mixture of both his parents, Alice was a mini Sylvia. Seeing the two of them sit side by side at the table, it was as if I were watching something out of *The Twilight Zone*. Sylvia was the blueprint that Alice would become in forty years' time. They looked, spoke, acted, and ate in exactly the same way. They had the same mannerisms, which I wasn't sure they were even aware of. Alice was as extravagant as her siblings and parents. She held herself with a great deal of grace for someone of her young age with the world at her feet.

The conversation had been easy, and they'd all seemed genuinely interested in what I had to say about how I'd built my business and how it was doing. It was like the many luncheons and dinners we'd had at the house for Daddy's business growing up, or the countless charity benefits mother had hosted. Ben was relaxed the whole time, constantly in contact with me, whether it was holding my hand or brushing his fingers in lazy patterns on my shoulder or leaving his arm draped across the back of my chair. Whichever method he settled on helped to keep me calm and anxiety free.

Cassie Gregg

When the topic came up of my family, and, consequently, my mother, they all seemed to be genuinely sympathetic to my situation. I loved that Ben leaned over and kissed me, not caring that his family surrounded us. While they were warm and welcoming, there wasn't enough ease with them that I felt comfortable enough to let my guard down completely. They were truly lovely people, but it seemed that all the puzzle pieces just didn't fit.

Thankfully, Ben and I had the rest of the day to ourselves after brunch, and it was just what we'd needed. Just as Ben was finishing the tour of the family's estate a storm front had rolled in, bringing with it the threat of a heavy afternoon storm. Ben and I barely made it back to the guesthouse before the sky opened up and warm spring rains fell from the heavens. Ben got a call from work shortly after we arrived back at the house, so I decided to head upstairs to catch up on e-mails and work.

Climbing the stairs, it dawned on me that I hadn't checked my phone since before we'd left Savannah. I reached into my clutch from the wedding and found that I had seven missed calls, six text messages, and three voicemails. I didn't know how I'd forgotten to check my phone for so long, but I had.

I unlocked my phone and opened up the calls first to see I had two from Dad, one from Jessica, and the rest from Ethan. It didn't seem to be a good sign that I had that many missed messages. I opened my text messages next and saw that I had one from Maddie and one from Jessica, each demanding to know what was going on between Ethan and me. There was one from Louis, updating me about shift coverage and that everything else was fine at the café, and the last three were from Ethan. I ignored them all for now and called up my voicemail, where I found one message from Daddy and the next two from none other than Ethan. Daddy asked if everything was okay because I'd seemed upset at the wedding, and he subtly hinted that he knew it had to do with Ethan. I shot him a quick e-mail that I was all right and everything was fine and he didn't have to worry. Next I sent Louis a thank-you text and my ETA on Monday as the voicemails from Ethan automatically begin to play.

In the first one he was angry with me for not telling him what was going on and for acting childishly. By the end he was yelling at me about friendship and loyalty, but I couldn't listen to it anymore. I hit delete before it was over and threw it down on the bed next to me. Never in all the years of our friendship had he ever spoken to me like that or said such hurtful things. I had noticed that some of his words ran together. He'd clearly been drinking when he called, which was so unlike Ethan—to get that drunk and call me ranting. Taking a deep breath, I picked the phone back up and clicked on the next message from him.

Cassie Gregg

At first there was nothing but silence. Figuring he'd accidentally redialed, I moved the phone from my ear to delete the message when suddenly the sorrowful tone of his voice came through the speaker. It nearly broke my heart to hear him like that. He sounded so miserable that I could hear the weariness in his voice as he begged me to tell him what was wrong. He apologized over and over so many times I lost count. I'd been upset listening to the first message, and surprised by his emotion, but this was worse than drunk, ranting Ethan. He'd apologized before; we both had. With a friendship that spanned almost two decades, there had been the minor argument here and there, but never had he sounded so defeated and dejected. His usual strong, confident tone had been completely replaced with sadness and pain. I didn't know what to do, so I deleted the message.

I opened the text messages from him and the first two were much like the calls that started angry then turned apologetic. The third one, however, gave me pause. It had been sent at three in the morning, with four simple words: *"Please Lee not him."* Although he left out the context of the message, I had a feeling I knew what it was about, and it all felt wrong. I was so confused, but most of all, I was hurt. Hurt by what he'd done, hurt that my oldest and best friend was in pain, and hurt that I was the cause of that pain. The last thing I ever wanted to do was cause him harm.

I had no clue what do to about Ethan, so I sat in the middle of the bed and stared at my phone in my lap. I don't know how long I'd been sitting there, but that was how Ben found me.

"Babe? You okay?" The concern in his voice broke through the spell I was in.

"What? Oh, yeah. I'm fine, just checking my messages. I have to make a couple calls, then I'm all yours."

"All right, I'm just going to wait out on the balcony to give you some privacy."

"'Kay." I smiled, trying to hide all the warring emotions that tore at my insides.

He turned hesitantly and, with one last look over his shoulder, left through the balcony doors. I called Jessica and Maddie back, and both calls went similarly, with both of them wanting to know what was going on between Ethan and me. I wouldn't—couldn't—tell them what Ethan did, just that I needed some space from him and if they would respect that, I'd appreciate it. Maddie readily agreed, but Jessica was hesitant, eventually agreeing to drop the topic if I promised to tell her what had happened when she got back from her honeymoon. I told her I would, but deep down I knew I wouldn't tell her.

Sighing, I walked through the balcony doors and found Ben leaning against the railing as he looked out at the grounds below. I moved in behind him and wrapped my arms around his waist.

"Hi," I said softly into his shoulder.

"Hi back," he said as he placed his hands over mine on his chest.

"Want to tell me what was bothering you before?" he asked.

I sighed and said, "Yeah. I checked my phone, and needless to say, that showdown with Ethan didn't go unnoticed by his family...or mine. And he left a bunch of messages on my phone last night. I forgot I turned it on vibrate for the ceremony," I explained, in hope that he'd understand why it had taken me so long to come out.

"I don't know what to do about him, Ben. I've never seen him like this, and he sounded so angry with me, but then broken, like I'd broken him." A tear rolled down my cheek at the realization of what I'd done.

He squeezed my hands tighter and then turned in my arms. "No, Char, you didn't break him. Whatever is going on is not your fault. He made his own decisions, and he hurt you, plain and simple. We don't know why he did what he did, but I know I don't need to know. I just need to know if you're okay. I will always stand by you, babe, no matter what."

Promise

I gave him another hug as he wiped the tears on my cheek with this thumb. "Thank you, really. You've dealt with a lot in the last couple of days, and I'm beyond grateful to have you. I love you," I said, sealing my statement with a kiss that left no doubt in his mind that I meant every word.

Phone and Ethan forgotten, we crawled into bed and watched as the thunderstorm outside raged on. We lay there for hours, laughing and talking while we snuggled in each other's arms. It was the perfect afternoon.

Sunday morning arrived, and the charity gala was upon us. It was a masquerade ball to support the local children's hospital, and apparently, it was *the* event of the season, and to be invited to it was the utmost honor and privilege. I was poked and prodded all day getting ready for the night, and I hadn't seen Ben since breakfast that morning. It was strange how much I found myself missing him. I was stepping into my shoes when I heard a knock on the door to the room I was getting ready in. All three Wentworth women strutted in, looking more stunning than I'd ever seen anyone look before.

"Wow! Y'all look amazing!" I exclaimed as they stood at the entrance to the room and stared back at me. What was it with this family and staring?

"Oh my..." Mrs. Wentworth said with a gasp.

"Darling, you look—" Sylvia started, only to be interrupted by Alice huffing, "—way better than me!" I looked down at the intricately detailed beaded-and-lace Alexander McQueen gown and nearly five-inch Follies Lace Louboutins.

"I look okay?" I smoothed self-consciously. "It's not too much?" I asked the room at large. All three women exchanged a look, and then all nodded excitedly.

"Benjamin won't be able to take his eyes off you. You look absolutely stunning, dear," Sylvia stated with what I thought was awe in her voice.

"Thank you, ma'am. Will one of you help me with my mask so we can get going? I don't want to be late."

"Nonsense, the men have already gone ahead to check us in and get things situated at the gala, and the limo goes when we tell it to. We ladies are traveling together, and there is no rush." Sylvia smiled at me as she approached to help fix my intricately laced mask, which matched my dress perfectly, to my face. Alice had helped me pick it out after she'd seen the dress I'd brought.

Ten minutes later, we were all piled into the limo, and my nerves started up again. I fidgeted with the scandalous slit in my dress that ended halfway up my thigh, pulling it closed so the bare skin of my leg wasn't showing. God, I hoped Ben liked the dress and hair and makeup. I'd never worn this kind of stuff around him before, and it was more than what I'd had on for the wedding. I'd never been one to wear a lot of makeup, even at my junior cotillion or any of the many events that my father's company hosted. I was much more at home in a pair of jeans, a T-shirt, and my Chucks, much to my father's chagrin. He never understood how someone of my status could dress so meagerly. I always told him that I liked to be comfortable and didn't see the point in ruining nice clothes baking all day. He'd grudgingly agree and let the topic go, but I knew it still bothered him.

More than anything, I wanted to call Ethan to have him calm me down, but I knew I couldn't do that now. Would I ever be able to do that again? Would we ever have our old friendship back?

God, I hoped so.

Chapter 8

WE PULLED UP TO A sprawling estate similar to the Wentworths', and again, I was in awe of the extravagance. All the lights twinkled, and the beautiful flowers dotted the immaculate landscape. There was a line of luxury cars and limos that led up to a grand entrance with no less than a white-carpet entry. Hanging lanterns illuminated the walkways and grounds, and the distant sound of a band hummed through the air. There were more people than I'd imagined there would be, and I wondered if I'd be able to find Ben in the masses. I'd decided to go with a very stylish but very impractical clutch and left my phone at the house, so I'd have to rely on sheer luck to find him. Not realizing that I'd spoken my concerns out loud, I was startled when I heard Mrs. Wentworth speak close to my ear.

"Don't worry, my dear. I'm sure he'll find you," she assured me. We pulled up to the start of the long entry carpet, and each of our doors were quickly opened as young men in jester costumes escorted us from the car.

"Thank you." I smiled politely at the young man whose hand pulled me from the limo.

Promise

"My pleasure, miss," he drawled in a too-smooth Southern voice. His brown eyes lingered a bit too long to be appropriate on my leg where my dress was slit. I quickly pulled it closed to cover myself and saw his smile grow wide as I hurried to continue on with the other women.

"See?" Sylvia pushed. "Any man would be lucky to have your attention tonight. Ben will be no different. And he'd better keep his eye on you," she added with a wink.

I followed the women to the mouth of the entrance and spared one last glance over my shoulder at the jester valet. He stood where I could see him and stared directly back at me with a look that sent chills racing down my spine. I quickly turned back around and continued walking down the carpet. The walk into the palatial house seemed to take forever, as so many of the journalists and photographers along the path continually stopped and asked the Wentworths for their picture. It was much like the events my family attended. The society pages loved to snap pictures of us at any and all outings. This was, unfortunately, nothing new.

Once we arrived inside, we were escorted with the other guests to the east wing of the mansion, which housed the ballroom and outdoor entertainment. I was struck speechless yet again by the beautifully decorated entry. The ballroom was filled with impeccably dressed men and women, their faces concealed behind exquisite masks. Some stood around talking, and some gathered around the bar ordering drinks. There were linen-covered tables looped around the dance floor in a horseshoe where more guests sat, and others moved around the dance floor to enjoy the band. Bustling waiters in top hats, white gloves, and tuxedos served champagne in the finest crystal flutes and carried platters of hors d'oeuvres. There was no way I was going to be able to find Ben in the sea of people. There had to be over three hundred people in attendance, and I scanned the room, but all I could see were hundreds of unfamiliar, half-hidden faces.

I saw Sylvia and Mrs. Wentworth break away to join a group of very handsome men, all ranging in age by the looks of their hair, and upon closer inspection, I could just make out Ben's sandy-blond hair. I turned to take another glass of champagne from a passing waiter, and when I spun back around to see if Alice would go with me across the room, she was no longer at my side. I'd lost sight of the other group, and no one around me looked familiar, even if I could have seen their faces. Luckily, in my heels, I was more than a few inches taller and was able to see more of the room than I would normally have been able to. I decided to head in the direction I'd last seen the men, and when I finally saw Sylvia again, relief washed over me.

I approached, and my eyes caught on a tall man with wide shoulders and a lean frame, casually talking with the

Promise

group before him. He scanned the room, but I couldn't move. Once his face was turned toward me, I could see that the man I was shamelessly ogling was Ben. I'd thought he was handsome at the wedding, but apparently I hadn't seen anything yet.

In a tux that was made for him, his toned body stood coolly waiting for what I hoped was me. A plain black mask covered half his face but accentuated the beauty of his strong jaw, high cheekbones, and sensual lips. My gaze seemed fixated on the plumpness of his bottom lip and his slightly thinner top lip, knowing what it felt like to have those beautiful lips pressed to my own. A slither of heat slid from my chest and settled into my lower abdomen. As he spoke, the flash of his perfectly straight white teeth appeared and captivated me further.

Someone passing bumped into me and shook me from my blatant appraisal. I sucked in a deep breath that I hadn't realized I'd been holding and squared my shoulders. But I couldn't seem to move, mesmerized by his easy movements and dashing good looks. After what seemed like an eternity, his eyes passed over my face and paused, with interest glowing in them, but he quickly continued to scan the faces around the room. He hadn't recognized me the first time and passed over me a second time, but paused longer than the first. I smiled my usual shy smile, but his eyes kept moving. Then, almost in slow motion, his eyes drew back to me.

"Hi," I mouthed.

Nothing. He didn't move a single muscle as his eyes trained onto me. I laughed to myself and thought that we couldn't keep doing this to one another or one of us was going to have a stroke from lack of oxygen. As if in one of those cheesy love movies I made Ethan watch, I slowly made my way through the crowd of people between us. They seemed to part the way for me as I moved through them. Men and women alike stared as I passed by until I finally arrived in front of him.

"Charlie?" he asked in awe.

"Hi," I said quietly.

"Hi back," he replied, breathless. We stood there looking at each other until the gentleman to his right cleared his throat, breaking us both from our trance.

"Wow, Charlie. I'm at a loss for words. You look absolutely stunning," he gushed. I felt the heat of my blush crawl up my chest to my face, coloring my cheeks a deep shade of red. Luckily, the mask hid my embarrassment, but I averted my gaze from all the attentive eyes.

After taking a moment to compose myself, I looked up to see that Ben still stared at me. Deciding to be as daring as the dress, I took a step closer to Ben so that my body just barely grazed his, and said, "Well, Mr. Wentworth, you look positively handsome in this tuxedo," looking up at him with lust-filled eyes. "We're being incredibly rude, Ben," I whispered as I ran my hand down the lapels of his tux.

"Right." He cleared his throat before continuing, "Tom, Richard, this is my girlfriend, Charlie Montgomery. Charlie, these are my good friends, Tom Avery and Richard Miller." He gestured to the men respectively.

I shook both their hands and offered a greeting in return. "Nice to meet you both." I smiled, delighted to meet some of Ben's friends. Tom and Richard were equally dashing in appearance—and from the cut of their tuxes, it was safe to assume that they were successful in whatever career they followed. It was easy to see the many openly interested and appreciative looks the handsome group of men gathered around me received from women around the room.

"Believe me—the pleasure is all mine," Tom replied, earning a glare from both Ben and Richard.

I laughed and said, "I appreciate the sentiment, but if you'll excuse us, I'm going to steal him away for a bit." I reached for Ben's hand, lacing my fingers through his, and led him outside to the beautifully lit veranda, where a handful of couples and groups were out enjoying the breezy spring night. From there we could hear the melodic hum of the band's music floating gently through the night air without all the pressure of everyone watching us dance. We found a space on the patio that was close to the music, but far enough away from the other dancing couples to have some privacy.

As soon as we'd settled in a spot, I turned and pulled his head down to meet mine. Stunned, Ben at first stood stock-still but quickly recovered and moved his warm body into mine, running his hands down my open back and pulling me closer, deepening the kiss on a groan. Heat trailed along my skin where his hands blazed a trail. A shiver worked its way across my heated skin, alerting us both to the effect he was having on me.

"I've been waiting to do that all day," I whispered breathlessly.

"I'm glad you did. I missed you today."

"I missed you, too. You really do look very handsome."

"Not a single person here can hold a candle to how beautiful you look tonight. I think my lungs stopped working when I realized that the stunning woman walking toward me was you. My tongue just about fell out of my mouth," he laughed.

"Mine did too," I chuckled. "I stood there and stared at you for a couple minutes when I saw it was you and realized that you were mine."

"And you're mine, Charlie. You could be in rags, and I'd still be drawn to you." He kissed me sweetly.

Promise

"You really know what to say to a girl." I blushed, loving his sweet words.

I fell comfortably in step with Ben as he began to sway and turn me around and around. He was such a graceful dancer, his strong arms holding me close as we began to melt into an easy rhythm and conversation. We were laughing and smiling, completely carefree and unaware of the outside world.

"You're smiling like a loon," Ben whispered.

"That's because I'm really happy," I mumbled into Ben's shoulder as he moved to turn us around again.

"I am, without a doubt, the envy of every man here," he said, whispering into my lips as he kissed me every few words. I smiled into his and returned the kiss.

After a few more songs, my feet began to throb in my fashionable but ridiculous shoes. Ben, being the chivalrous man that he was, led me over to a table and ordered us both a drink from the bar. We sat holding hands, talking, and observing the people around us. We talked more about our families and the things we did growing up. I was slightly saddened by the fact that all of my stories included Ethan, but since we weren't speaking, I quickly turned the conversation back to Ben.

He told me more about his family's business and the plans he had for the company now and when he took over for his father. He told me about his favorite childhood memories and college. We ordered another round of drinks when the emcee announced the winner of the silent auction items. The custom-baked goods package I'd offered went for much more than I'd ever imagined, but it was for charity, and I loved being able to help. The hosts, Regina and Harold Hamilton, stepped to the podium after the auction to thank everyone for their attendance and generous contributions, and announced that with plate and ticket sales, auctioned items, and pocket donations, the foundation had raised an astounding four million dollars. When the boisterous applause settled and Regina stepped to the microphone again, she revealed that the Wentworth family had pledged to match whatever was raised, effectively doubling the foundation's donation to the children's hospital. Ben stood along with his family, and they waved to the room, accepting their praise. More bright flashes went off around the room, memorializing the moment. After a final word of thanks, the Hamiltons encouraged everyone to stay and enjoy the rest of the evening.

Finishing the last of our drinks, we got up to find Ben's family but only made it halfway before reporters stopped us to ask Ben and me for a photo. Ben looked down to me as I looked up to him, and we just smiled at one another. A flash went off, and the man thanked us both, by name, for the picture. As much as I didn't appreciate the press's

Promise

intrusion into our personal lives, I couldn't stop the smile that took over my face as I looked into Ben's dancing eyes.

"Why don't we head out a bit early? I doubt we'll be missed, and we've been here for all that's really needed," he whispered in my ear as he placed a soft kiss just below it.

"Lead the way," I answered, a bit breathless, a shiver of awareness simmering along my skin. Lacing our fingers, he pulled me through the crowd until we were outside by the valet stand. The brown-eyed Southern jester from earlier was all too eager to help us. He rushed to grab Ben's ticket and brushed his arm along mine. I pulled closer into Ben as a shiver of a different kind ran down my spine. Ben felt me move into him but misjudged my reaction when he slipped his jacket off and draped it over my shoulders.

Touched by his thoughtfulness, I leaned up and kissed his cheek. "Thank you."

Our car arrived, and the shady jester jumped from the driver side and jogged around the front of the car to open my door. As he held his hand out for me to take, I looked hesitantly at it, but before I could make the decision, his eyes flashed, and he reached forward and grabbed my elbow.

"Here, miss, lemme help ya inta yer car," he drawled through his teeth, a sneer more than a smile occupying his face.

"I'm fine, thank you. I can manage," I replied quickly and tried to pull my arm from his clammy grasp, which only caused him to tighten his grip on me. Ben was preoccupied with small talk, unaware of what was transpiring. I looked over at him and finally caught his eye as the valet's grip on my elbow tightened more. In a flash, Ben was over to my side of the car, his face hardened and eyes chillingly cold.

"Remove your hand from her arm, immediately," he said coolly. The kid eyed Ben, looking like he was about to make a terrible mistake.

"I would take a step back before you do something you'll regret," Ben warned. The kid took another moment to decide but finally released my arm and took a step back. I scrambled into the car, squeezing my hands together to hide how badly they trembled.

I chanced a glance out the window and saw the young man standing there staring at me like he had when I first arrived. Ben stood a moment longer, blocking the valet's view of me through the window, and gave one last parting comment to the man, sending him walking back to stand with the other waiting valets. Ben briskly walked around the front of his car, keeping the man in his peripheral vision, and slid into the driver side. He roared down the long driveway, putting distance between the jester valet and us, as quickly as possible. I was still shaking when he

Promise

reached over to hold my hand and caused me to jump at the contact.

"Hey, it's okay. I'm sorry I wasn't paying attention. He never should've had his hands on you," he said angrily. I reached over across the center console and brushed my hand over the side of his face and into his soft hair.

"It's okay, Ben. It wasn't your fault. You can't be with me every second of the day to protect me from every little thing. But I love you for wanting to try," I said with a swipe of my thumb over his temple.

"I know that, babe, but I made you and your father a promise to look after you. From now on, I intend to do just that," he vowed.

For some reason, it didn't settle me to know that Ben had made that promise. I wondered if it was the promise that bothered me or if it was the person who made it.

Chapter 9

OVER THE DURATION OF OUR drive back to the house, Ben's tension seemed to lessen with every mile we put between the party and us, as did mine. When we arrived back at the house and Ben seemed to be himself again, we quickly remembered why we'd left the party early.

"Come on, let's get you to bed." He opened my car door, and I stepped out much more gracefully than I would have thought possible, what with his low-riding sports car and my tight dress and sky-high heels.

"What if I'm not ready to go to sleep?" I asked in the sultriest voice I could manage.

He looked down at me for a long moment before he said, "I don't think I mentioned anything about sleeping," he replied, his voice deeper and rougher than normal.

Heat seared through my belly, pooling low in my stomach. It was an entirely new feeling, and the surprise must have shown on my face.

"Char, we don't have to do this. We have all the time in the world. I can wait, I swear. I want to do this when you're ready. I don't want you to do something you're not ready for because you think it will make me happy," he said to me most earnestly. I smiled at him, knowing he'd just solidified my decision to take the next step with him that night. I'd been mentally planning this night for weeks.

"I know, Ben, and this is something I've thought a lot about, and I want to do this. More importantly, I want to do this with you," I replied. By now we'd made it as far as the steps leading to the upstairs master bedroom.

I could tell that he'd stopped us there so that I could make the decision of whether we would go upstairs together or stay down for a nightcap. Having already made my decision, I slipped the shoes from my feet, letting them dangle from my fingers, turned on my heel, and walked up the stairs, leaving Ben to follow behind me. I'd made my decision; it was his turn to make his. I walked into the bedroom, and he closely followed me in, gently closing the door behind us.

"Are you sure about this, Charlie? You can say no at any time," he assured.

"I know, but I won't." I smiled.

We stood there staring at one another for a few moments until I finally saw his reluctance dissolve. He took one large step to cover the distance between us and reached for me. "Thank God," he breathed reverently.

His strong hands held me to him as our mouths met in a heated seal. One hand held my head in place as he devoured my lips, while the other slid up my exposed back, sending shivers down my spine and goose bumps across my skin. His fingertips began a torturous descent down my back, lightly tracing along my spine to where he skillfully undid the zipper and flattened his warm hand to the base of my spine, bringing me closer into his body. The warm, hard weight of him pressed into my stomach let loose a moan from me into his mouth. Spurred by my sounds, a low growl escaped his chest as he pulled the dress from my shoulders and pooled it at my feet, leaving me in nothing but my panties. He released my hair from the low chignon that confined it and gently ran his fingers through the strands to loosen the curls into soft waves.

I unbuttoned his shirt one at a time and replaced each button with a soft, openmouthed kiss, feeling the soft hair on his chest against my lips and tasting his warm skin on my tongue. He groaned softly and pulled my head back to his and kissed me, angling his head and mine to deepen the already consuming kiss. My head swam with the intense passion of our connection. This was what I'd waited for.

Soon we were both lying on the bed, the warmth from his solid body engulfing me. Hard, smooth muscles moved over me as he pressed me deliciously into the bed. He was hard as steel but soft like velvet as I ran my fingers over his chest and shoulders, pulling him onto me so we were touching from lips to toes. I could lie there for hours and just touch his perfect skin. He looked into my eyes, asking silently if I was ready for what happened next. I took in a deep breath and nodded, waiting for the inevitable pain everyone talked about.

"Charlie, you have to relax. I'm going to go slow. I don't want to hurt you, but you have to let me in, babe. Just tell me to stop and I will, but try and relax. I promise I'll make it feel good."

I let out the breath I'd been holding, and after seeing, once more, confirmation in my eyes, he entered me, achingly paced, only to stop at the telltale sign of my virginity. As I took another steadying breath to ease the discomfort of his intrusion, he waited for me to relax yet again.

"Just breathe, baby," he cooed softly, his lips brushed against mine, tantalizingly soft. He began to kiss me deeply and as he sealed his mouth over mine, he pushed into me completely and stilled. A sharp twinge shot through my core as I gasped into his mouth. I squeezed my eyes shut, willing the discomfort away.

"Open your eyes. Charlie, look at me," he ordered softly. "You are absolutely beautiful," he breathed when I looked up into his shimmering hazel eyes. He hadn't moved since he'd made his final intrusion, but where there was once pain, the low hum of pleasure melted my insides and pulled at me to move, to ease the ache. I ran my hands over the strained muscles of his shoulders and back and tilted my hips toward him.

"Jesus, Charlie," he gritted out. "I'm not moving until you're ready, but you're going to kill me if you keep wiggling around like that." He reopened his eyes and looked down at me. "Just tell me when you're ready," he breathed.

I looked up at him and could see the restraint in his features, the slight throb of his pulse at his neck. Overwhelmed by the full feeling inside me, I no longer felt the initial pain and moved my hips slightly, testing the feeling of the movement. The feel of him inside me was unlike anything I'd ever felt before. He reacted quickly and stilled my hips with his hand, and I shifted up just slightly and pressed my lips to his neck and whispered huskily, "Move."

And move he did. The pain I felt before was a distant memory as his hips pushed in a rhythm that made all coherent thought escape me. Slow at first, he kept a steady pace, building up a fire that simmered low in my belly. The only thing I could focus on was the feeling of pleasure that coursed though my body. I cried out incoherently as he quickened his pace once more and I wrapped my arms tightly around his shoulders. What started as a slow, hypnotic rhythm had intensified to an overwhelming urge to complete one another. My body matched his as we moved together as one. A foreign feeling built low in my belly as my breathing accelerated. He stroked in and out of me, long and deep, and all I could do was moan in the

Promise

complete pleasure of the feeling. We were both panting in search of sweet relief as the pressure mounted, taking me higher and higher. I closed my eyes to the world around me and climbed farther until I couldn't take any more.

"Oh God, Ben! I... Oh God!" I stammered as the pleasure became too much, and I fell over the edge and into infinite bliss on a long pleasured moan.

"That's it, baby... God you feel so good... I've got you," he panted into my neck. And with one final thrust, every muscle in my body pulled tight as we both found our release. I felt Ben go still above me, both of us calling out each other's names as I felt my body languidly seep into pleasurable delight.

I came back to myself a little while later with the heavy weight of Ben's relaxed body still on top of me, warming me deep into my bones. Both of us caught our breaths, and I subconsciously began to hum. With his forehead resting on my chest, his arms wrapped tightly around me, I didn't realize I was still humming until he placed soft kisses to the hollow spot of my neck and sternum. Running my fingers through his impossibly soft hair and down his shoulders, I resumed my humming.

"I like that," he said with satisfaction.

"What?" I asked.

"You were humming. I like your humming," he said as he placed kisses to my neck and shoulder.

"Mmm...I like that," I said, squeezing his sides, still cradled between my legs.

"I mean it. Why haven't I heard you sing before?" he asked innocently. I was somber suddenly with the memory of my mother's soothing, angelic voice.

"My mother taught me how to sing," I answered, still brushing my hands through his now thoroughly messy hair, rhythmically soothing both him and myself.

"I'm sorry. I didn't realize it was about her. You don't talk about her much."

I smiled as the thought came to me: "She would have liked you." My voice was thick with emotion as a tear slid unbidden down my cheek.

Tracing his warm lips up the trail of tears, he soothed, "Shh, it's okay."

"I'm fine, really. These are happy tears. I'm just thinking about all the times I heard her sing." Settling beside me, he pulled me close and brushed the hair from my face and then softly ran his hands up and down my arm as I continued my story. "She used to sing us to sleep if we'd had a nightmare or couldn't sleep. She sang when we got hurt or we were sad. But my favorite of all was when she sang while she cooked. Sometimes she'd sing along with the radio. Sometimes she'd just sing from her memory. The smile she'd have on her face while she mixed ingredients and sang was the most beautiful thing I had ever seen; it was pure happiness. We'd be in that kitchen for hours on end just cooking and singing."

I paused, unsure if I should share the rest of the story. "Ethan was the first person outside my family to ever hear me sing. Eventually he convinced me to sing with our friends, but it took a lot of coaxing every time. It's been a long time since I've sung for anyone, but I do find myself humming when utterly happy." I smiled reassuringly at his concerned eyes. I couldn't bring myself to tell him that even though friends surrounded us, I'd always sung to Ethan.

"Well, I'm making it my life's mission to be the reason you are this happy. And maybe one day you'll sing again… for me."

I laughed as he tickled my ribs and cleared the last of my somber mood away. "Don't you dare, Ben!" I warned between gasps of laughter. We were both rolling around laughing when the incessant buzz of a phone broke through our laughter.

"You may as well answer it so it'll stop buzzing," he said, rolling off of me after a chaste kiss to my lips.

Sliding from the bed, I pulled the comforter around me to search for my phone. I padded across the polished wood floors and stepped over our discarded clothing in search of my vibrating phone. The phone quieted briefly, but quickly began to ring again, helping me to find it on the floor under Ben's pants. I reached down and quickly grabbed it up.

"Now that's a view I could get used to," I heard Ben comment as I righted myself and turned to see him lounging in bed looking hungrily at me. Girlishly giggling, I answered my phone without bothering to look at the caller ID.

"Hello?" I chuckled.

"Lee?" Ethan. "Lee, you there?" he asked again.

"Yeah, I'm here." My voice stilled Ben and caused him to sit up on his elbows and watch me intently. Even from across the room I could feel his heated gaze on me, but I couldn't look at him knowing what I'd just done and be on the phone with Ethan. Trying to escape the awkwardness, I tucked a blanket around myself and moved across the room to the large window wall.

"What do you want, Ethan? It's the middle of the night," I said in a hushed and irritated tone.

"Why are you whispering? Never mind. You never called back, and I got worried. Then no one would tell me where you were or what was going—"

"Because I told them not to, and you know where I am," I interrupted. "What do you want, Ethan? I'm being rude talking on the phone, and it's late," I added, getting more and more agitated. The hurt from earlier seeped back into my heart and darkened my post-coital glow. Glancing

Promise

at the clock, I saw that it was past two in the morning, and by the slur of his words, he'd been drinking...again.

"I just wanted to hear your voice," he said somberly. "I feel like something happened, and I'm losing you, Lee."

"Ethan, it's late. You've clearly been drinking, and it's been an emotional day. I'm not in the mood to talk about it right now. Besides, I know you're back to work tomorrow, you need to sober up and get some rest. We'll talk when I get back in town." I looked up to see Ben had quietly walked over to me.

"Char, just listen, please! I'm sorry about whatever I did. Just please tell me what it is so that I won't hurt you again. I never want to hurt you, Charlie. This is killing—"

"Babe, come back to bed," Ben said, his chin resting on my shoulder opposite the phone. I didn't miss that he'd done it on purpose, and it angered me that he was trying to make Ethan jealous. I shot him a look that sent him standing straight.

"Are you kidding me, Charlie?" Ethan practically yelled into the phone, causing me to wince. "I thought you were better than this," he spat disgustedly.

"Excuse me?! Who do you think you are, Ethan?" I yelled back, anger surging through my veins. I was so riled up that I hung up on him for the first time in our entire friendship.

"What happened?" Ben asked hesitantly.

127

"He... he..." I stuttered, still unsure of what had just happened. "He basically just called me a slut! He heard your voice and put it together that we slept together, and Mr. Man-Whore himself just called me a slut! He said he thought I was better than this!" I yelled in one breath, waving my hand between the two of us.

"He said that to you?" he asked in a dark voice.

"Yes, he said that, but calm down. I'm sorry I upset you. He can say that to me, and it hurts, a lot, but your opinion of me is all that matters now," I said pleadingly. "Please, babe, let's just forget it, and forget him. I don't want him ruining what we just had," I plied, holding my hand out to him as I sat on the edge of the bed. After he stood there for a minute, I saw his shoulders relax, and he slipped his hand into mine and joined me back in bed. As we crawled up toward the pillows, Ben pulled me closer to him and kissed my nose tenderly.

"Thank you," I said, snuggling deeper into his chest. "This right here is all that matters right now," I said, kissing his chest.

"Good, because you're not getting rid of me."

"Good, because I don't want to get rid of you."

"Good." He smiled warmly down to me. Because of his earlier comment about singing and wanting to make me happy, I realized that I was still holding parts of myself back from him, and after what we'd just shared, what I'd just given him, it only seemed fair that I truly share all of myself with him. Placing a soft kiss on the corner of his mouth, I disentangled myself from his arms and retucked the blanket around my body as I slipped from bed.

"Where are you going?"

"It's a surprise. There's something I want to do for you."

"I love surprises, but there's nothing more you have to do for me." He smiled secretively.

"Oh, shush." I smiled, blushing.

"You're pretty when you blush," he laughed.

"You have to behave if you want your surprise," I mockingly threatened.

"Do I have to?" He smiled wickedly, causing more heat to flood my face. To hide my embarrassment, I turned and walked to the piano sitting in the corner. Ben lay silently in bed as I settled myself on the bench and opened the fallboard, revealing pristine white and black keys. Testing the tuning and feel of the keys, I caught Ben in my periphery, sliding up and settling against the headboard. Taking one last glance his way, I was captivated by the image he created: his chiseled muscles on a long lean body, sitting relaxed against the soft pillows at his back, the white sheet pooling in his lap, exposing one defined leg and the perfect "V" of his hips. My mouth dried at the sight of him. His eyes heated at my perusal and took time to appreciate me in kind.

"Are you going to play something? Or just sit over there torturing me?"

I licked my lips. "Right." I turned back around to face the piano and laid my fingers atop the cool keys. Contemplating which song to sing, I ran through my go-to songs, jazz classics and contemporary songs. Then a current chart-topper popped into my head, and it seemed perfect for the situation. Stripping the song down to just a piano and my voice would be difficult, but the words spoke to me and would poignant for Ben and me. The opening notes flowed through my fingers, and I let the melody roll over me and closed my eyes and let the lyrics slip softly from my lips. While I might not be Alicia Keys, I knew that Ben was amazed by what he heard because he got up and sat on the end of the bed closest to me, his gaze fixated on the piano and me as I sang.

I looked directly at him so he knew that I felt that way about us. I wanted him to understand that Ethan didn't get to have a say in our relationship. What happened between us in bed tonight was ours and no one else's. He sat there silently, watching me play and listening to me sing, and it felt like another piece of the puzzle tried to fit into place. It felt good to share this with him, but again, it felt like it just wasn't the same...because he wasn't Ethan.

Promise

When I finished the song, Ben got up off the bed, walked to me, scooped me into his arms, and kissed me deeply, walking both of us back to bed.

"You are unbelievably amazing, Charlie."

"You're an unbelievably amazing man, Ben," I replied as I settled into his arms on his chest and fell asleep.

The next morning at breakfast, Ben and I sat at the dining room table after harmoniously cooking breakfast together in the kitchen. Just before we finished, Ben set his fork down and turned to me. "Charlie?" he probed.

"Hmm?" I mumbled around a bite of food.

"Have you thought more about getting married?" he asked intently. I stilled, my fork halfway to my mouth as my gaze shot up to his.

"I'm guessing by that shocked look on your face that you haven't," he offered. I regained some of my composure and set my fork on my plate.

"Honestly, Ben, no, I haven't thought about it. I'm still young and thought that I'd have more time to consider it," I answered. He grew quiet at my answer. "But I'm not opposed to talking about it," I amended.

"I'm not asking you to marry me, Charlie. I'm just wondering if you've ever considered marrying me. I know you're still young, but I'm almost thirty. I'm ready for that next step in my life, and I know I want to take that step with you. I just want you to know that."

Cassie Gregg

"Wow," I breathed lamely. "What I mean is, that's amazing, Ben, it is, and while I'm not ready right now to give you an answer if you asked, I know that if you gave me some more time that I could see myself saying yes." I smiled.

He let out a deep breath. "Okay, good."

"Good." I grinned.

Chapter 10

OVER THE NEXT FEW WEEKS, things fell into a comfortable pattern with Ben. I'd wake up early, go for my run, and then make him breakfast before I went into work, most times before he even got out of the shower. At night, we'd have plans for a dinner if we both weren't working late, or to spend a night in at either of our places. We spent nearly every night together, mostly at my place so that I could be closer to work in the morning.

While his contemporary penthouse was gorgeous, it was a further drive to get to work, and I'd have had to fight the morning work traffic into downtown. Another reason was that when I was there, I just didn't feel at home. If by chance Ben saw Ethan on his way to my place, it usually sparked some kind of argument between Ben and me. For some reason, Ethan was always a topic of contention for us, as was the topic of marriage. I had a feeling more of the pressure was coming from his family, but as much as I loved Ben, I just wasn't ready to say yes if he asked.

When we'd first gotten back from Charleston, Ethan had tried to come over a few times, but Ben had been there, and I'd told Ethan to leave. I knew we needed to talk, but the pain was still fresh, and if I was honest with myself, I didn't want to admit why it had hurt me so bad. Ben asked many times why I was still so upset and wanted to know why I couldn't just let it go, and I told him it was because he'd broken our trust and betrayed me.

What I never told him was that it was more than that, that deep down I knew the real reason I was mad at him was really because I was still in love with him. But I couldn't bring myself to acknowledge the jealousy and hurt from that broken love—to Ben or myself.

The more time that passed, the more Ben brought up getting married. While he never outright asked me, he continued to ask me if I'd warmed up to the idea, or he'd bring up a friend's wedding or engagement. I'd always tell him that I wasn't ready but that I loved him and we could consider it soon. I hoped that I wasn't lying to either of us when I said that. Everyone had always said we'd have a honeymoon phase, but we didn't. There was no desperate need to have the other person all the time, nor a deeply intense want for one another after that first time, but whenever it did happen, it was equally as special and amazing as the first.

I tried to ignore what Jess had said the day we'd spoken on the phone during her honeymoon, but I couldn't.

"All I'm saying is that when Grant and I finally did the deed, we couldn't keep our hands off one another. I finally understood the word lust. I couldn't get enough of him, nor did I want to be away from him. From what you've told me about you and Ben, that isn't the case. I don't want you to settle, Char. You are always saying you want the forever kind of love. You deserve that kind of love. You deserve the kind of love that reflects who you are, which is passionate and wonderful."

"I'm not settling, Jessica. I love Ben. I'm happy with him, and I see a nice future with him." I sounded like I was trying to convince myself, too.

"Is that what you want? A nice future?" The way she said it, it didn't sound at all like what I wanted. I wanted the passionate, can't-keep-your-hands-off-each-other lust she talked about. Maybe Ben and I would find that one day.

"I just want you to be happy, and I don't think, long term, he is that for you. But hey, what does an old married woman like me know anyway?" She laughed.

"He's talked about getting married. It feels like every week he brings the topic up. I keep telling him I'm not ready, I'm still young, but he says because he's older he's ready and basically just waiting on me. I don't know what to do about it."

She was quiet for a long moment.

"Jess?"

"I'm here. I'm just trying to absorb this new bit of news. Why didn't you tell me about this earlier?"

"I guess I didn't think it was that big a deal at the time since he didn't actually ask me."

"Not a big deal?"

"Well, it's a big deal now because I feel like all we do is argue about it."

"Well then, I guess the honeymoon phase is over with," she said with a chuckle.

"Speaking of, how is the honeymoon, Mrs. Foster? Where is Grant whisking you off to now?" I asked, hoping to distract her from her current topic. It worked and she sighed.

"Nice subject change, real smooth. And Grant is wonderful, Charlie, really wonderful. Married life is amazing, and the sex! Whew, girl, let me tell you. Mind. Blowing." She giggled. *"We're at the airport now, headed to Greece. Paris was exciting, but I'm ready for some relaxing sunbathing. I miss the sea air."*

"I hear you on that. I haven't been to the beach in ages."

"Have you talked to Ethan?"

"No, I haven't."

"Why not?"

"I don't know, Jess. I just haven't found the right time. Besides, every time his name comes up, Ben and I end up

in another argument. Ben thinks that Ethan has a hand in why I won't commit to marrying him."

"Interesting," she said vaguely.

"What do you *mean* interesting?"

"Oh, nothing," she said cheerfully. "I've gotta go. The pilot has the jet ready."

"Well, be safe and have fun!"

"Oh, I definitely will." I heard her giggles and the low rumbling of Grant's voice in the background.

"Give Grant a kiss for me."

"You bet I will! Love you!"

"Love you too. Bye."

She didn't know how Ben and I were. We were great together. Yes, we had our share of arguments, and we weren't burning up the sheets every second of the day, but we loved each other, and I had nothing to worry about. Right?

* * *

It was the middle of my busy season, with multiple wedding cake orders every week as well as the regular flow of café patrons. In other words, I was exhausted. It felt like I couldn't get enough sleep, no matter how early I went to bed. I'd cut my daily runs down to a couple times a week, and since walking and biking to the café took much longer than usual because of fatigue, I often found myself driving to work instead.

Cassie Gregg

I hadn't talked to Ethan since that first week we were back from Charleston, and it was starting to feel like a piece of myself was missing. I'd caught glimpses of him around the neighborhood, but we never seemed to cross paths. We used to run together in the morning, but after a couple weeks of him not showing up to run, I figured he'd changed his routine, just as I'd changed up the time and the route I'd been running at first in hope of avoiding him, until I realized I hadn't seen him out running at all since. I only caught a glimpse of him out walking Reese, but even then he seemed to be avoiding my area of the neighborhood.

I'd see the occasional woman leave his place when I ran by his street in the early mornings, but even that seemed less frequent than usual, so I assumed he was working on a new project and didn't have the time to pick up women. I was glad not to see Rebecca again and didn't know what I would have done if we'd run into one another again.

Ethan and I hadn't talked in over three months, and I felt his absence painfully, like something was missing. I missed him greatly, and my anger had turned to disappointment, which then morphed into sadness after a month of no contact, and I knew I only had myself to blame. Days turned into weeks and weeks into months. I thought it was getting easier, until something would come up that I wanted to talk to him about, but I knew that I couldn't. If I hadn't been so stubborn and had just talked to him, we could have worked it out—probably.

I'd been feeling under the weather the week before my birthday, and came down with a terrible cold that kept me in bed all week. Ben came and checked on me every day, but I was afraid I'd get him sick, too, so I limited our visits, and he didn't spend the night. Once I finally started to feel better, Ben thought a weekend away for my birthday was just what I needed to celebrate. Plus, he thought the time away would be a good chance for us to reconnect, seeing as lately we hadn't been on the same page.

I thought the lingering fatigue would be cured with a romantic getaway with no work and lazy afternoons in Ben's arms. He planned to take me to his summerhouse on Tybee Island for a long weekend. His idea of a summerhouse was a multimillion-dollar sprawling beach house set back on the Tybee River, surrounded by trees and water. He'd shown pictures to me and said it was one of his favorite properties because of the views. It looked like the perfect setting for a relaxing time together.

We'd planned to leave first thing Friday morning to beat the weekend traffic, and made reservations for a birthday dinner with Daddy after work on Thursday at one of my favorite restaurants. Ben planned to stay at my place so we could get up and go first thing, and I hoped that it would be a promising start to a great weekend.

Thursday came around, and I was tired to my bones. The morning had been an especially hectic one, and by lunchtime, I'd decided to take the rest of the day off and head home. I thought that since I'd skipped my run the previous two days, I'd go for a long one when I got home before I took a nap and got ready for dinner. I thought a little exercise would do me some good and get me out of the funk I was in.

I'd made it about two miles before my lungs started to scream. The first mile had been just what I'd needed. But around the two-mile mark, I couldn't seem to catch my breath for anything and decided to just turn around and walk home. As I rounded the corner of my street, a hazy feeling swept over me and slowed my steps further. As I approached my front gate, a wave of nausea hit me just before a loud ringing sang through my ears. I leaned over and heaved what little I had in my stomach.

When I stood straight again, the dizziness had renewed, and my vision blurred around the edges. Suddenly the traffic on the street behind me sounded distant and hollow as I reached for the porch railing. Halfway up the steps, dizziness swarmed me, causing my hand to miss the rail completely. One second I was looking at the ornate glass of my front door, and the next, the world seemed to

Promise

tilt on its axis, and I looked up at the sky. A sharp pain raced down my side, and there was a flash of agony in my head before everything went black.

Chapter 11

BEEP... BEEP... BEEP... BEEP...

The steady ring of the machine filtered through my ears. I tried to open my eyes when I heard a voice I hadn't heard in months...Ethan. What was he doing here? Where was here? And what was that incessant beeping? I tried to focus on the voices around me, but the more I tried to bring them into focus, the further away they sounded. I couldn't make out any words, but Ethan sounded agitated, and I wanted to know why. I tried again to lift my weighted eyelids, but my efforts were fruitless. The blackness crept back in, and I was pushed into complete darkness again.

I didn't know how much later it was that I felt someone holding my hand and heard muffled sounds as they talked to me. Suddenly, loud alarms sounded off and blared into my ears. The steady beep from before had ramped up to a rapid pace. The noise matched the panic inside me, and the longer I heard it, the more anxious I felt. I didn't know what was going on or why I couldn't move.

"Charlotte, can you hear me?" a strange voice called to me.

Promise

"Charlotte, if you can hear me, you're okay. You're in the hospital, and you're okay, but you have to calm down," the strange voice came again. The hospital? Why was I in the hospital? What had happened? Why wasn't anyone answering me? Why couldn't I talk or open my eyes?

"We're goin' to have to sedate her if she doesn't calm down, sir." The voice spoke again, but that time it was further away from me.

"Charlie, if you can hear me, I need you to calm down, sweetheart." Ethan! Thank God, a voice I recognized. I pushed all my focus onto his voice and tried to calm my racing heart.

"That's it, sweetheart. That's it," he crooned. I felt a hand move over mine in a calming rhythm. He was calling me sweetheart. He'd never called me that before. Why was he doing that? I wanted my questions answered, but I felt so tired. I felt myself drift back off to sleep, but instead of blackness closing in, it was just a restless sleep.

I felt my eyes peel open, striking pain through my skull as bright lights flashed into my vision before I could snap my eyes shut again. Groaning, I blinked rapidly and opened my eyes completely. Then a small, concentrated light moved over both my eyes and shot pain to the back of my head, causing me to wince. The movement caused the once-dull throb in my body to surge into sharp pains in my ribs and hip. I sucked in a sharp breath of air through gritted teeth to ease the discomfort.

"Charlotte, I'm Dr. Meadows. You're at St. Joseph's/Candler. You had an accident, but you're okay. You've sustained a bit of trauma but nothing life threatening."

Accident? What accident? I looked up at the stranger beside my bed questioningly. He was handsome for an older man, his gray hair cut short. He had warm brown eyes that sat underneath bushy, gray eyebrows. He had the calming demeanor of a lovable grandpa. "Do you remember what happened?" Dr. Meadows asked while looking down at my chart.

"I left work early because I was feeling tired, but decided to go for a run when I got home, hoping the fresh air would do me some good. I didn't run very far before I was too out of breath to continue so I turned back home. I remember rounding the corner of my street when I felt sort of funny. After that it all gets fuzzy, and then nothing until just now."

"You fell."

I knew that voice, except I didn't recognize what emotion filled it. He sounded almost haunted.

"Ethan?" I asked, looking around the room for him, which shot a searing pain into my head. "Ouch!" I winced as the pain throbbed incessantly.

Promise

"Can't you give her something now?" Ethan asked angrily as he rushed to my side.

"Now that she's awake, we can. We'll be able to better monitor her—"

"I'm awake and I can hear you. Don't speak as if I'm an invalid and can't understand you. I don't need anything. It's fine. Now, will someone please tell me what's going on?"

"Charlotte—"

"Charlie," I interrupted angrily. I heard Ethan clear his throat beside me. He knew I didn't like being called that. Only Mom called me Charlotte.

"My apologies, Charlie. You had a pretty bad fall this afternoon—"

"What time is it?" I asked, puzzled by the darkness outside my window.

"It's just past midnight. You've been unconscious since they brought you in this afternoon, about"—he checked his watch—"ten hours ago."

"Ten hours!" I exclaimed.

"Charlie, calm down. You shouldn't get too excited," Ethan interjected. I shot him a look and told the doctor to continue.

"As I was saying, Charlie, you had a bad fall this afternoon, which seems to be caused by a fainting spell. While we don't yet know what caused you to faint, we now know what made you fall. We will run some tests to determine the cause of your fainting spell. When you fell, you took quite a hit." He continued as Ethan flinched beside me. It must have been bad if Mr. Tough Guy himself flinched at the thought of it.

"You fell backwards down your front steps. Luckily, you must have been unconscious when you fell because you didn't brace yourself, you just fell loosely, which was the best thing to do. Regardless of that, you still took quite a hard impact and have a couple bruised ribs and quite a bit of bruising on your right side. Your hip and shoulder are going to be sore for a while, but nothing was broken, and there's no permanent damage. Our biggest concern was your head wound. The cut required a few stitches, and you've got a concussion, but since you've woken up and you seem to be alert and functioning normally, we're much less worried about your condition. Your CT showed a bit of swelling in your brain, which has since reduced, as evidenced by your consciousness. You'll need to be monitored for a few days, but all in all, I'd say you're a very lucky young lady."

Dr. Meadows smiled, the lines around his mouth deepening. Then he cleared his throat and began again, "Now, our biggest concern at this point would be to determine what caused you to faint. Has it ever happened to you before? How has your health been recently?"

Promise

"I had a really bad cold last week, but I've been feeling better, just lingering fatigue. I haven't eaten all day and I'm sure it was just low blood sugar."

"Charlie, you own a café. How can you go all day without eating anything!" Ethan asked, exasperated.

I shot daggers at him, and he silenced immediately. I turned back to the doctor when he looked up from his note taking. "Please continue, Dr. Meadows."

"It very well could just be from not eating, but I'll be more confident after we've run some tests. You'll need to stay here the rest of the night and, barring any complications, we'll discharge you in the morning. Your test results will take a few days, as it no longer appears to be an emergency situation. I'll give you a call when I get those results."

"Thank you," I whispered, thinking about all that had happened. I'd been here so long that I'd completely missed my dinner with Ben. *Oh God, Ben!* Where was Ben? Was he with Daddy? Where were they? I found it strange that I was in the hospital and only Ethan was there.

"Just rest up, Miss Montgomery. A nurse will be by later to check on you." Dr. Meadows smile and nodded before he exited the room and quietly closed the door behind him.

"Has anyone called Daddy? Or Ben? They must be freaking out. We were supposed to have dinner at—"

Cassie Gregg

"I'll call when we're done here," Ethan reassured me. I smiled a small smile at him in gratitude, happy to finally see him even under the circumstances. I didn't know what was wrong with me or why I had fainted, but I knew it wasn't low blood sugar because I'd had many days when I'd been too busy to eat and I'd never fainted because of it before.

"Where's my phone?" I asked Ethan as I looked around for any of my belongings.

"Umm...it didn't make it." He grimaced, holding up my shattered phone.

"Well, that's not good. Can I borrow yours? I really need to call my dad and Ben to let them know what's going on." With a look of displeasure, he grudgingly handed me his phone. I dialed my dad's number, and on the first ring, I heard the panic in his voice. The sound squeezed my heart in a vise grip.

"Ethan, thank God! Have you heard from Charlie? Ben and I can't get ahold—"

"Daddy," I interrupted.

"Christ, Charlie! Where are you, honey? Are you okay? I've been worried sick!"

"Daddy, slow down. Yes, I'm okay, and don't freak out, I'm in the hospital." Wait for it...

"You're what? Charlotte Elizabeth Grace Montgomery!" he roared into the phone so loudly even Ethan heard

Promise

him, making him shift uneasily in his seat. My father may have been the gentlest man with his daughters, but his temper was legendary. It came in handy when you were president and CEO of a Fortune 500 Company. I was lucky to have gone most of my life without incurring his wrath, but him using my full name now meant that my luck had just run out.

I sheepishly looked over at Ethan, who wouldn't make eye contact with me. "Daddy, I told you I'm okay." I paused. "I'm a little banged up, but Ethan's here with me, so there's no need to worry. You know I'm in good hands. Don't worry," I said genuinely, which made him look up and finally meet my eyes.

"Don't worry? I have been worrying up a storm about you, young lady, wondering where you are and if you're okay," he said. Quieting his voice, he added, "You're my baby girl. Telling me not to worry is like telling water not to be wet. I also have a very frantic young man here in my office that I'm sure you've aged about ten years in the last few hours from all this nonsense."

"I'm sorry, Daddy. Tell him I'm fine, and if you two want to come see me, I'm at Candler. I'll let you talk to Ethan now. I'm really tired," I said.

Without waiting for a response, I handed over the phone to Ethan, who took it from me questioningly. I pointed to my head and winced. His eyes softened imme-

149

diately with understanding, and he covered my hand with his own. I sank further into my pillow and drifted off to sleep as I listened to Ethan's deep voice talking to Daddy.

Chapter 12

WHEN I WOKE AGAIN, LIGHT had just broken across the sky, and my room was quiet. I moved my hand beside me and felt a solid object. Turning my head slowly, I continued to feel until I touched the soft hair of the man I loved.

"Ben?" I croaked. His head lifted quickly, and I took in his rumpled clothes and tired eyes.

"Charlie! Oh, thank God you're awake. Baby, I've been worried sick, but the doctor said I needed to let you rest and I shouldn't wake you." He gently ran his hands over my nonbandaged arm.

"I'm sorry. I didn't mean to scare you. I'm okay, Ben, really. Is my dad here?"

"He was, but I sent him home a while ago when it was clear you weren't going to wake up anytime soon. I told him I'd call in the morning once you were coherent again."

"You are seriously the greatest man in the whole world," I said with a smile.

"Flattery won't get you out of this one. You had me scared to death, Charlie. I couldn't find you anywhere, not at home or the café, or even Ethan's. Your father and I looked everywhere and called everyone we could."

"I'm sorry, Ben. I don't know what else you want me to say. Please don't be mad at me."

He let out a deep sigh. "I'm not mad, babe," he said. "I was just so worried. I didn't know what to do," he added somberly. "I wasn't there. I wasn't there for you when you needed me." At that he clasped my hand in both of his and kissed it over and over.

"Hey now, there will be none of that. I had an accident, but everything is fine. I'm fine. Look at me," I said urgently as I lifted his face to look me in the eyes. "I'm a little bruised here and there, but I'm still here, and I promise that I'm stronger than I look. I'm not going anywhere."

"Good." He exhaled loudly.

"Good," I reiterated, just as we had in the past. I shifted the best I could on the bed, attempting to make room.

Bewildered, Ben looked at me and asked, "What are you doing, crazy girl?"

"I'm moving over so you'll come up here with me. It's been too long since I slept in your arms, and I don't want to go another night without you," I answered honestly.

Smiling, he climbed gingerly up into the stiff hospital bed, careful not to bump into any of the bruises on my right side.

"You know I'd do anything to trade places with you right now," he whispered softly.

Promise

"I know you would, but I wouldn't want you to. I don't want you to hurt either." I smiled up at him and snuggled deeper into his arms.

By late morning that day, I was discharged with strict instructions from Dr. Meadows to take it easy and rest until my body had healed completely. The results for the different tests they'd done were going to take a few more days, but Dr. Meadows felt that it was all right to send me home and would call with the results. I was just glad to get out of there. I'd hated hospitals ever since my mom got sick.

"Glad to be getting home?" Ben asked, breaking into my train of thought as he drove me home.

I smiled over at him. "Absolutely. You have no idea how much I hate that place. Plus, I have so many things I need to check on and get done," I said absently as I made a mental checklist of all the things that I've neglected the last few days.

"All in due time, Char, but you heard what the doctor said. You need to take it easy for a bit before you go full throttle back at work."

"I know. I'll be careful. Plus, I think Louis loves his newfound authority. He's drunk with power." I giggled to myself, thinking of the hilarious text messages I'd received from Megan about what a tyrant Louis had become.

Those two bickered like an old married couple, and it always provided entertainment.

We rode in comfortable silence the rest of the way until we pulled up outside my house, where Ethan sat on my front steps waiting, and I turned to Ben. "What's he doing here?"

"I called him. Listen, I know you guys are going through a rough patch right now, and you know he's not my favorite person, but he's the one who brought you to the hospital. Apparently he found you and called an ambulance when he couldn't wake you up, and when he arrived at the hospital, he was in a fit when they wouldn't let him see you. He harassed the hospital staff the whole time you were being looked at. I think the only reason they didn't kick him out was because the wing you were in had his last name on it." He paused. "I'm not saying you have to forgive him for everything, but at least give him a minute to talk." I'd already forgiven Ethan, but I didn't tell Ben that. I'd found my forgiveness somewhere around week three of us not speaking to one another, but again, I hadn't said that to Ben. Or Ethan.

"He never told me that," I said instead.

"What's that, babe?"

"Ethan. He never told me that he did all of that, or went through that for me when I woke up the first time. He was there, and I was just so relieved to not be in the darkness anymore that I forgot to ask why he was there. Honestly, I was a little relieved to see my best friend again. He didn't say anything to me before I fell asleep again," I answered, not sure how I wanted to handle the impending encounter. We had a lot to work out.

"Just give him a few minutes. If for nothing else, do it for the years you two spent being best friends," he added and leaned over and gave me a sweet kiss on the lips before he opened his door to help me out of my seat. I stepped onto the sidewalk and looked up at Ethan, who stood waiting a few feet away.

"I'll take your bag in and give you two some privacy." I watched him disappear into the house, leaving me on the sidewalk with my best friend.

"Hey, Gray." I tentatively smiled at him.

"Hey, Lee." He smiled back. "I'm glad to see you vertical again," he laughed dryly.

"Very funny," I said, equally dry. "I guess I owe you a debt of gratitude for what you did. Ben told me, and I really appreciate it, you didn't have to especially—"

"Is that what we've come to?" he interrupted me angrily. "Platitudes and pleasantries over something that was once second nature? Hell, something that a complete stranger would do for another? This is ridiculous, Charlie," he huffed out.

"Whoa! Hold on, all I was trying to say was thank you for what you did, because you didn't have to...but I'm glad you did." I tried for humor to ease the tension that'd wedged itself between us.

"Didn't have to—" he grunted, exasperated. "Charlie, you're my best friend. You've been my best friend since I was seven years old. Why in the world would you think that I'd just leave you lying on the ground, bleeding and unconscious? Even if you weren't my friend, I'd still do something! How callous do you think I am?" he practically yelled at me, his face contorted with anger and hurt.

"Look, Ethan, I didn't mean anything by it. I was just trying to say that after everything that's happened, you didn't have to go to all that trouble for me. Especially after the way I've treated you." He looked at me again with a look that was equal parts anger and hurt. Then suddenly, without another word, he stormed off down the sidewalk in the direction of his house.

"So much for playing nice," I mumbled under my breath.

I'd made it to the top of the steps when that now-familiar feeling of dizziness washed over me. Maybe my concussion was worse than Dr. Meadows thought and I was still affected by it. Scared that I'd fall again, I took a seat on the porch landing and leaned sideways to rest my head on the large pillar. I'd clearly overestimated my abil-

Promise

ity for physical activity so soon after leaving the hospital. After about ten minutes, I heard my front gate open and clatter closed.

"Charlie?" he asked hesitantly.

"I thought you left," I retorted, exasperated.

"Yeah, I did, but just to get coffee around the corner and clear my head. What are you doing out here? Have you been out here the whole time?" He looked quizzically at me sitting in a pathetic lump.

"Just thinkin'," I offered, shrugging my shoulders. Unable to muster the strength to cover up what was going on, I added, "I'm tired. That walk's a killer," indicating the pathway from the street to my house. "I was just resting before I made the rest of my journey into the house...far, far away," I joked.

He looked intently back at me. "Charlie, what's going on? You love walking everywhere. The only time you use your car is when it rains. And for someone who runs at least five miles every day, I don't think a fifty-yard walk should tire you out."

"Yeah, well, it's more like two these days, and I think this concussion is worse than Dr. Meadows thought, because I feel like I'm tipping over every time I stand up." At that, his face turned grim.

"Why didn't you say something? I could have helped you inside. Better yet, where's Mr. Perfect to help you?"

"Stop right now, Ethan Grayson. I don't know what's gotten into you. I don't have the energy to argue with you right now, but I'll use whatever I've got left to kick your butt if you don't knock it off." I made to stand, but Ethan was there to help me before I was all the way up.

"Whoa there, Tiger. Why don't you let me help you the rest of the way?"

I shook from his grasp. "I'm fine. I can handle it without you," I spat at him like a petulant child as I slowly moved the rest of the way to the door. Ethan followed closely behind, just in case, and I was grateful for the assurance, even if I'd never tell him so.

By the time I crossed the porch to my front door, my ribs throbbed from my labored breaths and efforts to hold myself upright. My head had started to pound with a terrible headache after I stood up that made my eye twitch with every incessant beat.

Ethan looked over at me from beside the door. "Are you sure you're okay, Lee?"

"I'm fine, Ethan," I snapped a little too harshly, but I was tired of everyone asking if I was okay. Until I got the results from the doctor and had a resounding answer that I was fine, I wouldn't really know if I was.

He nodded and silently retreated down the porch. I all but sagged into the doorframe in relief of not having to hold myself up any longer. I didn't even have the energy to open the door, so I mustered what energy I had to knock on the door with my foot and waited for it to open. I heard Ben on the other side as he moved quickly toward the door. It swung open suddenly to reveal my concerned boyfriend.

"What are you—are you okay, Charlie? You don't look very good." That was it, the last straw. I'd had enough with people telling me I didn't look right and asking if I was okay.

"*I am fine!*" I yelled with the last of my energy.

"Charlie, calm down. What's gotten into you?"

"You know what, Ben? I don't know what's gotten into me, but I'm done. I can't stand one more person questioning me or asking how I am or telling me what I should and shouldn't do. If that's all you're going to do, then just leave because I don't have the energy right now to deal with it," I added angrily and marched (somewhat) into my downstairs guest bedroom and slammed the door shut.

I hobbled over to the bed and collapsed onto the comfort of its softness. I knew I didn't have the energy to make it up the long flight of stairs to my bedroom on the second floor, so the guest room would have to do for now. Forget the pain meds. I just wanted to sleep. Soon after my tantrum, I heard the front door open and click closed, and I knew that Ben had left.

What had I done? Why had I snapped at him? He hadn't done anything wrong. If anything, he'd done everything right. He'd given me space to talk to Ethan and then he'd just asked if I was all right like the concerned boyfriend he was. I was a terrible person. He'd been so worried, and I'd done nothing to make it easier on him. I was officially the worst girlfriend ever. So before I fell asleep, I texted him that I just needed a few days alone to recuperate and I'd call him soon. He replied quickly that he understood and that I should take some time, there was no rush, as he wasn't going anywhere. I told him I loved him, and he replied the same.

For some reason, even then I knew something wasn't quite right.

Chapter 13

THE NEXT DAY, AFTER A good night's sleep, I felt more myself again and really wanted to get back to work. Unfortunately, with bruised ribs and stiff muscles, I'd have to leave the heavy lifting and cooking to my staff. I'd be able to catch up on as much paperwork as possible with my limited mobility, so I decided to let Louis continue to run things as he had while I'd been in the hospital.

This being in conjunction with when I'd been sick, I'd been away longer than I ever had before or wanted to again. I knew that Louis was capable of running things, but Monty's had been my dream for so long that it was hard for me to be away from it, and I was afraid that if things didn't change, I'd have to give it up. I didn't know what I'd do if I did.

After a slow start to the morning, I walked through the doors at seven thirty, and the place was already buzzing with the morning commuters. The rich aroma of coffee and baked goods wrapped around me as I walked back to my office, welcoming me to my second home. Monty's had been a dream of mine since I was a little girl, but it was more than that. It was for my mother. It was my way of keeping a piece of her near me and sharing that little piece with the world. After years of planning and working, I'd finally made it come true.

Once I dove into the piles of papers on my desk, the day flew by, and at four p.m., I'd managed to get through all the stacks of papers and could see my desktop again. I'd placed the necessary orders for the week and signed all the checks that Louis had left for me to pay vendors and payroll. With all the covering the staff had done for me over the last couple weeks, I'd redone most of their checks to add a little bonus to all of them as thanks for their hard work.

As much as the café was my dream, I knew I didn't do it alone. I sat back and realized how tired I was, even after only doing paperwork all day, so I decided not to overdo it on my first day back and packed up my bag to head home. As I shut down my computer, I heard a knock on my office door.

"Come in!" I called.

"Hey, how was your first day back?" Louis asked. He walked into my office and stood in the middle of the small room appraising me.

I could tell he wanted to talk to me about something but didn't know how to bring it up. Knowing him all too well, I asked, "What is it, Louis?" A knowing smile played on my lips.

Promise

"Thank God! I thought you'd never ask," he exclaimed, causing me to chuckle at his predictability.

"What are your plans this weekend? Since you missed your birthday, I want to take you out for a belated birthday celebration."

Right...my birthday. I'd assumed that Ben had already cancelled the romantic getaway weekend because I'd been in the hospital and then thrown him out. Now I just didn't feel like celebrating anymore. Besides, who cared about turning twenty-six anyway? There wasn't anything exciting about it, and I'd rather spend a quiet night at home relaxing.

Ben had texted to see how things were going, but it had been a few days since then, and I hadn't heard anything from him since. My dad had called on Tuesday and rescheduled our usual birthday celebration of a pancake breakfast for that morning. I was glad that I'd gotten to see him and settle his worry that I was doing okay. It had taken some convincing, especially after I'd only been able to eat half my breakfast, but eventually he'd let it go, and we'd enjoyed a wonderful brunch at the house.

I hadn't heard anything from Ethan, which hurt more with every day that passed. We had our own birthday traditions, but I hadn't even gotten so much as a hello from him until later that day, when he texted a lame "*Happy Birthday.*" He'd avoided me even more, but I didn't blame him, or couldn't. I'd been a terrible friend to him, and after I'd iced him out after the wedding, I couldn't hold it against him for doing the same to me.

"I don't have any, Louis. I'm more than likely going to catch up on work and do some things around the house," I answered honestly.

"Fantastic! We're going out. Get all dressed up, I'm taking you for girls' night out!" The excitement in his voice warmed my mood to the idea. It did sound kind of fun. I couldn't remember the last time I'd just gone out with friends to enjoy a good time. The last time I'd let loose was four months ago at Jess's wedding. A night out with Louis would be much-needed fun.

***

This most definitely was not fun. My head pounded, and I felt lightheaded and all out of sorts. I'd say it was the alcohol, but I'd only had a few drinks. Louis was off dancing with his newest boy toy, Rico, Megan was over at the bar with her boyfriend, and the other women from our group were all out on the floor enjoying the heavy beat of the music while I sat at our table alone, trying not to fall asleep or run home to make my head stop throbbing.

After twenty more minutes of sitting alone, I decided to call it a night and called for a cab, but they said it'd be an hour wait. I just wanted to go home. Maybe the alcohol

Promise

was getting to me more than I thought, and I knew he'd come get me without question, but I hated to call. Shaking my head, I dialed anyway.

"'Ello ?" he answered groggily.

"Hey, Ethan, it's Charlie. Sorry. Did I wake you?"

"Charlie? What's going on? It's after midnight."

"Do you think you could come get me?" I asked hesitantly and waited for the inevitable no.

"Where are you?" he asked instead, all sleep cleared from his voice as alertness took its place.

"Um...some new club Louis brought me to," I slurred. Okay, so the alcohol was playing a bigger role than I thought.

"Jesus," he breathed. "You just got out of the hospital a week ago, Charlie. What are you doing going out?" He said briskly.

I heard the rustle of sheets and the distinct voice of the woman I loathed: "What's going on, baby? Why are you getting dressed?" *Rebecca.* I couldn't believe that after everything, he was with her. Of all the women in the world, he'd chosen to go back to that vile woman that broke us apart. How could he be with such a horrible person? Anger sank its devilish teeth into my mind.

"Actually, never mind, Ethan. You sound busy, and I don't want to burden you. I'll see you later," I added quickly and hung up before he had a chance to protest.

Cassie Gregg

He was now the last person I wanted to see. Forget him. How many chances did I have to give him? I knew it was on me to reach out and try to mend our friendship, but just when I tried, he plunged the knife I'd just pulled out right back in. I tried to convince myself I didn't need him.

I'd wait for the cab to pick me up, but I needed another drink to do that and wash the displeasure from my mouth and mind at Ethan's decisions. I couldn't bring myself to go back into the boisterous club to get that drink, so I walked a couple blocks and entered my favorite bar.

Forty-five minutes and three drinks later, James, the regular bartender whom I'd gotten to know over the years, walked me outside to the cab he'd called for me after I'd missed the other one, with his big tattooed arm wrapped around my shoulders for support and his scruffy, full beard tickling my forehead as I leaned against him.

I'd screened at least four calls from Ethan, and despite my efforts, my headache hadn't gone away. I was glad to be headed home. I stepped out into the night air and breathed in the crisp freshness of cooler temperatures and fragrant magnolia blossoms. It helped clear some of the haze from my clouded mind, but the lingering effects of the alcohol weighed heavily upon me. James helped me slide into the back seat and gave the driver my address from my license. As he pulled away from the curb, I sank back into the vinyl seat and drifted off to sleep.

Promise

I didn't remember falling completely asleep, but apparently I had, because I was jostled awake as my body was shifted gently into the air. Was I dreaming? When my mind cleared of sleep, the realization that I was in a cab and now being carried shocked me awake. Fear that I'd been so stupid as to fall asleep in the back of a cab and was now being carried away to God knew where had me struggling to free myself from the arms that held me in a tight grip.

"Easy," a voice whispered.

"Ethan?" I stilled and asked, confused, when my eyes focused on his strained face. "What are you doing? Put me down." I tried to fight free of his hold on me, but his grip only tightened more.

"Charlie, stop moving or I'm going to drop you," he warned. "You fell asleep in the cab. Don't you know how unbelievably dangerous that is? You know better than to do that. What were you thinking?" he admonished, but his voice held no harshness. "You're lucky I was waiting outside."

"Why were you?"

"I'd been pacing out front for the last hour, praying you'd come back. I half expected to get a call from the hospital. When I couldn't get ahold of you, I looked up recent club openings and went to the few that were on the list. I finally found the one you were in, but the bartender there said you'd left. It wasn't until a few minutes ago that I got a call from James that he'd put you in a cab and to look out for you. Swear to God, this was the longest twenty minutes of my life waiting for your cab to show up."

"I didn't mean to fall asleep. I don't actually remember going to sleep," I yawned.

"How much did you have to drink?" he asked. I thought about it, but it didn't seem right. I'd had two drinks at the club and three at the bar. I shouldn't have been as out of it as I was with only five drinks, two of which were really watered down.

"Two weak cocktails and three beers," I answered.

"Yeah, right, since when does five drinks take you down?" he huffed gruffly.

"I don't know. It just did," I said petulantly. "Will you put me down, please? You can't carry me all the way inside."

"Says who? And have you been eating? You feel like nothing in my arms, Charlie," he admonished. This time there was an edge to his voice.

"I'm eating." I yawned again. "Is there anything else you want to scold me about, *Dad*? Not that it's any of your business," I added sleepily and snuggled into his neck. He smelled distinctly of Ethan, and memories of us flooded my mind as I drifted back to sleep.

Promise

"Lee? Charlie." I woke again to gentle circles being rubbed into my back.

"What?" I asked groggily, realizing that Ethan had laid me down on my bed. He'd carried me all the way up to my bedroom without complaint.

"Where's Ben?"

"I don't know. At home, I guess," I answered, sadly thinking of Ben's hasty departure from my life last week.

"What's going on, Charlie? You're not eating. You're not running. You and Ben apparently aren't talking. What's going on with you?"

"Nothing's going on with me. I'm fine!" Calming myself, I added, "Really, I am. He didn't just leave. I asked him for some space. Had I known he'd take it so seriously, I wouldn't have said anything."

"Well, if he's stupid enough to stay away from you, he doesn't deserve to have you at all." Something in my stomach fluttered at his words. I rolled over to face him sitting on the end of my bed.

"And who does deserve me, Ethan?" I asked expectantly. He sat there still as a statue, clearly warring with himself over the answer. Then, very suddenly, he moved up the bed and leaned over me. His beautiful face lined up with mine and hovered just inches away. He looked deep into my eyes, searching.

"Me," he whispered right before he dropped his head and kissed my lips with a touch that sent my heart into overdrive. Every nerve in my body simmered with awareness as his mouth moved over mine, urging my lips open. I hungrily obliged as his tongue dove into my mouth, reaching tantalizing depths. His tongue slid along mine before pulling both back into his mouth. Our tongues danced in long slow licks, as harmoniously as if they were made to do so. Until reality crashed back in, and I pulled away, pushing him from me to get more space between us.

"What—" I tried, staring wide-eyed up at him. "Why did you do that?" I asked, breathless.

"Because I've wanted to for so long and figured now was as good a time as any," he stated nonchalantly, as only Ethan could.

My mind was spinning. Ben and I were still technically together. Rebecca had just been with him. What had I done? How could I have let him kiss me? But that kiss. What I wouldn't give to have another. I sat up and dislodged him from my body.

"You should go," I finally said.

"Lee," he started.

"No, don't call me that. Why would you do that? I love Ben, and you have Rebecca. This was all a big mistake. I've had too much to drink, and you're nostalgic for what we used to have, but don't anymore. You were my best friend, Ethan, and this was a mistake."

"Stop saying that! This was not a mistake! And what do you mean we *were* best friends? You're still mine, and you can't tell me how I feel, Charlie. It doesn't work like that. You don't just get to dictate how people feel for what suits you."

"Just stop, Ethan! I don't trust you anymore. Don't you get that? You broke my trust...and my heart."

"What are you talking about, Charlie?"

"The wedding!" I exclaimed as tears began to fall from my eyes. "Your little flavor of the week cornered me in the bathroom and threw it in my face that I was a virgin and that I'd never be able to satisfy Ben or you. Then she called me Charlotte and told me the only reason that you were my friend was because you pitied me because my mom died! She practically grinned when she said you told her everything." By then I was up and pacing as tears streamed freely down my face.

"I'm so sorry, Charlie. I didn't know. God, I didn't mean for her to do that to you. You have to believe—"

"Yeah, I know you're sorry. But you were my best friend, Ethan. You knew how I felt about that, and you knew what it meant to me. You knew how vulnerable I was to that, and you told a random girl! You told her about Mom! How could you do that?" I yelled at him.

Cassie Gregg

"She wouldn't leave me alone!" he yelled back at me. "She just kept bugging me and asking me about you and our relationship, and she wouldn't take my word that you and I were just friends. So I got angry and told her that nothing had or ever would happen between us because you were a virgin and you didn't love me like that. I don't know how she found out about your mom and your name. I swear to you, Charlie. I never told her those things. Had I known she was going to do something like that, I never would have kept her around. I would have been more careful. And stop saying we're best friends in the past tense. You *are* my best friend, Charlie. You always will be."

"You should have been more careful to begin with, Ethan. I trusted you. I trusted you with my heart and that, as my best friend, you'd protect me. You spent six years out there protecting the damn world, but when it mattered the most, you failed to protect me. Instead you fed me right to the wolves." I shook my head. "I can't, Ethan. I can't do this with you anymore. Get out."

"Charlie—"

"Just get out, Ethan," I said in such a defeated tone that he didn't bother to fight anymore. He got up off the bed and walked to the door. He paused at the threshold, his hand on the doorknob, and spared one last painful glance my way before he walked out the door.

Promise

Of all the times I'd dreamed of kissing Ethan, never could I have imagined it would end like this. Never could I have imagined we'd ever end.

Chapter 14

ON MONDAY, DR. MEADOWS CALLED and left a message about wanting me to come to his office. I figured it was for my results, but I felt good, better than I had in weeks, minus the emotional turmoil I had rolling around inside me. My injuries had healed nicely, and the scar on my head faded a little more every day, so I decided to postpone another visit to the hospital. For one, I hated them, and secondly, I was so busy catching up at work, I didn't really have the time to make an appointment and miss another day. I'd resolved to call if things changed and I didn't feel good again.

By Thursday, he was calling me every day, and I had no choice but to call him back and set up an appointment. I told Louis I'd be out half a day Friday and planned to come in after my appointment.

Friday morning, I made my way up to Dr. Meadows's office and felt an eerie chill pass over me. It left me feeling like I was running out of time. I couldn't seem to shake it for the duration of my journey down the hallway to his office. God, I hated hospitals. I arrived at his door right on

Promise

time and took a moment to settle myself before I knocked on the solid wood door.

"Come in," he called from the other side. I opened the door, and instantly I knew something was wrong. There were two other doctors standing in his office, poised calmly on either side of his desk.

"Charlie," he greeted me warmly. "I'm glad you made it. Please come in and have a seat. This is Dr. Allan Sharp, and over there is Dr. Bennett Williams."

"Hello," I offered softly in greeting. Both doctors smiled politely back, but I could tell there was sympathy in their eyes.

"Well, there's no way that we can make this easier for you, Charlie, but we want you to understand we are going to do everything we can to help you." He paused, waiting for me to acknowledge what he'd said. I nodded, wanting him to explain further. "Your tests came back, and there are some concerns. I've brought both Dr. Sharp and Dr. Williams in to look over your test results as well. We've found some abnormalities in your blood test that indicate that you have leukemia."

Wait. Did he just say leukemia?

"I know this is a lot to process right now, and I'm sure you have a lot of questions. We're here to answer them for you."

Cassie Gregg

Nothing. My entire mind went blank. Cancer. I had cancer. Oh God, no! My dad, what was he going to do? And Maddie? They couldn't go through this again. I couldn't put them through it again, especially if it ended like my mother. Suddenly, a peace settled over me. I'd get to see her again. We could bake and sing together. It had been so long since the last time we'd done that together. I swore I could hear her singing to me, soothing my worry and fear. If I just closed my eyes...

"Charlie? Charlie, can you hear me?" My eyes fluttered open, and I saw Dr. Meadows's brows pulled down in concern.

"Are you all right, Charlie? How are you feeling?" Dr. Meadows asked as Dr. Sharp moved around the desk and took my vitals.

"I feel fine. I was just...processing." I paused, realizing what I was about to say. "I'm fine. I just haven't had the chance to eat today. I should go have lunch or maybe just a snack." I cut myself off, realizing that I'd just rambled. I smiled up at him. "I guess it just runs in the family then," I added.

"What does, Charlie?" Dr. Sharp asked.

"Dying young," I whispered. "My mom passed away when I was young, breast cancer," I added.

"I'm sorry to hear that, Charlie. We're not saying that you're going to die, but we need you to take this seriously."

Promise

"Of course, I know that," I answered distractedly, looking out the large window. The outside world continued to move along, but I felt like mine was standing still.

"While you seem to be handling this rather well, Miss Montgomery, is there someone we can call for you? Family? A friend?"

"No," I stated adamantly. "I don't want them involved in this at all. I'm fine. I can do this on my own. I went through this when my mom was diagnosed, and I know what to expect. I just need to know what your plan is." Seeing that I was serious about not asking anyone for help, Dr. Sharp, an oncologist, continued.

"Right, well, you'll need a bone-marrow biopsy as soon as possible, so that we can determine the type and progression of the leukemia. We can schedule you first thing Monday morning. That will give you the weekend to get things settled before the procedure. From there, we'll be able to determine the best course of treatment. Do you have any questions?"

Monday. Monday was the beginning of the end. It was the day all the needles and hospital stays and sicknesses began.

"Monday is fine. Will I be able to work?" I asked hopefully.

"Not on Monday and probably not Tuesday. My recommendation would be to return to moderate work

Cassie Gregg

Thursday at the earliest, but you should really take it easy while you recuperate. As for during treatment, I don't recommend it; however, that will be up to you." I had to be prepared to take a lot of time away from the café. I needed to remember to talk with Louis and Megan. I knew that once chemo started, I'd be gone even more.

"Fine, make the appointment, and I'll see you Monday." I got up to leave and felt a wave of dizziness flash into my head. I shook my head to bring the door into focus and stood upright when it passed. I left the office quickly so as not to give anything away. They'd warned me about possible symptoms to look out for, and if they were recurring and prominent, I was to come back to the hospital immediately. I couldn't afford to do that just yet. I had too many things to get in order first. I also couldn't let them see the tears that threatened to fall.

I made it through my front door before I felt hot tears stream down my face. I collapsed to the floor, sobbing at the realization of my situation. I had cancer. That ugly word I'd learned all those years ago had come to take over my life again. I was twenty-six years old, and I had cancer. I'd never backpacked through Europe or gotten married or had children. I wondered if this was it for me.

Chapter 15

ALL WEEKEND I'D PREPARED FOR my upcoming biopsy, and by Saturday, all of my injuries from the fall had healed. I'd found a bit more energy in my day-to-day activities. Having seen the many procedures my mother had gone through, I knew I'd be in pain for a day or two, so I stocked up on food, movies, and paperwork from the café that needed to be done. I also set up a car service that would pick me up from my appointment and told Louis I'd be out of town for a few days. He seemed suspicious that I was going to be gone again, but he thankfully let the issue go.

Monday came around, and I felt as prepared as I could be. After taking a cab to the hospital, I checked in at the surgical reception desk and sat in the waiting room with old vinyl chairs and old magazines scattered around the room. It would be a fairly quick procedure, but my whole life depended on it. God, I wished Ben was here. But even more, I wished Ethan was here. He'd hold my hand and tell me a happy memory that would take my mind off what was happening, but that wouldn't happen. He could never know; no one could know. It would be too hard for them to go through this again. I didn't want to be the one to hurt all of them.

And Ben hadn't signed up for anything like this. He had such a vibrant life ahead of him. He didn't need the hassle of dealing with a ticking clock. He wanted marriage, kids...forever, and now, more than ever, I couldn't promise that.

I knew I'd have to face everyone eventually. If the worst happened, I'd have to have arrangements made for Monty's, my house, and every other aspect of my life. Plus, everyone would start to notice if I was too frail to move or get out of bed. And there was the possibility that I'd end up in the hospital because my immune system crashed. Given all of that, it just seemed better if everyone in my life didn't know.

A nurse in pale-pink scrubs and a bright smile that was set to comfort any patient called me back into a procedure room. She did her preop checks, gave me a gown to change into, and left me alone. I sat in the cold, sterile room and waited for the doctor to come in and begin the biopsy. The longer I waited for the doctor, the more my leg bounced up and down. After what felt like an eternity but was really only ten minutes, Dr. Williams came into the room.

"Are you ready to begin, Miss Montgomery?"

"Yes," I answered as strongly as I could manage.

Promise

"Lie down on your side and hug your knees to your chest. I'm going to give you the first injection. That will numb the area, and the next needle will be the one extracting the bone marrow from your pelvis. The needle will go in through the back of your hip and retrieve the marrow from there. I'm not going to lie to you: this is going to be painful, even with the numbing agent, but I assure you, Miss Montgomery, that I will do my best to try and make you as comfortable as I can. After the biopsy, you're welcome to rest here for a while, and when you feel that you are ready, we'll escort you out. Do you have a ride arranged? You won't be able to drive afterwards," he asked.

"Yes, I have a car that'll be waiting for me when I'm done."

"Very well, Ms. Montgomery. I'm going to begin now," he warned gently as he placed a calming hand on my shoulder.

Two hours later, after the procedure ended and then the numbing agent lessened and the excruciating pain reduced to a dull throb, they discharged and wheeled me down to the lobby. Outside, a large, black-tinted SUV sat in the drop-off circle, where a man stood waiting outside the passenger door, holding a sign with my name on it. The orderly wheeled me up to him, and he smiled politely down at me. "Miss Montgomery?" he checked.

"That's me, but you can call me Charlie." I threw him a half smile as I shifted to get out of the wheelchair. The movement sent shocks of pain though my hip, leg, and back, causing me to wince and suck in a large breath. The driver saw my struggle and didn't hesitate as he moved to my side in just one step, his solid arm wrapped around me as the other reached for the door handle. Very deftly, he opened the back passenger door and gently lifted me into the seat.

"Wow! First-class service, thank you." He was very fit for a man his age, and his strength surprised me.

"Of course, Miss Charlie. My name is Joe Fletcher. Is there anything else you need?" he asked through a healthy dose of Deep South accent.

"Thank you, Mr. Fletcher, just home please," I answered genuinely. I smiled at the fact that he'd called me Miss Charlie.

"No need for the mister. Just Joe is fine." He smiled in return.

"I'm sorry if you had to wait long, Joe. I didn't realize the timeframe would be so much longer," I offered apologetically.

"No need to apologize, Miss Charlie. I didn't mind 'tall." He smiled.

There was something about him that I liked instantly. Where others would have felt intimidated by his size, I felt instantly safe and knew that I could trust him from the moment he stepped to my side to help me into the car. I leaned back and relaxed into the plush leather seat as best I could, trying to keep the weight off of my hip. I took deep breaths after every bump and hole we hit along the way, counting the minutes until I could get off my feet and into bed.

When we pulled in front of my house, I had a light sheen of sweat on my forehead. Joe put the car in park and came around to help me out as the car idled in the no-parking zone in front of my house. He opened the door and must have noticed my pained expression, because his eyes filled with concern, but he said nothing about it. After my feet were safely on the pavement, Joe looked up at the house questioningly, as if he expected someone to come out and help me inside.

"There's no one else here. I live alone." I smirked as Joe let out a quiet breath. If I had to guess, it was a sigh of worry and frustration.

"Well if it's all the same to you, Miss Charlie, I'd like to escort you up to your door. Just to make sure and all." I smiled at the sincerity in his voice and accepted his offer. He was a true Southern gentleman, with manners to boot. I looked up at him and scrutinized him more fully. The man looked like a rugged bodyguard, but underneath the hard exterior, I saw that he was really a good, kind man.

There was a softness to him that was both contradictory and comforting.

We got about halfway down the walkway before I had to take a break from the pressure on my hip. After patiently waiting a few minutes, we continued on, but Joe was carrying more of my weight than I was by the time we reached the tall porch steps. When we finally arrived at my door, I sighed in relief. "Thank you, Joe. I really don't know how to thank you for this."

"It was my pleasure, Miss Charlie." He waved me off.

I turned to him after I unlocked the door. "You know the café down on Bull Street?" I asked, knowing that if he lived in the area, he probably did. Almost all the locals knew about Montgomery's.

"Sure do. Monty's has the best coffee and muffins I ever had!" he cheered happily.

"Well, I'm glad you think so. Next time you're in there, it's on the house. Just give them your name, and I'll be sure to make a note of it with the staff. Matter of fact, from now on, everything's on the house," I said with a light smile, as the pain in my hip kept mounting with every minute I stood on it.

"Oh no, I couldn't possibly accept that, Miss Charlie. It's too much."

"Nonsense, I live to feed good people. And I can tell already you're good people, Joe."

Promise

"Well, Miss Charlie, that's awfully kind of you." He paused and pulled a card from his breast pocket. "In case you are ever in need of a ride again, just call me, and I'll be there."

"Thank you, Joe, I'll be sure to do that. Have a good day."

"You too, Miss Charlie, and feel better," he offered before he descended the stairs.

I waved and closed the door tightly behind him, sinking to the floor. I didn't know how long I sat propped up against the door, but by the time I'd mustered the strength to move, the sun had set, and I felt utterly exhausted. I texted Ben to tell him I loved him and that I'd like to see him over the weekend. We hadn't spoken in a long time, but I knew I had to tell him about Ethan kissing me, and we needed to work some things out.

I set my phone down on the kitchen island and slowly walked up to my bedroom, and as soon as I lay down, I drifted off into a dreamless sleep.

Chapter 16

A LOUD BANGING SOUND WOKE me, but I didn't know where it came from. I reached for my phone, but it wasn't next to me. I remember that I'd left it charging on the kitchen counter that morning. I looked over at my bedside clock and read two o'clock. I'd slept the day away, but I felt much better than before. My head no longer throbbed, but my hip still smarted if I moved too quickly, and when I looked down at it, I saw an ugly bruise starting to bloom from where the needle had been injected, expanding over the side of my hip.

I slowly made my way into the kitchen and grabbed a bottle of ibuprofen from the cabinet. Just as I swallowed down the pills, the banging began again in earnest, and I realized it was coming from my front door. I didn't know who it could be. Most people I knew had a key to my place, so I assumed it was an unknown visitor. I quickened my steps to get to my front door and pain shot through my hip at the exertion and faltered my progress. I threw the deadbolt and pulled the door open, angry at both the intrusion and the pain in my hip.

"What!" I yelled, and was suddenly pulled forward and engulfed in strong, familiar arms.

"Thank God! Where have you been?" Ben exclaimed. "I've called you at least a dozen times, and I've been knocking on your door for the last twenty minutes. Have you been here the whole time?" All these questions and I was still confused as to why he was here.

He must've read the confusion on my face because he set me away from him and added, "I got your text Monday, but I couldn't wait until this weekend to see you. But when you didn't answer yesterday, I went to the café, and Louis said that he hadn't seen or heard from you since Sunday and he was worried about you too. So I got more worried and thought maybe you'd had another accident. So I came over here to check on you, and you didn't answer again. I even went over and asked Ethan if he'd talked to you. When he said he hadn't, I got really worried."

"Wait, what day is it?" I asked, confused.

"It's Tuesday," he said slowly. "Are you sure you're okay, Char? You look a little pale. Why don't you sit down, and I'll make us some lunch?" Food did sound really good, so I opened the door wider to let him pass. Just as we walked into the kitchen, my phone rang and "Dr. Meadows" flashed on the caller ID. I snatched it up before Ben could see.

"Glad to see it still works," he mumbled. I looked over at him questioningly, but he kept moving toward the pantry.

"Hello?" I answered.

"Hello, Charlie, it's Dr. Meadows."

"Hi, how are you doing?"

"Just fine, Charlie, but shouldn't I be asking you that?" he laughed.

"I'm doing well, thank you."

"Glad to hear it. I wanted to call and set up an appointment for you to come in. We have your results from the biopsy, and I'd really like to meet with you as soon as possible. Can you come in this afternoon?" No. I finally had Ben back, and I didn't want to lose him just yet.

"I can't today, how about tomorrow?" I offered.

"That will work, Charlie, as long as you're going to take this seriously. This isn't something to be put off. We really need to discuss these results and a treatment plan," he warned.

"I know. I understand. Are you available tomorrow afternoon? I'm free at four."

"Yes, that will be fine. I will see you then." *It couldn't wait.* That wasn't a good sign. Right then, Ben appeared in front of me with two plates of food, but my appetite had suddenly vanished. Not wanting to alarm Ben, I smiled and joined him at the kitchen table.

Promise

That night, I lay awake and listened as Ben breathed evenly beside me. Having him next to me distracted me from the trepidation growing inside me. I hadn't told him about Ethan, because I knew if I had, he wouldn't have stayed the night. I didn't know if it was having him that settled me or if it was just having another person beside me that mattered. I was happy to have him back, but a newfound nervousness had settled inside me about him finding out I was sick. I also felt a pit in my stomach that I knew had to do with Ethan. That kiss had meant something, no matter what I'd tried to convince him and myself of. That kiss both wound me up and settled me down. It changed me. No matter how hard I tried to deny it, it had. I looked over at Ben's beautiful, relaxed face and resolved right then that I couldn't keep him. He deserved better, especially now.

I woke up to strong arms wrapped around me, warmth at my back. It felt just like old times, but somehow different. I wasn't sure if I cherished it more knowing that I'd have to let him go or if I was relieved it would be ending soon so that I didn't have to keep secrets from him anymore. I turned over slowly to look at his face in the morning light and just absorb his features. He was just so handsome I could've stared at him all day, but he began to stir and pulled me closer into him.

Cassie Gregg

"G'morning, beautiful." I smiled at my favorite endearment of his.

"Morning, handsome. How'd you sleep?"

"Better than I have in weeks."

"Me too," I lied. My dreams had been haunted most of the night by Ethan and Ben and my mother, but it was just another thing I kept to myself.

"Don't give me so much space next time," I joked as I poked his stomach. He squirmed and dug his fingers into my ribs, causing me to laugh and wiggle as he tickled relentlessly. I winced when his elbow hit my biopsy hip and he stilled instantly.

"Damn, Charlie, have you been eating? You feel like you've lost weight," he said gently as he felt my ribs. Before I could stop him, he pulled his shirt I was wearing up and saw the garish bruising on my hip from the biopsy.

"Jesus, Charlie!" he yelled as I yanked at the shirt to cover myself back up.

"It's nothing, I'm fine," I tried.

"That is not nothing. What the hell is that from?" he asked as he sat up and tried to get another look at it.

"I said it was nothing, Ben. It's just an old bruise from when I fell. It's fine, really. I'm fine." I got up to get dressed and examined my body more closely for the first time in weeks.

Promise

I hadn't realized how much weight I'd lost, and the dark circles under my eyes would have to be covered with a little bit more makeup. The bruise from the biopsy was an angry black-and-blue splotch the size of a softball surrounded by a purple-and-green maze of bruising that covered nearly my entire hip. I could see other bruises on my back and arms from where I'd bumped into things and broken blood vessels. It would have been better to keep them covered, but he'd already seen my hip, and it seemed silly to try and hide now.

I was thankful he hadn't seen them last night when we were making love. There were a couple times I'd thought I was going to scream out from the pain of him gripping my hip, but I'd pushed it aside and focused on the pleasure.

Thankfully, the weather had started to cool, so I could get away with layering and thick clothing. When I finished getting dressed, I turned to find Ben still sitting on the side of my bed, looking down at his hands. I walked up to him and took his head between my hands and swallowed as I prepared myself for the lie I was about to tell.

"Everything is fine, Ben. I promise you I'm okay. Please don't worry about this. I'm sure it'll go away in a few weeks. It hardly hurts at all." The lie tasted like vinegar in my mouth, but I knew it was the best thing for him.

After breakfast, Ben left for work, and I spent a few hours straightening up and cleaning the house. My dad still found it shocking that I preferred to clean the house myself instead of hiring staff to do it. I told him that I'd had enough of it growing up and I enjoyed the peacefulness of cleaning. By lunchtime, I'd exhausted myself again and decided to take a short nap before my appointment with Dr. Meadows.

At three o'clock, I was out the door and on my way to the hospital for my diagnosis appointment. Knowing that parking was tight at the hospital, I decided to leave the Tahoe out front and pulled my baby from the garage. It was a beautiful, sleek all-black Audi R8 that I'd bought last year as a one-year opening-the-café anniversary gift to myself, and I loved driving it.

It was decided that Dr. Meadows would remain my primary doctor, but Dr. Sharp would take over as my oncologist, and Dr. Williams would be the surgeon should I have a need for any more procedures. When I arrived for my appointment, I could tell by the looks on my doctors' faces that the news they had wasn't very good.

"Hi, everyone," I greeted.

"Hello, Charlie." Dr. Meadows spoke up for the group, as he usually did.

"How are you feeling today?" Dr. Sharp asked, like every other time we'd talked on the phone. One of those times I should have told him the truth about my symptoms.

Promise

"I'm doing good today," I said instead. It wasn't a complete lie, but it was one heck of an omission.

Dr. Sharp cleared his throat. "Charlie, we need to discuss your course of treatment. Your test results show that you have AML, acute myeloid leukemia. While leukemia doesn't have a stage one through four like other tumorous cancers, it does have subtypes, and your biopsy confirmed which subgroup of AML you have. This type of cancer progresses quickly, regardless of the subtype, and your diagnosis is called M0, which is undifferentiated acute myeloid leukemia. It's treatable, but we must be very aggressive, as it seems that we aren't catching this as early as we would have liked to."

"What do you mean?" I asked. Okay, now I was worried.

"What I mean, Charlie, is that your cancer has developed further than we had hoped in an already destructive condition. We will need to start an aggressive course of treatment immediately if we have any hope of slowing it down and putting it into remission. AML is common and treatable, but it becomes more aggressive the longer it is allowed to go untreated. There is also a risk that it will spread to your liver or spleen. Then it will get much tougher to treat."

"And what does that mean?" I squeaked again.

Cassie Gregg

"I know that these are a lot of big words, and this is a life-changing conversation that we are having, but I want to assure you that we are going to do everything in our power to help you fight this. We'll start you immediately on oral antivirals to boost your immune system. By next week, we'd like to start you on a chemotherapy program."

Two weeks? That was all I'd have left of my old life? Two weeks? It all seemed so surreal.

I left the doctor's office with antivirals and a date to start chemo. I felt like it was all moving so fast and I couldn't catch up. I wished I could call Ethan but knew I ultimately wouldn't. I would, however, try to reconnect with him, because with everything that was going on, I knew that what limited time I had left I wanted to spend with my best friend.

I drove from the hospital on autopilot and didn't really come out of it until I pulled into my garage. I got out and just started to walk, needing the fresh air and space to think. I kept walking until I'd reached my favorite part of Forsyth Park, the tree-lined sidewalk that led to a beautiful fountain that sparkled in the shining sun. I sat down on a bench and watched the water cascade and splash in a hypnotic cycle. I watched families around me enjoying the beautiful weather, couples waking arm in arm enjoying the landscape. Everything looked picture perfect all around me, but it felt like I was falling apart.

Promise

I thought about what I'd do with the café, knowing that I'd have many long absences when I started chemo. I'd have to figure out a reason to give the staff for why I'd be gone so much. They were so used to me being there around the clock that it would have to be a good enough reason to convince them why I was suddenly spending so much time away from them. I would be out for at least one week every month, and maybe more, depending on how I handled the side effects after the first few treatments.

After long consideration and warring with myself about lying to everyone I loved, I decided I'd tell Louis I was helping a sick aunt in Atlanta, and I'd tell the family I was helping a sick friend if they asked, but I didn't know what I'd do about Ethan. He'd be able to tell if I was home, especially since he usually walked Reese past my house on his way to the park, so I'd have to be careful.

Then there was Ben. I could lie to him that I was out of town, but in my heart I knew that I shouldn't drag out the inevitable any longer and hurt him more. He'd be my first call, and I'd invite him over to handle it as soon as possible. Like a Band-Aid, the sooner I ripped it off, the sooner it would feel better. But who was I kidding? A broken heart was a broken heart, and it would hurt no matter what.

* * *

Cassie Gregg

The next night I sat across from Ben and tried to get my thoughts in order as I picked at my dinner. Even though I'd convinced myself I needed to break things off with him, I couldn't bring myself to say the words to him out loud. The way he looked at me had me second-guessing if I wanted to end it. He made me want to be selfish with him.

"Stop looking at me like that," I admonished.

"Like what? How am I looking at you?" he retorted.

"Like I just hung the moon," I quipped.

"Maybe because you're the most beautiful girl I've ever known, and every time I look at you, you take my breath away."

At that, I crossed the table and sat in his lap in the blink of an eye. Ben stood effortlessly and walked to my room, all the while never letting my feet touch the ground. He sat me on the edge of my bed and leaned down and captured my lips in a hungry kiss. We stripped each other of our clothes, and then he was inside me.

Both of us were caught in a hungry urge for one another. We found our rhythm together, and I climbed higher and higher. I wanted to savor this moment with him, knowing that it was probably my last, but our urgency pushed all notions of slow from our minds. All my worries melted away as Ben and I reached bliss together.

Promise

A while later, I rolled over slowly and stretched the sleep from my muscles. Ben was on his back as he looked out the window, his face illuminated by the moonlight.

"A penny for your thoughts," I interrupted the silence.

"Just thinking is all," he replied, pulling me closer to his side.

"You looked like you were thinking pretty hard. Want to tell me what it was?"

"Want to tell me what's going on with you?" he answered coolly. The hostility came out of nowhere, but I shouldn't have been so naïve as to think that he wouldn't notice I'd changed.

"I don't know what you're talking about. Nothing is going on with me," I lied.

"Right. You're just so stressed out that you've lost, what, twenty pounds? Twenty pounds you didn't have to lose in the first place. You're so tired you can't make it up the stairs without getting winded, and you don't run anymore," he accused.

He had been paying attention. I guessed the idyllic love bubble was about to burst. "I don't know what you're talking about, Ben. I'm fine," I tried again.

Even though it was a blatant lie, I couldn't bring myself to tell him the truth. He was giving me the chance to come clean and I couldn't do it. I knew he'd choose to stay with me, and I couldn't put him through what was to come for me. In a huff, he stood from the bed and pulled his clothes on haphazardly.

"What are you doing?" I reached for him, but he snapped his hand away. "Ben? What's going on?"

"I'm leaving. I can't take you lying to me anymore. I don't know what it is you think you can't tell me, but I'm done waiting for you to trust me," he said angrily, shoving his foot into his shoe. "I damn near asked you to marry me, Charlie, and you've been avoiding the topic ever since. You've gotten secretive. and you're lying to my face. I don't even know who you are anymore."

"Don't say that, Ben. You know exactly who I am. I told you that I wasn't ready to give you an answer."

"And when will you be ready, Charlie? Will you ever be? Is it the idea of marriage that scares you so much, or the idea of marrying me?" he spat angrily.

"I'm not scared of marriage, Ben. That's not what this is about."

"And what is it about? Because I sure as hell don't know anymore."

I was silent, unsure of how to tell him the truth.

"I don't know. Maybe we just need some time to think about things. I don't know," I answered lamely.

"I don't know either, Charlie. I don't know what to do about you anymore. I'm twenty-nine years old and ready to start a family. I was ready to marry you, but I can see

Promise

now that it was wrong of me to try and make you ready too."

"Ben—" I started, but I was interrupted as he retreated downstairs to the main level, where he threw on his coat angrily.

"Save it. I'm sick of your excuses, and I don't want them anymore. I'm done."

With that, he grabbed his keys and walked out the door and slammed it shut with a loud thud. I stood silently in the foyer, then fell to my knees, and let loose uncontrollable sobs that wracked my body. Everything seemed to hit me all at once, and I curled into a ball there on the floor and wept. I cried for the future I'd lost, the uncertainty of my life, the unfairness of my disease, and I wept for the man I loved. I wept for the love we'd had, the love we'd lost, and the love we'd never have again.

Chapter 17

SOMETIME LATER, A HAND RUBBED up and down my back, and I woke completely to find I'd moved onto the couch, my head in someone's lap and my favorite blanket wrapped around me.

"It's over," was all I managed before tears flowed down my cheeks again. I couldn't put into words all that I felt was over, but I let him assume that they just meant Ben's and my relationship.

"Shhh," was the only thing Ethan murmured as he continued to rub my back.

"You came back," I whispered into the dark. His hand stopped its rhythmic pattern and came up and tucked the hair away from my wet face.

"I never left," he said, and for the first time in months, I felt whole again as I drifted off to sleep in Ethan's soothing embrace.

The next morning, I woke up in my bed with Ethan sprawled on a makeshift bed on the floor next to me. I quietly climbed out on the opposite side of the bed so I didn't wake him up and made my way into the kitchen to start a pot of coffee. I looked through the fridge and saw I had the makings for pancakes and got to work mixing the batter. My heart was heavy with the sadness of having lost Ben, but I told myself over and over that it was inevitable we'd break up. I just didn't know it would hurt this bad. While I poured the coffee into two mugs, Ethan came into the kitchen looking rumpled and sleepy and strangely breathtaking.

"Mornin'," he yawned.

"Morning, sleepyhead. Sleep okay?" I smiled, but I knew he'd be sore today from sleeping on the floor.

"Yeah, I slept okay," he answered, rubbing out a kink in his neck.

"You know you could have just slept in the bed or one of the guest rooms."

"I was trying to be respectful. And you kept having nightmares or something, so I wanted to be close by in case you needed something." I hadn't realized that I'd had nightmares. All I remembered was crying and crying some more.

"I'm sorry you had to deal with all that."

"It was nothing. I'm glad I was there. You needed me." He smiled, like it was that simple.

"I guess you're right."

We ate in comfortable silence before Ethan's assistant called with a problem. I packed up a few of the extra muffins I'd made for him to bring to Ethan's assistant, Perry and Dan.

"Are you going to be okay here by yourself?"

"I'm going to be fine, Ethan. I think I got it all out of my system last night. Besides, I have a lot of work to catch up on, so I'll be busy and at the café most of the day anyway."

"All right. Well, call if you need anything, okay?"

"Okay. Have a good day and be safe," I added, unsure if he'd be going to an active build site or not.

"I always am." He smiled and winked at me as he walked out the door.

***

I'd finally gotten Ethan back, and it was a slow readmittance into my life that started when he'd come over for coffee in the morning a couple times a week. Then he'd stopped in the café for lunch a few times, and then he was over for dinner almost every night two weeks after Ben left. We'd gone back to our normal selves, for the most part. I didn't run with him anymore, and I caught him staring at me intently sometimes. We had an unspoken understanding that we didn't talk about the night that Ben left, but each passing day it got easier to ignore the sadness of losing him.

Before I knew it, the week of my first chemo appointment arrived, and an overwhelming feeling of a

Promise

winding-down clock consumed me. I thought about postponing my treatments for a week or so. I knew the doctors had said I needed to start fighting this immediately and aggressively, but I wasn't ready to give up my life or accept that there were things that I'd always dreamed of that I'd never have.

I'd always wanted to have a family with my forever love. Chemo would make that next to impossible. My life would effectively be put on hold for the next few years, or for however long this battle took me, and there would always be the fear that it could come back at any time. It just all felt like too much, too soon.

Plus, Ethan and I had taken up some of our old routines, and it was like the knot I'd had in my stomach for months had suddenly untangled. We had a movie-marathon weekend, takeout Tuesday, and we met for lunch on Friday at our favorite bar. The last week had been perfect. I didn't think it was too much to ask for a few more perfect weeks. I canceled my appointment with Dr. Sharp and figured I'd start the following week, after Halloween. Ethan and I'd be able to pick pumpkins and have one last good weekend. A knock at the door pulled me from my daydreaming.

"Coming in!" he warned as he walked into my house. I was glad he'd gotten used to using his key again.

"Hey! I'm in the kitchen, looking for the menus!" I called out.

"Top drawer, left of the stove!" he called back. I pulled open the directed drawer and found the stash of takeout menus.

"Got 'em! Thank you!" I heard the low rumble of his laughter from the living room. He always laughed at me when I misplaced things. I was afraid my time with Ethan was coming to a close like it had with Ben, and after the weekend I'd have to start avoiding him again. He'd eventually be able to tell that something was wrong, just like Ben had. I'd be able to hide it at first, but not for long, and I knew that he couldn't find out.

My family had been through enough, and I couldn't put them through such pain again. I also knew that losing Ethan would cause more pain than the disease ever could. Besides, Maddie's baby was due soon, and I hoped that everyone would be too preoccupied with the new family member to notice too much about me.

I'd never called Dr. Sharp back to reschedule my appointment, and two weeks had passed since I had been supposed to start. I avoided his calls regularly, but I enjoyed living in the fantasy world where cancer didn't exist in my life. It wasn't that I didn't want to get better; I did. It was more that I didn't want things to change more than they already had. I'd gotten back to my old routine of

Promise

being at the café every day, and Louis and Megan were as glad to have me back as I was to be there.

Ethan and I were better than ever, and while I felt lethargic at times, I hadn't experienced any more nosebleeds or dizzy spells. I wasn't deluded enough to believe that the cancer would just go away because I didn't want to deal with it. I knew I needed to start treatment, but if I was honest with myself, I was putting it off because I was scared out of my mind.

It was Saturday afternoon, and I'd been busy at the café all morning, but the afternoon had slowed down. After I finished all the necessary paperwork for the week, I closed up early and gave everyone the afternoon off. Just before dinnertime, I realized I hadn't heard from Ethan all day and decided to call him and invite him over for dinner and a movie.

My call went to voicemail, so I asked him to call me when he got my message. By seven I still hadn't heard anything from Ethan, so I went ahead and started making dinner. I'd just finished making the spaghetti sauce when there was a knock on my door. Moving quickly, I looked through the clear glass window beside the door and saw Dan standing there, looking disheveled with his head hung low.

I pulled the door open wide. "Dan, what are you doing here?" My heart dropped into my stomach as I took in his appearance and the absence of Ethan. He had a busted lip and a bruise bloomed on his jaw. "Are you okay? What happened to you? Where's Ethan? Is he okay?" My voice rose with every question.

"Whoa, there, Charlie, slow down. I'm okay, and so is Ethan. I just brought him over to his place, but I wanted to see if you'd check in on 'im. Deb is worried and wants me home, but I didn't want to leave Ethan alone. He got banged up rather good tonight. I got into some hot water with a mouthy foreman, and Ethan stepped in as usual to play hero. The guy put up a real good fight. I'm fairly certain he's got a mild concussion and some cuts and bruises. Ethan refused to go to the hospital, but I'm sure he'll be fine in a few days. I ordered him to take a few days off to rest up, but we both know he's too stubborn to listen to me, so maybe you can talk some sense into him. I know you've taken care of him before, but I didn't want to assume."

"Of course! I'll head over there right now. I've cleaned him up after a fight before, I just haven't done it since before he left for basic." I trailed off, thinking of all the times Ethan had gotten into a tussle with someone.

He was usually levelheaded and calm, but when he saw that someone needed defending, he was the one to step in, with no regard for himself. When he really lost his temper were the times that some guy said something asinine about me or to me, and he'd go at it full steam ahead. I'd scold him while I patched him up and tell him to ignore their comments because they didn't bother me, and he'd argue with me about it. It would ultimately end when he'd promise not to fight for my honor anymore, but when I'd ask him to pinky swear on it, he never would. I knew it was because he knew he'd break it.

After the dust settled, we'd put in a movie and pop some popcorn and hang out until we both fell asleep on the floor in front of the TV. The times that he was noticeably banged up in high school, we'd stay in the fort for the night, because his parents despised that he got into fights. Sometimes he'd stay up there for a few days, until he'd healed enough to go back home to face his parents.

While he was overseas, I often wondered who patched up his wounds, if he had any. He never talked about it, but I'd always hoped he'd returned as perfect as when he'd left.

"There's spaghetti on the stove, Tupperware above the fridge. Help yourself and bring some home to Deb, and I'll head over to his place now. Just close up behind you when you leave."

"All right, thanks, Charlie. I know he'll be happy to see you." He smiled.

I smiled in return and stepped back to let him pass to go into the kitchen. I grabbed my jacket and scarf and slipped on my boots before I headed out the door. I walked down the street and breathed in the crisp fall air as I tucked my hands in my pockets to keep them warm. I got to Ethan's and saw that only a few lights were on inside the house.

I walked up the path quickly and knocked on his front door. Reese barked from within the house as he ran to the door. A moment later, it opened swiftly, and my breath caught in my throat at the sight of him.

His lower lip was cut, and a small amount of dried blood sat in the corner, where a nasty red welt bloomed on his jaw and cheek. His left eye was already bruised and swollen, and above his right eye a small cut bled down into his eyebrow. The left edge of his jaw was scraped and bleeding slightly, and his shirt was stretched out and torn in places. The worst, however, was the large gash at his hairline that bled through the Band-Aid that attempted to hold it together.

"I think you need stitches," was all I said after I stood there and stared.

"Probably, but I'll stick to a Band-Aid," he said stubbornly as he pulled the door open further. "Come on in. I know you're dying to get your hands on me," he said with a wink, and I would have laughed, if not for noticing the stiff way he walked into the living room.

Promise

"Ethan, what happened to you?" I whispered as I stood at the entrance to his living room and tried to stop the tears that welled in my eyes.

Noticing my distress, he walked up to me and hugged me close to him. When I wrapped my arms around him, he flinched and held his breath when I squeezed his ribs too hard. Not wanting to cause him any more pain, I pulled away quickly. "Sorry."

"It's okay. It wasn't your fault. I think my ribs are bruised, but nothing feels broken."

"How would you know? You refused to go to the hospital."

"Because I know what it feels like when they're broken, and it doesn't feel like that."

I realized that he was referring to when he was in the Marines, but it wasn't the time to push him for more information.

"Go sit down, and I'll grab the first-aid kit."

I walk into his bedroom to get the kit from his attached bathroom, when a picture on his dresser caught my eye. It was the two of us the day before he'd left for basic training, when his parents had thrown him a going-away party, after they'd accepted that he wasn't going to change his mind about enlisting. They invited everyone they knew to send him off. They were proud of him for deciding to defend our country, even if they didn't understand it completely.

Cassie Gregg

It was, as usual, an extravagant Southern garden party on a sunny fall day. I couldn't remember the picture being taken, but the longer I looked at it, the more captivated I became.

I stood next to Ethan with my arms around his waist and his arm around my shoulders. He'd nestled me under his shoulder, hugging me to him. I smiled brightly at the camera while Ethan had a big, bright smile on his face as he looked down at me. I'd never seen the picture before, but by the looks of it, it hadn't always sat neatly in a frame. There was a heavy crease across the middle of the picture, and the edges were slightly torn. It looked weathered and worn, but well taken care of. I reached out and touched the glass, treasuring the breathtaking smile on Ethan's face.

"I carried it with me every day."

I spun around, startled to hear Ethan behind me. "What?" I asked as he walked up next to me and picked the picture up.

"My mom sent it to me a few weeks after the party. I'd never been so happy to get such a simple thing in my life. It was like I had you with me, even though you weren't there. I kept it with me every day and never went anywhere without it tucked in my pocket."

"It's a beautiful picture," I whispered, looking up at him.

Promise

"When times got tough or I felt homesick, I'd pull it out and just felt this calm wash over me. I'd hoped that when I looked at it, you were thinking of me too."

"I thought about you every single day," I confessed, and he turned to look at me intently.

"Really?"

"Of course I did, Ethan. You're my best friend. I worried if you were okay, if you were happy, if you were safe."

"My unit always gave me shit about carrying that picture around. But after I finally showed it to them and told them about you, they all wanted to know more. I'm pretty sure they all wanted to meet you. They loved the stories about us growing up and hearing how you were doing in your e-mails. I'm pretty sure they were in love with you after the first batch of cookies you sent." He laughed and then sobered. "You were like this bright spot in all the darkness."

"I'd love to meet them all, too." I smiled and placed my hand on his arm. His features seemed to darken and turn somber, and I realized that it was because not all of them were around anymore.

"I'm sorry. I had no idea..." I paused. "You never talk about it, about being over there."

"It's because I know a lot of it would hurt you, and I don't want you to feel sorry for me or worry about what it was like for me. I want you to look at me and see me like you did before I left."

"Ethan, I see you as I always have. If anything, I admire you even more, just like I told you the day you enlisted. I can't imagine what it must have been like, and I have no clue what you went through, but for you to come home safe and be able to wake up each day and continue to try and make the world a better place, I don't have the words to describe how proud of you I am." I smiled as I hugged him to me. He flinched again from the contact, and I was reminded of why I'd gone into his bedroom to begin with. "Take a seat and let me clean you up."

I returned quickly from his bathroom with the first-aid kit and a washcloth and found him sitting on the end of his bed. I knelt on the floor in front of him and cleared away the blood from his mouth, eyebrow, and jaw with the damp washcloth before I cleaned the open cuts with antiseptic. I cleaned the cuts on his hands and elbows and wondered the whole time what had happened to him.

I worried that I'd hurt him further if I pressed too hard, so I cradled his hand in mine like I held a baby bird. He only flinched a couple times, and I saw the muscles in his jaw tighten only a few more, but he hadn't said a word since I'd returned back from the bathroom, so I worked in silence, concentrating on his wounds and not the increasing rush of my pulse.

Promise

Finally, I stood up and moved between his knees to clean the gash on his head. After I staunched the bleeding and disinfected the wound, I held the edges together and applied a couple butterfly strips to keep it closed. Cradling his head in one hand, I reached up with the other, gently brushed my thumb over the wound, and then leaned down and softly kissed the skin beside it. I prayed it didn't hurt too badly. His hands moved from where they rested on his knees to the back of my legs, where he held me in place tenderly, his warm hands gently cupping the soft skin of my thighs.

I looked down at his eyes, and in them I saw a reflection of the love I'd once buried deep inside my heart. "Ethan—"

"I love you, Charlie."

I stilled immediately. With the three simple words, my whole world stopped and started again. Ethan loved me. He was in love with me. Oh no... Please God, don't let me lose him. I have to beat this disease. I have to be all right.

Chapter 18

I BRACKETED HIS HEAD IN my hands and slowly tilted it back up to mine, but the rest of his body sat rigidly.

"Gray?" I asked softly.

"Yeah, Lee?" he answered.

"Do you mean that?" I asked hesitantly.

In the silence that followed his reveal, the idea that Ethan loved me had taken hold of my heart, and it hadn't once let go. The fear I felt before telling Ben I loved him wasn't there when I thought of loving Ethan and telling him so. I only felt relief. Relief that I had never really known before left a peace inside me that told me he was my true love, the elusive one—my forever.

"With all my heart, sweetheart," he said, and reached behind my head and pulled my lips down to his. He kissed me so passionately I didn't think I'd ever recover. I pulled away from him ever so slightly and rested my forehead on his and looked into his beautiful blue eyes.

"Promise?" I whispered, our lips brushing with the word.

"Pinky swear," he whispered back before he sealed his lips tightly to mine once more.

Ethan stood suddenly and wrapped his arms tightly around me, crushing me to his body, while I looped my arms around his neck. I couldn't seem to get close enough to him. I wanted to feel every inch of him on me. His hands ran up and down my back as I dove my fingers through his soft hair. His hands slid down over my butt and squeezed gently, causing me to gasp, giving his tongue admittance to slip past my lips and find refuge inside my mouth.

As our tongues danced, a fever began to rise inside me, and with one more squeeze, he lifted me effortlessly off the ground. I wrapped my legs around his solid waist. Coherent thought had gone out the window as we kissed each other harder and harder, desperation setting in. We tore at one another's clothes and laughed when we fumbled with buttons or pieces of clothing got caught on limbs. Finally, with nothing between us, he leaned over the bed and gently laid me down but held off, his body hovering just inches above mine.

"What is it, Gray?" I asked as I looked into his expressive eyes that had darkened to the color of a midnight-storm sky.

"God, it's good to hear you call me that. I was afraid I'd never hear you call me that again."

"You have nothing to worry about. You'll always be my Gray." I smiled sweetly up at him.

"Are you sure you want to do this?" he asked hesitantly.

I placed my hand on his cheek and reassured him, "Yes, I'm sure. I've never been more sure of anything." I pulled him closer to me and felt the hard planes of his body against the soft curves of mine.

"You are so damn beautiful," he whispered reverently.

He kissed a path down my neck to my shoulder, then down between my breasts, over each of my ribs, and down to my hips and back up again. Each flutter of his lips on my skin was another stroke of heat to the fire that burned inside me.

"Ethan," I breathed as he kissed the sweet spot just below my ear. Raking my fingers over his chiseled shoulders, I gasped in surprise and pleasure as he entered me for the first time and moaned my name in prayer. "God, Charlie."

I hugged him to me and soaked in his power and strength. With him inside me, I felt unimaginably full and complete. Without a word, he began to move in slow, smooth strokes, pulling me, inch by inch, closer to the edge.

"Ethan!" I panted harder as he began to move faster above me and inside me. Soon his breaths and my moans harmoniously echoed through the dimly lit room.

"Oh God, Ethan!" I gasped as I clung to his shoulders. I couldn't take anymore.

Promise

"Please," I begged. "Please, please," I pleaded, my fingers digging into the muscles of his back, my legs hugged tightly to his ribs.

"Just let go, Charlie. Let go, sweetheart. I've got you." And with one final thrust he locked his lips to mine in a searing kiss as we both fell headfirst into endless pleasure.

When my eyes fluttered open, dusk had slid through, and bright stars filled the night sky. I was cradled on my side with Ethan tucked around me like a blanket. I ran my fingertips up and down his arm, relishing the feel of him. He stirred behind me and pulled me closer to his chest, his heat soaking into my bones.

"Hey now, I was having this awesome dream. Why'd you wake me up?" Ethan whispered in a husky voice.

"I just wanted to touch you to see if this was real or if this was a dream," was all I managed before a knot choked my throat.

I closed my eyes and began to sing. I didn't realize I'd sung out loud until I was halfway through Etta James's "At Last" and Ethan kissed my neck and shoulder. I stopped singing to revel in the feel of his warm lips on my skin.

"Don't stop," he protested, "I love it when you sing. You used to sing all the time, a habit you picked up from your mom." He stated it plainly, but the fact that he remembered warmed my heart to its deepest parts. "I think it's a very fitting song for us. Don't you think?" he grinned and I laughed at his teasing tone.

"I can't believe you remember that," I said as I turned over to face him.

"Of course I remember. I remember all the good times...and the bad," he said as he pulled me closer to him. Bad times? Like when we watched my mom slowly wither away in front of us.

Suddenly, it was too hot. I had to get up, out of the bed. I didn't know if I was running away from the memory or him, but before I could get far, a strong hand reached out and stopped me.

"Hey, what's wrong? Is it your mom? I'm sorry I brought it up. I just remember all the times you sang to me in the fort whenever I got upset," he cooed as he attempted to coax me back to bed. "Or when I coerced you into singing at the bonfires," he teased, and I smiled back at him.

"It's not about Mom. I love that you remember her too. I just needed some water. You dehydrated me," I laughed as I hopped across the cold floor on the way to the bathroom, scooping up Ethan's flannel shirt as I went.

In the bathroom, I looked at myself in the mirror and felt different. I didn't feel like I had after Ben and I slept together. I felt more whole. Like the final puzzle piece of my soul had fallen into place.

I turned an appraising eye to my body and noticed that I'd managed to put on some weight in the last couple weeks. I could still use more, but it was a start. I had more color in my skin, and I didn't look exhausted anymore. Postponing chemo hadn't been as bad as I'd originally thought it would be. I'm not sure if I expected to start looking like the walking dead, but I hadn't expected to start looking better. I slipped Ethan's shirt back on and ran from the bathroom and launched onto the bed to Ethan's waiting arms with a giggle.

He pulled me in and wrapped his arms and blankets around us both. I lay there listening to the steady beat of his heart, and then I turned my head into his chest and placed kisses on his sternum and over his heart.

"I love you, Charlie. I always have," he whispered. I smiled into his chest as tears fell from my eyes.

"That's good, Gray, because I've always loved you too," I replied truthfully as I drifted off into the second most peaceful sleep I'd had in weeks.

* * *

Ethan coaxed me awake in the middle of the night with soft kisses to my neck. His strong body pressed into my back while his hand ran over my hip to my stomach. He trailed his fingers up my stomach and cupped my breast in his very capable hand. I arched my back into him and reached up and pulled his head down to mine. His lips demanded and gave, pushed and pulled.

I moaned in objection when his hand moved from my breasts but sighed when it trailed down my side and over my hip. His fingers slid intimately down the inside of my thigh, and he grasped my knee and opened me to him, pulling my leg back over his hip. I panted in anticipation of what he'd do next. I was his instrument that he played to his will, and I loved every minute of it. He slid inside me with exquisite slowness that stopped my breathing.

"Ethan," I moaned. His warm, labored breaths beat at the back of my neck and sent shivers across my skin.

"God, Charlie, you feel so good," he exhaled. His chest vibrated against my back with a groan.

"Don't stop," I gasped.

With a strong thrust he whispered, "Never, sweetheart, never." He slid my leg forward, looped in the bend of his elbow, his hand braced on the mattress, and he rolled us slightly and sank deeper inside me, eliciting a passionate moan from both of us. I squeezed him intimately, loving the feeling of him inside me and provoking a growl from his chest that quickened his pace. The only sounds that filled the room were our heavy breaths as we enjoyed one another's bodies. We came slowly and together in a heated passion that overtook every part of my being.

Promise

Sometime later, I lay there in Ethan's arms, his fingers softly running up and down my back. He hadn't fallen asleep yet, and something had been on my mind that I'd wanted to ask him.

"Gray?" I asked quietly.

"Yes, Lee?" he replied just as quietly.

"What changed your mind?"

"Changed my mind about what?"

"About me, about us."

"I don't understand."

"What changed in your mind that you realized you loved me and didn't want to just be friends."

"I had a feeling I'd have to confess sooner or later," he sighed, and I turned over to face him, his face hidden in the shadows of the room.

"Confess what?" I probed.

"Back in high school, you wouldn't put your books down long enough to realize that every guy wanted to be with you."

"They did not!" I exclaimed, and he laughed and kissed my nose.

"Oh yes, they did. Sunshine, trust me. I had to sit there and listen to them talk about wanting to be with you, and somewhere inside me it didn't feel right that you were with someone else. I didn't know why I felt like that. We both know I was busy enough with other girls, but for some reason I felt like I had to keep them from you. So I did. When someone expressed interest in you, I deterred them. None of them deserved you, but somehow Billy Woodall slipped through the cracks. Before I could stop him, he'd asked you out, and there wasn't anything I could do about it."

"Wow, I didn't know you did that."

"Well, I did. And it followed me all the way to Yale, but I didn't have the power there I did at St. Andrews."

"I don't know what to say, but that doesn't really answer my question."

"I know. I'm getting to that." He paused. "When I got to basic, I realized that the real reason I didn't want any of those guys to be with you wasn't because they didn't deserve you, well, not entirely, but because I loved you, that I'd always loved you. Being away from you for so long, it made me realize that I didn't ever want to be apart from you like that ever again, and I vowed that when I got home, I'd tell you how I felt."

"But you didn't." I traced my finger over his cheek down to his jaw, and his eyes closed appreciatively.

"No, I didn't. I got home, and you'd grown into this beautiful woman. I didn't know how to see you that way. You'd always been Lee, my best friend. But when I set eyes on you that first day home, you were the woman I loved, and it scared me shitless," he chuckled. "You seemed to have everything figured out, and you'd followed your dreams, and it all seemed to be going just as you wanted it to. I didn't know if I fit into that plan anymore. I thought I couldn't have you, so I tried to bury my feelings with other women, but it never worked. You were always there, and I knew that I had to have you. So I waited until I thought you were ready to hear what I had to say. But I waited too long, because Ben came along, and I got jealous as hell."

"I remember the first time you met him. I didn't understand why you were being so rude to him. It all makes sense now, all of it. That weird mood you were in before the wedding. The cryptic words you said to me when you called after. It was all because you were jealous of Ben."

"Yes, it was. He had what I wanted more than life itself, and I didn't know how to get you back. Then I royally screwed things up with us, and I swear my heart ached every day that I didn't talk to you. I'd been so afraid to tell you I loved you, but that was overshadowed completely by the fear that you'd never speak to me again."

"I'd never have let that happen. The wedding was partly my fault, too. I overreacted completely and was childish not to forgive you, but my heart was broken, too. I realized that my love for you that I'd buried all those years ago wasn't as forgotten as I'd thought, and it hurt so bad to think that you didn't feel the same way."

"I definitely felt the same way. I had for a long time. I was an idiot not to have told you years ago."

"To be fair, I realized I was in love with you while you were deployed, too."

"Really?" he asked, surprised.

"Really. You'd missed another one of my birthdays, and something inside me just clicked. Then you got home, and I thought that there was no way a man like you would date a girl like me. You were way out of my leag—"

He interrupted my words with a searing kiss. "Don't you ever dare think or say something like that ever again. We're meant to be, Charlie. I think we always have been."

"I couldn't agree more," I whispered as I leaned up to kiss his enticingly soft lips.

Chapter 19

I WOKE LATE THE NEXT morning and stretched languidly beside Ethan's warm body. I turned to the bay window and watched the raindrops run together and streak down the glass. It was a hypnotic dance that brought a peace to the raging storm. I rolled over and saw that Ethan was still sound asleep on his stomach beside me. His beautiful profile was relaxed in sleep, and my eyes traveled over his sleeping form, admiring the man he'd become. His tan skin was smooth and soft and begged to be touched.

In the dim light, I saw all the imperfections of healed scars on his back and shoulders. His large, solid bicep was marked with the Eagle, Globe, and Anchor garnished with a *semper fidelis* banner. I'd seen flashes of it after he'd first returned and then saw it for the first time when he wore his old sleeveless Yale shirt when we went running. It shocked me at first that he'd gotten a tattoo, but now it seemed to fit him perfectly.

I traced my finger over the writing and placed a kiss to the symbol. I still felt such pride for his sacrifice and service. I slid flush into his side and ran my hand over the strong expanse of his muscled back. I leaned down and kissed the first scar that I saw. He moved when I kissed the next one, but I laid my hands on his waist to keep him from turning over and felt the raised skin of another scar on my fingers, but saw nothing.

"Shh," I whispered and pressed my lips to another scar on his shoulder. I sat up and straddled his hips, kissing every scar and every inch of his beautiful skin. "Will you tell me how you got them?" I asked.

"One day, just not today," he answered quietly. He rolled over but kept me straddled over him. When he turned over I got a fantastic view of his broad chest, chiseled abs, and narrow hips. I sat there, my hands braced on his stomach, and tried to only look right into his eyes, but mine were caught on a long, jagged scar that ran from his waist to his hip, jutting inward before swooping back around to his back. I ran my fingers over the scar as tears pooled in my eyes. His hands covered mine, sandwiching them to his skin.

"I worried about you every single day. I still worry about you," I sniffed as he reached up and caught a wayward tear I hadn't meant to let escape. I looked away from him to gather my thoughts, and my eyes focused on the metal of his ever-present ID tags sitting on the nightstand. His two tags shone in the early morning light, but the third tag that was chained separately to the bottom of his chain didn't catch the light, though it stood out nonetheless. This one was encased in a black rubber border, and when I flipped it over, it wasn't Ethan's name that I read but another man's. In a stark realization of its meaning, I felt tears clog my throat.

I'd seen the telltale ball-chain poke out of his shirt collar over the years, or the outline of the hanging dog tags showing through the fabric when he wore a tighter shirt. He never took them off, not even when we ran, since I'd heard them jingle as he ran beside me on our morning runs. I'd come to associate that sound with Ethan.

Shaking off some of the sadness that crept in, I turned my focus back to Ethan's beautiful body and came to another tattoo on his right pectoral that made my breath catch in my throat. Two boots sat side by side with a gun sitting between them, the muzzle facing down, and on the stock hung a Marine's helmet. A banner ran under the length of the tattoo that read, "*I am my brother's keeper*," and, in that moment, I knew that he'd lost people close to him.

"You don't need to worry, Charlie. You never did."

"But I didn't know that, and clearly I had some right to worry," I admonished, running my fingertips down the long, jagged scar on his side. "I'd sit there in front of the television and hold my breath as the list of names ran over the screen. I'd breathe easier only when I got a reply to my e-mails. I worried that one of those days, my prayers wouldn't be answered, and I'd have to sit there and read your name on a screen or get a phone call from your mother that you were gone."

"Charlie." He paused. "I won't lie that it wasn't dangerous. It's war. But no matter what I went through over there, I knew that everything would be all right."

"How could you have known that?"

"Because you told me it would be. When my faith was tested, it was your voice I heard telling me that everything would be okay. Telling me that you were with me. I was reminded of my promise to you that I'd return home safe, even though so many didn't." He grew quiet for a while, but he needed a moment to settle himself.

My eyes traveled his torso again but caught sight of another tattoo tucked under his left arm, along his rib. A purple bruise bloomed over his ribs that hid the fine lettering, but in the light I was able to make out the start of script letters. I leaned to the side and gasped when I read what was written there.

"Ethan?" I asked as I looked up into his eyes.

"It's not that bad, just bruised. It should clear up in a few days."

"Not that Ethan, this," I said as I ran my fingers over the initials scribed into his skin.

"Oh, that. I forgot you hadn't seen it."

Promise

"Ethan, I...I don't know what to say." I stared, speechless, at the beautifully scripted *C.E.G.M.* curved along his ribs over his heart.

"You don't have to say anything about it. I got it right after basic, before I got deployed."

"But...why?"

"I told you, Charlie. It's because I realized how much I loved you, but it didn't seem fair to tell you and then leave. I wanted you close to my heart no matter where I went."

Tears pooled in my eyes as I held my hand over his heart and mine. "It's beautiful, Gray, absolutely beautiful," I said as I reached up with my right hand and slid the ring that had held residence for the last five years from my left pinky. I looked down at the infinity symbol, stark in its dark color against my pale skin hidden from the sun behind my ring.

"On my twenty-first birthday, I realized that I didn't just love you, but that I was in love with you, and you were a world away. So I went out and did the most spontaneous thing I've ever done. I got this...for you," I added, looking down at his handsome face. He clasped my hand in his and examined the small tattoo bisecting the top of my pinky.

"I can't believe you did this. All this time..." He trailed off.

"I know it almost doesn't seem real, but it is, Ethan. This right here between us is as real as it gets." I leaned down and kissed him passionately, and he sat up and wrapped his arms tightly around me.

"You never have to worry about me being away from your heart, Gray. I'm not going anywhere, not without you."

"Promise?" he asked as I slid my hand into his and pulled it to my lips.

"Pinky swear." I smiled and kissed the knuckle of his little finger.

Chapter 20

THE FOLLOWING WEEK WENT FASTER than I would have liked. It seemed that most of my days went that way, slipping through my fingers. My chest felt heavy with the burden of my lies. I lied to Ethan over and over, and I made promises I didn't have a right to make. I didn't know what my future held, but I'd promised him there would be one. It seemed like time sped up, but I didn't know how to slow it down.

I noticed the symptoms that Dr. Sharp had warned me about were back with a vengeance. I was more fatigued, I'd lost most of my appetite, and my nose bled multiple times. It was like my body had put up one last front to ward off the disease the last few weeks, but now it was telling me that it was time to start getting help to fight back.

I knew the cancer had to have progressed, so I decided to stop hiding in fear and putting off the inevitable, and called Dr. Sharp to schedule an appointment to begin my treatment. He wasn't pleased that I'd avoided him for nearly a month when I called and was rightfully concerned of my regress, and I would require more testing.

I'd be tested that week, and the treatments would begin dependent upon the results.

On Monday, I went to the hospital to have my blood drawn and tested. I went between the morning and afternoon rushes, and after Dr. Sharp said he'd call when the results were in, I went back to work. I was a ball of nervous energy the rest of the day and glad that Ethan was working late. When I woke Tuesday morning, Ethan slept beside me, his arm wrapped tightly around me. He'd come in after I'd gone to sleep, and I smiled that he'd chosen to sleep next to me instead of alone at his place.

I wanted him to keep sleeping, so I slipped soundlessly from the bed and got ready for work. After I showered and dressed, I gave Ethan a kiss on his forehead before I headed down to the kitchen and made breakfast for myself and put a plate in the oven for Ethan. I left the coffee on and a note that told him I'd enjoyed waking up with him and that I'd see him for dinner if he had time, and, of course, that I loved him.

Work went both fast and slow. I was a nervous wreck as I waited for Dr. Sharp's call. He'd said he'd call Wednesday, so it surprised me when my caller ID lit up with his name.

"Hello?"

"Hello, Charlie, it's Dr. Sharp."

"Hi, Dr. Sharp, how're you doing?"

Promise

"I'm doing well, Charlie, thank you for asking. I'm calling because I put a rush on your results and just got them back, and as I said before, I'm concerned about your numbers. I'd like to begin your treatment as soon as possible. I don't want to wait another week to begin."

"That doesn't sound promising."

"It's not what we had hoped, but we're going to do everything we can to treat this. But like I said, my recommendation is that you begin as soon as possible."

"Okay. When would that be?"

"Very good, let's schedule you for eight a.m. on Thursday."

"All right, Thursday, eight a.m., got it."

"And, Charlie, it's imperative that you understand the seriousness of your condition. You cannot afford to skip these treatments if it is your wish to get better. If that is no longer your wish, then we need to have a discussion about how to proceed. If you want to beat this, then you have to fight. That fight starts now."

"I understand, Dr. Sharp, and I do want to get better. I want to fight this. I promise I'm ready now. I won't miss my appointments anymore."

"I'm glad to hear that. We'll see you on Thursday."

"Okay, good-bye, Dr. Sharp."

"Good-bye, Charlie."

Cassie Gregg

I knew I only had two days before my life changed, and I felt overwhelmed with the awareness that my time with Ethan had come to an end. He'd spent every night at my place since that wonderful Saturday two weeks ago. I wasn't sure what excuse I could give him that he'd believe as to why I couldn't see him for the next week. I gave a cover story to my employees but still didn't know what to say to Ethan. I figured I'd tell him what I'd told my staff, that I'd gone to help a sick friend. At least it was almost the truth.

I called Joe and scheduled him to take me to and bring me home from my appointment Thursday. Knowing I wouldn't be in any condition to cook for the shelter Thursday night, I messengered money to Jan, the shelter director, to get pizzas for everyone. It would do in a fix, but I'd have to come up with a better solution for the future.

It helped ease some anxiety that my appointment was when Ethan was at work, so I wouldn't have to worry that he'd see me. I told him over dinner Wednesday that I'd be out of town while I cared for a friend in Atlanta, and he kissed me and told me to travel safe and call if I needed anything.

On Thursday, I arrived at the hospital for my first chemo session, and the weather reflected my somber mood. A cold front had moved through, and the threat of rain hung dangerously in a cloud-laden sky. I sat in a treatment room with five other chairs set in a semi circle. A kind nurse, who'd introduced herself as Lisa, set up the IV for the chemo pump and offered me a blanket. I took it gratefully, and she sat down next to me while the chemicals pumped into my body. She chatted and made pleasant conversation, but my focus was scattered.

"I have a question, and you have every right to tell me to take my nosy old head and butt right out of your business, but I couldn't help but notice your last name. I've seen you before, at the donor's gala a few years ago. You wouldn't happen to have any relation to Mr. Jackson Montgomery, would you?" I smiled at her hesitance.

"That would be my father. I accompanied him to both the naming ceremony and the gala. I go every year that I can. It is one of my favorite charities."

"I'll say. The pediatric oncology unit is the most sought-after in the hospital, as well as across the nation. Your family must be so proud."

"We are. It has been a pleasure to see the program grow to what it has become." I paused. "I'm not one to throw the weight of my name around, so I'd appreciate if we kept that between us. There are plenty of other patients in need of care, and I don't want any special treatment."

"Of course, Miss Montgomery."

"Charlie, please."

She smiled warmly at me and patted my hand. "I have a few rounds to make, but press the button if you need anything at all. I'll be back in a little bit to check on you." I smiled up at her and settled into the chair more comfortably. She hesitated at the door and gave me one last glance. She looked like she wanted to say something more, but then thought better of it and left the room with a shake of her head.

I managed to get sick only once during my session and was glad that the other chairs had remained empty throughout my appointment. Lisa said I'd done really well and that most first-timers had a much more difficult time. I didn't know if I should have been proud of that fact or not, but thanked her anyway.

After she unhooked me from the portable pump, she helped me down the hall to Dr. Sharp's office. He explained what to expect over the next few hours as well as the next few days. Even though I remembered some of what my mother had gone through, it helped to know what to expect and when. The nausea passed as Dr. Sharp finished up his meeting with me, but lethargy had taken its place. They cleared me to leave with strict instructions to go right home and rest.

I took the elevator down to the main lobby, where Joe waited for me, and as soon as he saw me, he stood and came to my side. He gently held my arm and provided some

Promise

much-needed support. Unlike the first time, he helped me into the front seat of the tinted Escalade and said it was so he could keep an eye on me when I questioned him.

Honestly, I was just happy to have someone there. I'd thought doing it alone was what I wanted, but the whole time Dr. Sharp talked after my appointment, all I thought was that I wanted Ethan. I wanted him there in the hospital, and I wanted him there when the side effects hit, but because I was too scared, or too deluded, he wouldn't be. That made me heartsick more than anything.

Joe didn't ask questions, but I had a feeling he knew it was something serious. To break the silence, I asked if he had any family, and the infectious grin that covered his face said it all. He told me about all the members of his family and how he'd retired from the private security sector years back, but his loving wife had said he had to get out of the house and get a hobby. So he chose to start a lucrative car service.

He told me about his favorite muffin at the café, and the stories he told about his kids kept my mind at ease and the nausea at bay. We were a few blocks from my street when I asked him to pull over so I could throw up. He helped me back up into the truck and offered a handful of tissues as he pulled from the curb.

Joe parked as close to my walkway as he could, his Escalade just barely situated between the fire hydrant boundary and my Tahoe. I'd never thought the hydrant's location in front of my place to be inconvenient, but that had since changed. He gently but firmly held my elbow as I slid down from my seat. Joe escorted me up the walkway and paused at the base of the porch steps.

"You sure you're okay to be here alone, Miss Charlie?" Joe asked me for the tenth time.

"I promise, Joe, I'll be just fine." He grunted quietly as he ushered me up the long porch steps. "Same time week after next?"

"I'll be there, Miss Charlie," he answered grudgingly, then turned and left me alone at my door.

I walked through the vaulted foyer and into the empty kitchen. My movements echoed in the cavernous house and left me saddened by my self-induced solitude. I only had myself to blame. I grabbed the box of saltines and a can of ginger ale and brought them up to my room. From what the doctor had said, I knew that I'd need them later, and he'd warned about empty stomachs, but right now my biggest concern was resting. I returned downstairs to my living room and watched the Food Network while I dozed on the couch. I fell asleep there, curled onto my side, when a wave of nausea hit me so hard that it woke me, and I ran for the bathroom.

I kneeled there on the tile throwing up, over and over until there was nothing left in my stomach, and I dry heaved painfully into the toilet. I spent the night on the bathroom floor because the two times I tried to lie in bed, the nausea surged back through me. I went upstairs at some point and tried to eat the crackers and take down the soda, but it didn't last long, and I gave up trying to keep anything down. My stomach cramped mercilessly, and I felt feverish and restless. It was five in the morning before I crawled into my bed and slept the next day through.

I woke Saturday with a pounding headache, dry mouth, and intensely sore throat. The nausea was gone, but my body was so weak I couldn't muster the energy to get up. I lay in bed all day, in and out of sleep. By Sunday, I had enough strength to slide from bed and shuffle to the bathroom and shower. The hot water did wonders, but it zapped all of the energy I had left. I attempted to brush my teeth, but my arms were so heavy I used the counter to prop myself up. Ethan called a couple times, but I didn't have the energy to talk, so I sent his calls to voicemail and sent him texts about being unable to talk, but I loved him and would call soon. I didn't call him back until Tuesday.

Tuesday was a good day. I showered, brushed my teeth, and managed to make eggs and biscuits for breakfast and still had energy to clean the bathroom and change the sheets on my bed. I talked to Ethan at lunch, and he said he missed me and couldn't wait until I got home. I told him to come over Wednesday after work, and if he brought the movie, I'd cook dinner. He agreed, and I felt some of my worry ease, but I knew I couldn't keep the ruse up much longer. I couldn't keep lying to him.

* * *

"Hey, it's me!" Ethan yelled as he came through the door. "I brought your mail in. I'll set it on the table," he added.

"Thank you! I'll be down in a minute," I called back and took one last look at myself in the mirror. I'd covered the dark circles under my eyes completely and used a healthy dose of bronzer to be sure my face wasn't pasty white anymore. I smoothed the wrinkles from my off-the-shoulder cashmere dress and ignored how it hung off my body when it used to cling to it. I made my way downstairs, and my spirits instantly lifted when I saw Ethan standing in the kitchen.

"Aren't you a sight for sore eyes." He smiled as he picked me up. He set me on the countertop and kissed me deeply, and I sunk into his lips. "Damn, Lee, you feel like a feather. Have you lost more weight? I hope you're not forgetting to take care of yourself while you're taking care of your friend." Oh no. I'd put the thick dress and boots on in hope that he wouldn't notice, but of course he noticed—it was Ethan.

"Nope. But you're awfully kind to say so. Flattery will get you everywhere, Mr. Stone," I teased, kissing his beautiful full lips and hoping that I'd distracted him.

Luckily it took hold and he reluctantly let the topic go. "So action, comedy, or drama?" he asked as he held up three options.

"Hmm, I say comedy. And if we have time, action!"

"I knew there was a reason I loved you." He smiled and kissed the top of my head. I would never tire of hearing him tell me he loved me, innocent or otherwise.

Ethan set the movie up, and I made popcorn and drinks. I'd prepped a pizza earlier in the day and popped it in the oven as Ethan settled on the couch. I brought him a beer and our large bowl of popcorn.

"Mmm, that pizza smells amazing!" he hummed as I took my place beside him.

"Pepperoni, sausage, and black olive, your favorite!" I kissed his cheek and popped a piece of popcorn into my mouth.

He hugged me into his side and smiled as he started the movie. Twenty minutes later, the timer went off, and I hopped up to grab the pizza from the oven and stumbled slightly from a rush of lightheadedness. I looked over my shoulder, but luckily Ethan was focused on the TV and hadn't seen my falter. In the kitchen, I pulled the pan from the oven, but my muscles shook from exertion, and I rushed over to the counter and dropped the pizza onto it safely. At the loud clatter of the pan, Ethan turned on the sofa and looked into the kitchen.

"You all right in there?" Ethan called.

"Just fine! Be out in a second!" I called back to him.

My subconscious warned that he'd know something was wrong, if he didn't already. I had five more rounds to go, and after number four, I'd start losing my hair. The weight loss and fatigue would become more prominent with every session. Luckily, I had a little time before I had to go again. I wanted to make the time I had with Ethan count. Who knew what the future would bring?

Chapter 21

TIME SEEMED TO BE MOVING increasingly fast. My second session went much like the first, but I asked Joe to pull over three times on our way home to throw up. He was understanding and kind about the ordeal, but he did ask if he should go back to the hospital when the third time brought nothing up but dry heaves. I told him that I was okay and to get me home as soon as he could. I knew he hadn't signed up for all the complications, but I appreciated him all the more for staying on.

When we pulled up to my house, he opened my door and offered his hand in assistance, but I was already too tired from vomiting to move freely. He took one look at me and lifted me out of the front seat. He set me down on the sidewalk, and I leaned heavily into his side, unable to hold myself up. Joe looked down and wrapped his arm tightly around my waist and walked me into the house, nearly carrying me inside. He was much more hesitant to leave me alone, but I ushered him out with a batch of his favorite muffins I'd cooked before my appointment, telling him that I would be fine. I closed the door on his retreating back and pulled myself to the bathroom to prepare for the impending nausea.

When the effects subsided, I made plans with Ethan, and when he saw me, it was evident he noticed how tired I was. He looked at me with sadness and concern but didn't ask what was going on. He'd tell me how beautiful he thought I was and kiss me gently. I tried to reassure him and told him it was the stress from the café and worry over my friend that kept me from sleeping well. He took my word for what it was, but he didn't believe me completely. He was my best friend, for God's sake. How much longer I thought I could lie to him before he figured something out, I didn't know. But I knew that I had to do something.

A few days before my third session, Ethan took Reese and me to the park to enjoy the changing fall leaves and cooler temperatures. We languidly walked arm in arm through the picturesque park and tossed the ball for Reese when he circled our legs impatiently. We hadn't gone far before I had to stop and rest. I sat on the nearest bench and pulled Ethan down next to me. I tried to mask the true reason I'd sat down with the lure of soft kisses to Ethan's lips, but it only lasted so long before the cold seeped in, and I started to shiver.

"Do you want some hot chocolate or coffee? Your hands are freezing," he asked as he grasped my numb hands between his and breathed warm air onto them.

Promise

"I'd love some hot chocolate." I smiled.

I watched as he stood and walked across the way to a vendor cart. Reese sat beside me and stared up at me like he knew something was wrong. His humanly expressive brown eyes watched me closely, his head tilted intently. I lifted my hand and scratched behind his ear and was rewarded with a soft lick to my fingers when I pulled away. I looked around me and absorbed the beauty of nature around me. The leaves had changed and some floated to the ground; others clung to their branches and refused to bow to the wind's demand. I compared myself to the leaves and wondered if I'd be as strong as those that held on or if I'd be one of the leaves that let go and floated to the ground.

The morbid comparison sent a shiver down my spine that left me feeling uneasy at the thought that this could be the last time I enjoyed the fall. Sensing my distress, Reese laid his heavy head in my lap, and I was touched by the quiet comfort he offered in the small gesture. I ran my hand over his soft coat, rhythmically soothing the both of us.

He was a gentle giant but also a fierce protector. The day Ethan had brought him home, I thought he was crazy to have gotten a Rottweiler, but the moment I saw him, my heart melted. As I scooped the adorable bundle of fur into my arms, I told Ethan that he looked like a furry little peanut butter cup. The idea stuck and Ethan decided to name him Reese. He laughed at me and said only I would think a dog looked like a baked good.

By the time he was six months old, he was seventy pounds of sheer muscle, and I joked that he looked more like a tank, but to me he was just as sweet as his namesake. Ethan said with the proper training, he'd be just like any other dog.

But he'd been only partially correct. Ethan's buddy in the police K-9 unit trained Reese into a perfect protection dog. He was well behaved, followed commands, and never strayed far from your side. His leash was more of a formality that Ethan often just carried when he walked him. As promised, Ethan had turned a rambunctious puppy into a precision-trained protection dog. But I knew the intuitive nature of Reese hadn't been taught or trained. It was just who Reese was.

Ethan returned with two cups of steaming-hot cocoa, but I hadn't noticed, lost in my thoughts and the fear of the idea that this was my last.

"Charlie?" Ethan probed.

When I didn't reach for the proffered Styrofoam cup, he said my name louder and touched my shoulder. Startled, I jumped and gasped, dislodging Reese's head from my lap. His low growl caused Ethan to frown down at me.

Promise

"What's going on with you, Charlie? And don't say nothing because it's not nothing. For God's sakes, my own dog just growled at me. What's going on, Lee?" When I didn't answer, unsure of what to say, he continued. "Is it drugs?" he asked seriously. I almost spat all over my coat when I choked on a mouthful of cocoa.

"Of course I'm not on drugs, Ethan. Why would you even ask me such a thing?" I knew why but played dumb anyway.

"You want the list?" When I again didn't answer, he went on. "Fine. First there are the dark circles under your eyes you don't think I see. You're gone for long periods of time, and when you are here, you're not really here. You're exhausted all the time and you seem to lose more weight every time I see you." He paused. He looked unsure if he wanted to make his next point, but shook his head and trudged on. "I've seen the needle marks, Charlie. When you're sleeping sometimes I just look at you, watch you sleep. I've seen the marks on your arm a few times, and I want you to tell me the truth. Please, Lee, just tell me what's going on. Whatever it is, you can tell me. We'll figure it out. We always do. I'll always stand by you." He looked pleadingly into my eyes, and I almost cracked right there and told him. But then the image of him haggard and depressed as he tried to carry my burden flashed to the front of my mind and overruled all other thoughts.

"Ethan, I'm fine, and I'm most certainly not doing drugs. You know me. You know I would never do something like that, ever. I'm just tired and stressed out. If it were any more than that, I would tell you—you know that," I tried to assure him, but it didn't go far.

"I thought so, but I'm not so sure anymore," he whispered.

We sat there for a while, neither of us speaking. The only sound around us was the scrape of dried leaves shifting and the distant sound of chirping birds.

Then he cleared his throat. "You can always tell me anything, Lee. I'm not going anywhere." That was what I was afraid of.

"Promise?" I asked him.

"Pinky swear," he replied.

* * *

I approached the halfway mark of my treatment plan, and it was the week I most dreaded. Dr. Sharp had warned that physically, it would be the hardest one. Combined with the previous sessions, the progression of the disease, and the regression of my health, it was his suggestion that I stay in the hospital for the week while the chemo worked its way through my system, but I refused to spend more time than necessary there.

Promise

I promised to call if it got unmanageable or come back to the hospital if it was unbearable. He wasn't pleased with my choice of words, but unless he admitted me I wouldn't stay. And I told him as much.

Defeated, he prescribed a low dose of morphine pills to administer to myself on an as-needed basis. He called Lisa into the room and directed her to take me down the hall for my treatment. Both Dr. Meadows and Dr. Sharp had been pushing for me to tell my family, but I'd refused time and again. They strongly disagreed but ultimately respected my wishes.

Unfortunately, my iron levels were too low, and Dr. Sharp wanted to raise them before we continued treatment. We postponed the session a week so I could safely raise my levels. After Dr. Sharp prescribed an iron supplement to take with every meal, I was given a few bags of IV fluids because my other nutrient levels were also low.

Even though I was about to be halfway through my treatments, I felt weaker than ever before. I wasn't sure if it was from chemo or the cancer, but I found it exponentially harder to do everyday tasks. I hadn't baked in weeks, as the mixing bowls were too heavy and the batters required too much stamina. I hid in my office and did paperwork when I was at the café, and I knew my staff had questions, but I didn't want to be in front of the public too much. Many of the people who came in knew my family and Ethan's, and I couldn't risk someone saying something to them. I'd only managed to bring dinner to the shelter on the weeks I didn't receive chemo, and the weeks I did, I prearranged a catered meal for the house. Jan was ever grateful, but she too was suspicious and worried about me.

The following Tuesday, I had my iron levels rechecked in the morning and they were where they needed to be, so I was scheduled for my third treatment that afternoon.

When I arrived at my appointment, Lisa scrutinized me intensely. "You look like you haven't slept in days, child," she admonished.

"That's all I've done," I sighed.

She got me situated in a chair and hooked the portable pump up to my IV. She sighed loudly, like she did every time she was about to ask me a personal question.

"Go ahead and ask, Lisa. I know you want to."

"Well, Charlie, I've known you a good bit of time now, and you have every right to tell me to take my nosy old head and butt right out of your business, but not once have I seen somebody here with you during your treatments. Mr. Fletcher is the only person I see you with, and he's not family. I know your family, and I don't understand why they aren't here with you. They're huge benefactors of this hospital, but they won't be here when one of their own gets sick? I don't rightfully understand."

"I haven't told them."

Promise

"I'm sorry. My hearing must be getting worse in my old age, but I thought you just said you haven't told them."

"That is what I said, Lisa. They don't know."

She stood there speechless for moment, then sank into the chair beside me. I reached over and laid my hand over hers folded in her lap.

"It was my decision not to tell them. I didn't want to hurt them again." I paused and gathered my thoughts. "When my mom got sick, we tried to pretend that everything was normal. But when the treatments stopped working, everything changed for us. My dad took a break from work to stay home with her while my sister and I left school to do the same.

"My father loved my mother so much that he wanted to spend as much time with her as he could because they knew her time was limited. Every day he spent with her, watching her die, he died a little too.

"When she passed, he became this shell of a man. He went back to work, and he almost never came home. When he did, it was like he was a ghost. He'd slowly watched as part of his soul slipped away and he was powerless to stop it. This powerful man, who'd never lost before, lost the most important thing in his life," I explained and looked up when I heard Lisa sniffle beside me. I wiped at my own tears and continued. "I didn't want to be the one to put him through that again. My closest friends went through it with our family, and I don't know that I can ask them to do it again, and I couldn't stand the thought that I'd be the cause of turning my father back into that shell of a man.

"I know that it was selfish of me, to save myself from that hurt. And I know that it was selfish of me to keep this from them, because I know my family would want to be here, but I kept them from it for so long, I'm not even sure how to tell them now."

"But, Charlie, child, that's not your choice to make. Nor is any of this your fault. You didn't ask for this disease. You got sick, plain and simple. I know your family loves you. How could they not? You're a beautiful, vibrant woman who has so much life inside her. You have to believe that. You need to tell them."

"I know, and I was going to..."

"You were going to, but?"

"I don't know anymore."

"You don't know about what, Charlie?"

"If I'm going to live," I answered somberly. "I'm just so tired. Early on, I was optimistic and stubborn about not telling my family, thinking that everything would be all right, and I'd get better. I'd convinced myself that once I was out of the woods, I could tell them and they'd be okay because I'd spared them the worry. I would be fine, and there would be nothing left for them to worry about. But now..." I breathed around the thick tears that clogged my throat. "I can feel it inside me, like I'm fighting a losing battle. I don't know that I'll be okay anymore. I don't know how to tell them that I'm dying or that there is a very real chance that I'm going to die.

"How do I tell my father that his little girl may not live to see her twenty-seventh birthday? How do I tell the man I love that I can never have his children? I feel like I've missed my chance to tell them, because if I tell them now all it will do is bring them pain. I'm so scared, and I don't know what to do."

"A lot of people in your position feel this way. But you have to realize how lucky you are to have people in your life that will worry and be pained over you. Not everyone in your condition does. There is no way for us to know which way the chips will fall, and we don't have complete control over how they do, but what you do have control over is how you live the rest of your life, however long it may be. You still have fight in you, Charlie, I can see it, but you have to decide if you want to fight or not. If there is something worth fighting for, do it. Just consider what I said about your family. They'd want to know. Imagine if it were reversed." She stood from the chair, tucked a blanket around me, and left with that parting wisdom hanging in the air.

After Lisa left, I slept through the rest of my session, which thankfully kept the nausea at bay. The ride home

Cassie Gregg

with Joe was quiet. I think he could tell I wasn't in the mood to talk since I made no effort to engage in conversation. I thought about what Lisa had said about telling my family I was sick. Logically, it all made perfect sense—I knew what I should do, but my logical brain wasn't working. I was torn between wanting them to know and wanting to protect them.

I stared out at the blurred world beyond the window and wondered about what to do. Joe knew about Ethan and my family from our many conversations. When he drove me, he never opted for music. Instead, he elected to small talk his way into every detail of my life, and he did it effortlessly. He disagreed with me about keeping my family in the dark and often told me that I should stop lying to them so that I didn't suffer alone, because it was plain for him to see that I was suffering.

"But I'm not alone, Joe. I have you!" I'd retort, and that always seemed to make him smile. It was a sad smile, but a smile nonetheless.

I fell asleep halfway through the drive, unsurprisingly, which forced Joe to carry me out of the car and into the house. He gently laid me down in bed, and I felt him sit with me in the chair beside my bed. I was home a few hours before the nausea set in. When I woke the house was empty, but I saw that Joe had put my phone, my anti-nausea medication, and a glass of water on my nightstand.

I took the Anzemet right away, but it only put off vomiting for a few hours until the medicine wore off. I spent the next few hours in the bathroom throwing up. I lay on the cool tile floor until the queasiness subsided and I was able to get back in bed.

It was a short time later that the fever set in. I took my temperature and ibuprofen before I got back in bed to rest more. For a while, it felt like my skin was on fire, and I was burning up from the inside out. I put a cool washcloth against my forehead and neck and stripped down to my bra and panties in hope that it would help cool me down. Once the fever-reducer kicked in and my temperature tapered off, I was able to rest somewhat peacefully.

My fever broke in the early morning, and my body was wracked with uncontrollable chills. I put on a pair of sweatpants over my leggings and one of Ethan's hoodies over my nightshirt. My bed was covered in blankets, and I turned off my A/C completely and switched on my heat. No matter what I tried, I shook as the cold seeped deep into my bones. What I wouldn't give to have Ethan wrapped around me.

Around noon, I fell into a restless sleep as my body slowly began to warm and settle. I got up a while later and managed to make something to eat for dinner. I was incredibly thirsty and finished off two bottles of water before I finished my sandwich and brought a third with me to the couch. I sat up with my laptop as classical music played softly on the stereo. I paid my bills, answered e-mails, and even managed to get an hour of paperwork for Monty's done before my eyes slid closed for the night.

When I woke the next morning, I was surprised to feel somewhat normal. I cooked breakfast, did some laundry, and cleaned up my room. I walked into my study and inhaled the rich sent of mahogany and the distinct aroma of books.

I walked over to the corner of the room where my piano sat open, facing out the bay window to the garden. I pulled the bench back and sat comfortably in the middle of the seat and pulled open the fallboard. My fingers caressed the cool white keys and the familiarity of the motion settled my mind. With every note of *"La fille aux cheveux de lin"* that I played, the warring emotions and worries inside me drifted away. The contradiction of simplicity and complexity in the music drove me further and further into tranquility. I finished the piece and sat silently watching the sun dip lower and lower in the sky. I stood from the piano and went up to my bedroom to lie down before I made dinner.

I don't know how long I napped before a sharp pain sliced through my body and jolted me awake. It felt like the nerves in my body grated over a hot poker as fire burned through my muscles. It was pure agony. If I moved too quickly or breathed too deep, sharp pain coursed through my body, radiating down my spine as I lay in bed and whimpered as the pain beat relentlessly at my body. I forced myself to descend the stairs and stumbled into the kitchen, where I'd left the morphine Dr. Sharp prescribed.

I pulled the bottle from my purse and fell to my knees when a fresh wave of pain crashed through me. Unable to grip it properly, I struggled to unlock the safety lid. I gritted my teeth and pushed the pain aside long enough to get the lid off, shake out two pills, and swallow them down. I rocked back and forth on the kitchen floor, praying that it would be over soon.

Finally, after what felt like an eternity, my muscles, nerves, and joints relaxed into the floor as the morphine took over and blocked the pain. I pushed myself up off the floor and dragged myself to the guest bedroom and crawled under the covers. I couldn't have been asleep more than a few hours before the morphine wore off, and the pain pulsed back through my body. It wasn't as intense as before, but my head and joints throbbed with every beat of my heart. I curled my knees to my chest and cried as I prayed, again, for the pain to stop.

I passed out at some point, from pain or exhaustion I don't know, but when I woke it was still dark outside, and the clock read four. The aches were dull compared to before, and I was able to sit up and gulp the rest of my water bottle. My mind was foggy from the morphine, but the sense of dread was gone, and I knew I'd made it to the other side.

My stomach rumbled for the first time in days as it called for food, so I made my way into the kitchen and started cooking. As I finished the last bite of my omelet and potatoes, dawn was just breaking through the sky. I looked at my phone and saw that it was Friday morning. It was no wonder Ethan had left me three voicemails. I grabbed another bottle of water from the fridge and called him back as I went to sit at the piano again.

"'Ello?" he answered with a sleepy voice.

"Hey, Gray, I didn't mean to wake you."

"It's fine, Lee. Where have you been? I've left you a bunch of messages."

"I'm sorry. I haven't had time to check my phone, but I'm back now and completely beat. How about lunch today? I can bring something by the office?" I asked hopefully.

"I can't today. How about dinner tomorrow night at your place? I'll cook and we can just relax."

"You'll cook?" I laughed.

"Yes, I'll cook. I can do that, you know," he replied, exasperated.

Promise

"I'm sorry. I've just never seen it happen. You always make me cook."

"That's because you're better at it than I am. But I promise it'll be edible."

"All right. Saturday, my place, six p.m. Don't be late."

"I won't."

"Promise?"

"Pinky swear."

"I love you, Gray."

"I love you too, Charlie."

Chapter 22

AFTER I HUNG UP WITH Ethan, I found myself drawn to playing the piano again. I'd forgotten how much I loved to play and how soothing it was for me. Everything around me melted away, and all that was left was pristine notes and hypnotic melodies. I played for a while longer until my arms grew tired.

I stood from the piano bench and black swarmed into my vision from standing too quickly. I placed my hand on the piano to steady myself and waited for the dizziness to pass. I climbed the stairs to my bedroom and slipped off my clothes as I walked into my bathroom to take a shower.

Under the hot spray of the water, I felt my muscles finally relax fully, and I let the water wash away the memory of the last few days. I was standing under the spray with my head bowed, watching the mesmerizing drip of water from my body, when suddenly bright red splashes dotted the shower floor. I reached up and felt warm blood flowing from my nose and tasted the metallic tang on my lips. I straightened and pinched my fingers to my nose to stop the bleeding. It took several minutes before I got it to stop, and I felt dizzy from the blood loss.

Promise

Having already washed and shampooed, I turned off the water and stepped from the stall into the steamed bathroom. My movements were sluggish, but I got ready for work as quickly as I could. I hadn't been to the café in days, and I wanted to check on my staff and the place. I hoped that the normalcy of my routine would help shake the last of the fog that had settled in my head.

I was busy at Monty's from when I walked through the door until I locked it up for the night. The days seemed to fly by, but it helped greatly that I had dinner with Ethan to slow things down for me. I missed him more than I ever would have thought possible. I worried that he'd know something was wrong with me when he saw me since, despite my efforts to eat more, no food sounded good and I'd lost more weight.

My typical year-round tan had faded to give my face a pale, sickly color, and the fog that settled in my head days before thickened with each passing day. The determination I had to bake couldn't combat the sluggishness of my muscles. I managed to make a few pies and four batches of cookies before I felt too fatigued to do any more.

In my eyes, it was progress. After I closed up the café Saturday afternoon, I headed home to prepare for Ethan to come for dinner, but instead I shuffled my feet around the house, not finding the ability or energy to get anything more done. I was determined to put on a brave face for

Ethan, and it was easier than I thought it would be when true excitement coursed through me and gave me the boost of adrenaline I desperately needed upon seeing he would arrive soon. It seemed my heart was going to run the show.

Ethan came over around five, flowers in hand and a passionate kiss on his lips. I arranged the bouquet of daises in a vase and set them on the kitchen island. Ethan came back into the house with bags full of food and made himself comfortable in the kitchen and started cooking while I set the table for dinner. It smelled absolutely delicious, and I was relieved that my appetite had returned.

With the table set and Ethan banning me from the kitchen, I walked into the study and opened the French doors wide so that the sound would carry to Ethan in the kitchen. I sat down at the piano to play a classical piece like I had been but thought that maybe a little treat for Ethan would be nice since he was cooking dinner.

I thought about what song to play and decided on a newer one that Ethan probably hadn't heard yet. It was powerful and poetic and one of my new favorites that I hoped he'd like. I started to play the song, and, as I came to the first chorus, I felt the newfound peace settle inside me as the strains of the song flowed from my fingers and voice. The words, heartfelt and emotional, soothed the fear and uncertainty I felt warring inside me. I sang the words as

Promise

if they were my own and felt them floating around me, comforting me inside and out. As I finished, Ethan knelt behind me and wrapped his arms around me, grounding me to him.

"That was beautiful, Charlie," he whispered in my ear. "What song is that?"

"It's called 'Gravity' by Sara Bareilles."

"I like it. You sounded amazing. I love when you sing for me."

I turned my head and captured his lips in a meaningful kiss. "I love *you*," I whispered, emotion catching in my throat.

Ethan's eyes softened as he tucked my hair behind my ear and kissed my cheek.

"I love you too, sunshine," he whispered back before he touched his lips softly to mine. I moved my hands up his shoulders and around his neck and deepened the kiss. We pulled apart regretfully, both of us breathless.

"Don't distract me, or we'll have to order pizza."

"I like pizza," I teased and continued to hold him to me. He groaned and gave me one last kiss before he pulled away.

As he walked into the kitchen, he called over his shoulder, "Just hold on to that thought for later." He grinned mischievously.

My cheeks heated at the thought of what we'd continue after dinner. I wondered how quickly we could get through our meal. "How long until dinner is ready?" I asked huskily.

Ethan laughed from the hallway and told me to have patience. Laughter bubbled out of me for the first time in days, and I started to feel lighter, like my old self again. Turns out, he was exactly what I needed.

"Why don't you sing some more for me while I finish up dinner?" he called.

"I think I can do that," I replied as I turned back to the piano and started to sing my private concert for Ethan.

I sang another song by Sara Bareilles, a few of Ella Fitzgerald's, some Billy Joel just for him, and then one of my favorites: Nora Jones. I'd just started to play "Don't Know Why" when someone rang the doorbell and knocked on the door.

Without stopping, I yelled, "Could you get that? I'm on a roll in here."

I heard the door open, just as I started to sing the first verse. Angry voices carried from the foyer into the study and stilled my fingers.

"Gray?" I called. "Who's at the door?" I called again as I stood from the bench to see who was there. As I straightened, black swam into my vision and a loud ringing buzzed through my ears. I bumped into the bench

Promise

seat, and it toppled over, causing a crashing sound that seemed farther away than it should have been. I felt the warm trickle of blood as it slid down my nose and over my lips and chin. A commotion at the door tried to draw my attention, but all I could focus on was the bright red liquid that covered my hands and dripped onto the floor in a macabre scene.

"Ethan!" I panicked, calling out for him with the last of my conscious energy.

"Charlie!" I heard the voices yell in unison. I looked up and was confused at the sight before me. Ethan and... Ben were rushing from the entryway toward me. It looked to me that Ben was ahead of Ethan, and, when he went to grab for me, Ethan put himself between us and threw his hand away before he could touch me.

"Don't you dare touch her," Ethan warned.

"Don't tell me what to do," Ben slurred angrily as he shoved Ethan's hands off of him. "You don't know what she wants. You won't let me ask her. I have a right to ask her, and she has a right to know that I still love her!" he yelled.

"I don't care how you feel, and you sure as hell don't need to tell her. You don't deserve her," Ethan spat.

"And what does she deserve, Ethan? Because she sure as hell deserves better than you!" Ben countered as he shoved a hand into Ethan's chest.

Abruptly, Ethan lunged forward and slammed Ben into the built-in bookcase. In a flash, Ethan cocked his fist back and plowed it into Ben's jaw.

I heard myself yell for them to stop, but I was rooted to my spot, covering my nose to stop the incessant bleeding. With every passing minute, I felt myself get drowsier, and I knew I needed to stop the bleeding. I watched as Ben managed to shove Ethan off him and threw a haphazard punch that Ethan easily dodged. I continued to beg and plead with them to stop; whether it was out loud or just in my head I didn't know.

Suddenly I felt like I was on a tilt-a-whirl, and my vision clouded over. I reached out to steady myself, and my hand connected with the piano keys in a cacophony of violent sound. My knees gave out, and I slumped to the floor heavily before my whole body went into a spasm, and I shook violently, unable to control my shaky movements.

"Holy shit! Charlie!" I heard Ethan yell and then came a loud grunt.

"Oh God, Charlie!" That time it was Ben's voice.

Finally the shaking stopped, but it was getting harder to breathe by the second. It felt like an elephant was sitting on my chest, and I gasped for breath desperately as black crept into the corners of my vision. The voices became far away and hollowed like echoes in a long tunnel. I looked up and saw Ethan hovered above me. My body relaxed as the band across my chest released. Ethan repeated for me to breathe, but little air passed my lips. Ethan's fingers pressed to my neck, and he yelled frantically for Ben to call an ambulance. After all these years I'd finally gotten the man that I loved, and I was about to lose him—for good. The last thing I remembered before everything went black was Ethan's blurry face bent over mine, pleading, "Hold on, Charlie. Please God, hold on. Stay with me, sweetheart..."

***

Beep...beep...whoosh. Beep...beep... whoosh. The rhythmic cycle echoed through my ears over and over. I didn't know where I was or what was going on, but I wasn't scared by my scattered thoughts. The last thing I remembered was singing while Ethan cooked dinner, and then Ben was there, and they fought. Had Ethan been hurt? I knew he was very capable of defending himself, but he was also capable of getting hurt.

The once-rhythmic beep of the machine rapidly ascended with my concern for Ethan. I heard distant voices as they shouted commands. One voice rang through all the others, a voice I'd know anywhere. *Ethan.* He sounded scared, his voice agitated. I reached for him, but my body ignored the order. I wanted to comfort him and tell him everything was going to be all right, but my arms wouldn't move, just as my eyes wouldn't open, and the beeping became urgent.

Alarms sounded from the erratic rhythm, but I was indifferent. My mind vaguely registered panic but had blanketed itself in an eerie calm. A warm sensation spread up my arm and loosened all thought from my mind. The beeping around me gradually slowed as I gently floated back into a black abyss.

Chapter 23

Beep...beep...beep—whoosh. Beep...beep...beep—whoosh. Beep...beep...beep—whoosh. The foreign sound puzzled me as I tried to swallow, but something blocked my way. I gagged on the obstruction that choked me uncomfortably, and I wanted to grab whatever was there, but again my arms wouldn't move.

I heard Ethan's and Daddy's frantic voices join the assortment of sounds as they yelled for a doctor. I didn't know what I was choking on or why my eyes wouldn't open, but the warm sensation spread up my arm again, and it pulled me back into the blackness, and as the dark took over, I felt a warm hand slip into mine.

A while later, the steady beeping continued, but the rushing air sound no longer followed. I felt cool air in my nose, and something lay gently on my upper lip. I tested my throat and found the only difficulty in swallowing was due to dryness. I opened my eyes and blinked rapidly at the dim light of the room. When my vision cleared, I saw a head lying beside me and knew instantly whom it belonged to. Unable to resist touching him, I lifted my hand and rested it in his soft hair, comforted by the familiar silky, soft texture. I'd barely made purchase when his head came up quickly and two deep-blue pools stared down at me.

"Charlie?" His hoarse whisper choked from beautiful lips. "Charlie, can you hear me?" he asked more urgently, and in answer, I raised my hand to his unshaven cheek with all the energy I had. It started to slip from him, but he latched on to my hand and held it to his face reverently. My hand felt cold against the warmth of his skin.

"God, Charlie! Your hand is like ice!" He curled my hand between his and placed warm kisses to my knuckles. I smiled weakly up at him with gratitude. He always knew what I needed.

"Charlie, sweetheart, you're in the hospital. You really have to stop doing this to me," he added, exasperated. I smiled again, but stopped when I saw the look on his face. He was so wounded, defeated, that it hurt me to know I'd caused it. Warm tears spilled over my cheeks.

"Shhh, it's okay. You're okay," he cooed as I nodded my understanding.

"You?" The croaked whisper pulled from my lips.

"Me? Charlie, you're worried about me right now?" he asked incredulously. I nodded again. I knew by the look of him that he'd had a rough night. He hadn't shaved, his hair looked like he'd run his fingers through it countless times, and his rumpled clothes were the same ones he'd come to

Promise

dinner in. He looked like he needed a hot shower and a good night's sleep.

"Sunshine, as long as I get to see those beautiful gray eyes, I'll be just fine," he told me. He reached for my hand and laced our fingers together.

"So...tired...Gray," I rasped. I felt my eyes grow heavy with every minute they were open.

"I know. I'll let the doctor know you woke up, but for now just rest, sunshine. I'll be here when you wake up."

"Promise?" I asked as my eyelids slid closed.

"Pinky swear," he answered, and kissed my tattoo.

* * *

The next time I woke up, I was more alert but much weaker. I'd never felt weakness like it before, and just holding my head up was exhausting. As I stirred, my arm hit something warm and solid beside me.

"Ouch! Watch where you throw those things," he mumbled into my shoulder.

"Sorry," I offered with a shy smile.

"You're forgiven," he answered, kissing my shoulder. "You scared me," he added in a grave voice. I struggled to turn on my side to face him, but when I finally did I laid my head on his arm and looked up at him.

"I'm sorry. I didn't mean to," I said earnestly as I stroked his tired face. "How long have I been here?" I asked Ethan, as I took in his abnormally unkempt appearance.

"Two days," he said as he checked his watch. "Almost three." He let out a big sigh and briefly closed his eyes to block out the memory of the last few days. He rested his forehead to mine and said, "Two of the longest days of my life."

"So it's Tuesday?" I asked reluctantly as I remembered that I was scheduled for my fourth treatment.

"Almost, yeah, why? Got a hot date?" he teased.

"Something like that. Have you been home at all? Showered? Changed? Eaten anything?" I quipped, looking away from him.

"Slow down and stop worrying about me. We need to worry about you right now. I'm fine, Lee. Better now that you're awake." Pausing, he added, "So before the doctors and your family come barging in here, you want to tell me what's really going on?" He looked at me, and I knew I couldn't lie anymore. But I thought one giant Band-Aid would be better than multiple, so I asked Ethan to get the doctors and my family.

Despite his protests, he hesitated only briefly before he got up from the bed. I smiled to reassure him, and myself, but I could tell it did nothing for either of us.

A few minutes later, Dr. Meadows and Dr. Sharp came in and introduced two new doctors as Harold Mar-

Promise

tin and Eli Parish. They asked that everyone wait outside while they went over my chart and current condition with me. Each performed his examination and clarified what had happened.

Dr. Sharp explained that my situation, while not quite critical, was much worse than it had been. The cancer was acting aggressively, and they were going to increase my chemo dosage. I'd be admitted for the duration of my treatment. They were worried about my body's ability to recover from the side effects independently of an IV and close supervision.

I wasn't pleased to hear that I'd be stuck in the hospital for a few weeks, but after they explained that my body was growing too weak to fight the cancer and chemo alone, I accepted the situation. I didn't have the energy to fight them on the subject as well as the cancer, so I sat back and let them hook me up to more machines as they started me on IV fluids and steroids.

The neurologist said I'd experienced a nonepileptic seizure. Excessive fluid loss from both blood and dehydration caused my blood glucose to fall well below normal levels and triggered a seizure. The seizure had ceased both my breathing and heartbeat due to my body's already weakened state.

They said that CPR was administered right away and I'd regained a regular heartbeat in the ambulance. With everything that had gone on, they warned me that they would have to keep a close eye on my treatments and how I felt, because they didn't want me to have another episode. They added an antiseizure medication to my growing pile of pills, as well as an IV drip that would give me the proper nutrients to bring my blood glucose levels up and keep them up.

I listened to what they said, and I knew that the road to remission had just gotten a lot tougher. Even though my family and friends were outside the door, I didn't want to face them; I couldn't. I was right back in the middle of the same argument with myself.

One side of me knew I had to tell them, needed to tell them, but the other side still wanted to spare them and hide from the reality that lay before me. I didn't know how I'd tell them or what I'd say. They didn't deserve this, and they didn't deserve what was about to happen. Who knew if the chemotherapy would even work or if I'd survive it? The grave tone of the doctors didn't infuse me with much confidence, and I knew that I couldn't face them. I didn't want them to be stuck in the hospital too. They had their own lives to live, even if I couldn't live mine.

When Dr. Parish and Dr. Martin left, I asked that Dr. Sharp stay behind. Dr. Meadows said he'd check on me later, but he had other patients to see down in the emergency department. I thanked him and asked that he

Promise

send Ben in on his way out if he was still here. I knew my dad and Maddie would want to see me first, but I couldn't handle seeing them yet. I knew I had to face Ben and at least tell him the truth, so he wouldn't blame himself for us not working out.

I was surprised when Dr. Sharp questioned if I was sure I wanted to talk to everyone. He said he didn't want the stress to cause another episode, but I reassured him that it was a long time past when I should have. I didn't tell him I was going to tell only one person.

Shortly after Dr. Meadows left the room, there was a light knock on the door.

"Come in," I called out.

Ben entered slowly and stopped short before he approached the bed. I imagined how I must look and tried to hide my cringe. I felt like death warmed over, quite honestly, and I chuckled mirthlessly to myself at the irony of my statement.

"Hi," I said.

"Hi back," he replied. A smile spread across my face at the memory of our greeting.

"How're you feeling?" he asked, but I could see he instantly regretted it.

"It's okay. I'm okay," I offered. I waited until he looked back up at me. "Ben, can you sit down for a minute? I'd like to talk to you." I nodded my head to the chair beside my bed. "There's something I need to tell you, but first I need to apologize for the way I acted and the things I said to you and didn't say to you."

"You have nothing to be sorry about, Charlie. I'm the one who is sorry. I shouldn't have just shown up like that out of the blue. And I shouldn't have done it in that state," he interrupted.

"No, Ben, I'm the one who needs to apologize. I lied to you. I lied to everyone, for weeks. I let my fear and anger get the better of me, and I took it out on you. But when you came back, I was so scared that I'd lose you again that I kept up the lie so I didn't give you an opportunity to do it again."

"Charlie, what are you talking about? What's going on?" he asked me, his voice laced with concern.

"I'm sick," I stated plainly.

"Char, you're in the hospital. I just watched you have a seizure with blood running down your face," he deadpanned. "I know you're not well, but you have a team of doctors here working to make you better. It's going to be oh—"

"No, Ben. I'm *sick*."

"What do you mean?" He moved so he stood next to my head.

Promise

"I have leukemia," I blurted in a rush, and watched as the word sunk in. Shock, then disbelief, transformed his handsome features.

"But you're so young. You're only twenty-six for God's sake, Charlie! You're young and beautiful. You have so much life in you—" He stopped and looked at me. I could see that the tears that threatened in my eyes were also in his.

"Charlie," he started again, "how long have you known?"

"I found out a few days after I fell."

"But that..." He paused, thinking back, then swung his head back up to me. "That was months ago! We were still together! You lied to me for weeks!" His voice had risen considerably over the course of his sentence, but I deserved it. I'd hurt him. Dr. Sharp opened the door and checked on us.

"It's okay. Everything is fine, Dr. Sharp," I assured the concern on his face.

"*Fine?*" Ben screamed. "God dammit, Charlie. I hate that word!" At that, Dr. Sharp moved into the room and closed the door behind him.

"Sir, you need to lower your voice," he commanded calmly.

Ben turned to me, "Charlie, this is not *fine*, and you are not *fine*. All those times I asked if you were okay, you lied to me. You lied right to my face. Why didn't you tell me? Did you not trust me enough to tell me you were sick? Did you think that I wouldn't love you anymore?"

"It's not that. Ben. It's not that at all. It's quite the opposite. I didn't tell anyone. So far you're the only one who knows. I couldn't tell you, or anyone, because I wanted to save you the trouble and pain of going through this. I couldn't put my family through it again. You don't know what it was like for my mother and our family. We barely made it through, and we've never been the same. I didn't want that to happen again." I paused to gather my thoughts.

"I loved you so much I couldn't bring myself to hurt you like that. I didn't want this life for you, a life where you had to put your life on hold and take care of me—a life where your girlfriend was too tired to go out, too tired to be anything but a body next to you in bed, a life where the woman you wanted to marry and spend your life with couldn't give you the family you both dreamed of or the long future you'd planned.

"I didn't want you to have a life where the threat of cancer was a cloud that would hang over our heads for the rest of our lives. So I pushed you away before it was too late. But when you came back, I selfishly wanted to keep you even if it wasn't fair to you."

"But I loved you, Charlie," he implored. "You were supposed to tell me everything, especially the things you didn't tell everyone else. I was going to ask you to marry me, for God's sake." I could see the hurt and sadness that consumed his eyes.

"I never meant to hurt you, Ben. You have to believe that was the last thing I ever wanted to do. I thought I was doing the right thing, but looking back, I can see that it wasn't. I just wanted more time. I wanted more time with you, more time with my family, more time for normalcy, more time for life." I paused, breathless. Dr. Sharp came over and increased the flow on my oxygen tubes, and I smiled my thanks.

"You said that I was young and had a lot of life in me, but that's what I thought about for you. You're an intelligent, handsome, strong man who has so many great things to offer this world. I didn't want to be the reason you had to hide away or be the reason your view of the world changed. I didn't want to bring darkness into a life destined for light. And honestly, I wanted to be as perfect for you as you'd been for me. I knew when I got my diagnosis that I could never be that for you. So I did what I thought was best for you, and let you go."

"But that's not life. Life is messy and hard. The only good thing about it is when you find someone to go through it all with you."

"I know, and this disease helped open my eyes to who that was for me. I'm sorry that it wasn't you. I had so much fear that Ethan and I would never happen, or God forbid that it would and wouldn't work out. And then what would I do?" I paused. "But this diagnosis stripped away that fear and helped me to see the truth."

"I was the one supposed to protect you, not the other way around. God, Charlie, I'm so sorry. I'm sorry I couldn't protect you." He collapsed to his knees as his head fell to the bed. Dr. Sharp quietly left the room and gave us privacy once more.

"Shh...it's okay," I repeated over and over as I ran my fingers over his head. "Everything is going to be okay. You're going to go live the life you deserve with a woman who will be equally deserving. You're going to love one another and be good to each other. You're going to walk through the messy stuff together, and you're going to protect her as you've always protected me. This isn't your fault, Ben, and it isn't your future. You couldn't have saved me from this even if you'd tried." I smiled at him as he raised his head from the bed.

"I'm sorry, Charlie. I'm sorry this has happened to you."

I reached over and held his hand in mine as we sat in silence for a moment. Then he smiled sweetly at me and

Promise

pushed up from the floor to once again take his seat in the chair beside my bed.

"So...you and Ethan, huh?" he smiled ruefully.

I sighed and returned his smile. "Like I said, when something like this comes into your life, you're shown opportunities you might have never considered before or had the guts to follow through on. One of those opportunities for me was Ethan. He came back to me at a time when I needed him most, and he helped me unlock the love I'd hidden in my heart for all these years. I loved you, Ben. I still do. But I realized that I just loved you, but didn't *just* love Ethan. I was *in* love with him. That was the difference that I hadn't known for a long time. I'm sorry. You probably don't want to hear how much I love him."

"It's okay. I understand. I think I've always known that you loved him as more than just your best friend. I'm glad you've realized it because you deserve happiness, now more than ever, no matter what I said the other night. I can see the way your eyes light up when you talk about him. Please, please just promise me you'll fight. Fight to have all those things you said to me with Ethan. I know he loves you. I've always known he loved you. He looked at you the way I did, but you never saw it. I think that's why I didn't like the guy. I knew that if it ever came down to it, you'd choose him over me. I see now that that was the right thing all along, and I should have just stepped aside.

You two belong together. It's as clear as day." He paused before he leaned forward and said, "You'll call if there's ever anything you need?"

"I will, Ben, thank you. You've been an amazing friend, and I'm eternally grateful for it."

"You're welcome. I'll see you around, Charlie."

"You bet you will."

"Good." He smiled.

"Good." I returned his smile.

He stood quietly at the side of my bed, and I felt my body relax from the lifted weight of the burden I'd carried. It was the longest I'd been awake in days, and I'd completely exerted myself emotionally and physically. I yawned and felt my eyes slowly close. Ben leaned over and placed a gentle kiss on my forehead.

"Good-bye, Charlie," he whispered.

"Mmm," I mumbled after him. The door to my room closed, and I succumbed to the pull of sleep.

Chapter 24

First thing the next morning, I heard my family outside my door, demanding to know what was going on. Dr. Sharp tried to calm them down, but it was no small feat. I heard Daddy threaten to have him fired (and since he sat on the board of trustees he had the power to do it) and that he'd pull his donor contributions if they didn't tell him what was wrong with me, but Dr. Sharp didn't budge.

I heard Maddie calm him down, and he apologized for his threat but insisted he had a right to know. Dr. Sharp and Lisa tried to keep them out of my room, but Maddie managed to push into my room, quickly followed by my dad and Ethan. He looked slightly better than before but still ragged, and I had a feeling my dad had sent him home to shower and change at some point last night since he wore different clothing.

I hoped he'd gone to work in the last few days, or else I'd feel terrible that I'd kept him from his business. I looked out the open door and saw Jessica, Grant, Louis, Megan, and Mr. and Mrs. Stone standing in the hallway with Lisa.

"I see the gang's all here," I joked, and looked up at Ethan, who looked somber as he shifted behind my dad and Maddie.

"Dr. Sharp, I thought I asked to not have any visitors," I asked under my breath.

"I relayed your wishes to your family, but I have to do what's best for my patient, and I believe that that would be you telling them what's going on, Charlie."

I felt the tears clog my throat, and I couldn't look anyone in the eye, so I looked down at my trembling hands. Ethan stepped forward and reached his powerful hand over to steady mine. I tried to draw strength from it, but my mind raced with panic and indecision. My family called out questions in rapid-fire succession.

"What's this all about?"

"Are you okay?"

"What's going on?"

I couldn't find the words. I was overwhelmed by their presence and I was shocked to realize I didn't want them there. All I could do was shake my head over and over. Ethan squeezed my hand tighter, and I flinched, causing him to drop my hand immediately.

"Lee? Please, you're scaring me. What's going on, sweetheart?"

"Sweetheart?" my father asked.

Ethan ignored my father's scrutinizing stare and Maddie's open-mouthed gawk and asked me again what was wrong.

I looked over to Dr. Sharp, and he saw the fear and stress in my eyes. With a slight nod of acknowledgement, he stepped forward and spoke to everyone.

"If you would all please wait in the hallway, I need to speak to Charlie alone." His request was met with feverish denials and questions. Ethan's hand clasped mine again, and I broke.

He sat there supporting me while I'd done nothing but lie to him and all of my family for months. I thought about the night before and how freeing it had been to tell Ben the truth. Could I really do this to all of them? We'd barely survived my mother. Could I really make them go through this again? The voices of my family continued to run together as their worry poured out. Each demanded I speak, but I couldn't find my words. Tears fell from my eyes as I listened to their pleas.

Finally, I looked up to the faces of all the people I loved most in the world and felt my heart crack. They kept waiting for me to say something that would change their lives forever. I couldn't do it. I couldn't be the one who broke their hearts again. I couldn't be the reason for their pain.

"I can't," I whispered.

Cassie Gregg

"You can't what, Charlotte?" my dad asked angrily.

"I can't do this. I want all of you to leave. Now." The protests began in earnest, but I couldn't take it anymore.

"Now!" I yelled with all my might, causing my heart monitor to rise dangerously. I tried to breathe in more air and calm down, but I couldn't catch my breath.

Dr. Sharp stepped forward and began taking my vitals while Lisa came running into the room and ushered my family out. I still couldn't seem to catch my breath, and Lisa moved to help take the nasal cannula off and put an oxygen mask on over my nose and mouth. She turned and escorted my family from the room, and I saw the dawning look of understanding on my father's face and knew then that he knew what was going on.

He'd been at my mother's bedside every day, and it didn't escape him what was going on. The look of utter disbelief and grief that filled his eyes split my cracked heart in two. Ethan looked between the two of us, and the utter panic and shock on his face brought more tears to my eyes.

This is the best thing for them. I repeated the words over and over like a mantra. The chaos outside my room became deafening as I sank lower into my bed and let the tears I'd kept inside flow freely from my eyes, my heart, and my soul.

* * *

Promise

It was the third day after everyone had left my room that my dad finally went home. Shortly after he left, the rest followed—all except Ethan. I'd befriended another one of my nurses, Ami, and she kept me apprised of what was going on outside my room, whether I wanted to know or not. She was a kind woman, about my age, with a warm smile and beautiful chestnut hair. I enjoyed the talks we had and her sense of humor. She never missed an opportunity to tell me about Ethan.

Even if she hadn't told me he was still there, I knew he was. I'd hear his deep voice rumble as he spoke to nurses and doctors out in the hallway. He'd ask how I was, but they'd respect my wishes and wouldn't tell him what was going on. They told him I was doing fine and in good hands.

Some days I felt better; others I felt weaker. The doctors, however, said I was strong enough for my fourth treatment and would be hooked up to the pump that afternoon for my new dosage treatment. It was after this session that I'd lose my hair, and I'd prepared myself for it to happen, but how prepared could one really be? I'd shave my head at the first sign of it falling out, but decided not to worry about it yet.

I called Joe to let him know what was going on and that I wouldn't need him that week. He told me he'd see me tomorrow, and I smiled because I knew he'd come to make sure I was okay. Over the last few weeks, I'd come to see him as a dear friend. I loved our car rides and hearing about his family. He never talked about his time in the Army, but he let it slip on one of our trips that he was a retired serviceman. As with Ethan, I didn't push for information, but I could tell that whatever he'd done, he'd been good at it.

Lisa wheeled the chemotherapy pump into the room for my treatment and hooked up the bag. It dripped for three hours, and she sat with me for every minute of it. I got sick twice, and twice Lisa helped me into the bathroom as I threw up everything in my stomach. Both times she called for assistance to safely get me out of bed, and when Ami bustled into my room, I heard Ethan outside in the hallway, demanding to know what was going on. I prayed he didn't come in and find out what was happening. I didn't want him to see me like this.

"That boy out there loves you, you know," Lisa scolded as she took the plastic bin she'd placed in my lap with this last round of nausea. I'd been too weak to get out of bed the third time the nausea hit.

"Yes, he does," I agreed. "Almost as much as I love him," I added sadly.

"Have you thought any more about letting him in?" she asked hesitantly. I tried not to hear the hidden meaning in her words, but it was hard to do.

Promise

"I don't want him to see me like this. He doesn't do well with not having power, and in this situation, he's completely powerless. I don't want to hurt him." I paused, gathering my thoughts. "I want him to remember the old me. He loved that girl. Not this weak, sick one. I want him to go on with his life, live happily, find his forever."

"Have you considered he already has?"

"I don't want him in here," I stated firmly.

"Yes, Miss Montgomery," she replied pointedly in show of her disapproval.

If I hadn't heard it in her voice, I would have seen it in the stern, motherly look she gave me. What did she know? Ethan was better off without me holding him back, just as Ben had been better off too. He'd find another woman soon, and I'd be remembered as the girl who was once his best friend. I lay back after she left my room and waited for the next battle.

Like with the last treatment, the fever struck first, and Ami came in and gave me a fever-reducer through my IV line and hooked up an extra bag of fluids to keep me hydrated. She sat with me for a while and patted my head and neck with a cool towel. My temperature was still high, so she called for a couple ice packs and put them under my arms and behind my neck. When the fever finally broke, my body, once again, swung in the opposite direction and sent me into severe chills. Ami swaddled me with blankets and put a heating pad down for me to lie with. Lisa sat next to me again, and held my hand while my body shivered uncontrollably.

The next morning, I threw up again and again over the course of a few hours. I dehydrated myself, so they reattached the IV fluids and antinausea medication.

Lisa and Ami were angels, especially Lisa. I didn't know how she managed to be there and move so quickly for a woman her age, but I was impressed and grateful. She did everything she could to make me as comfortable as I could be, and I was indebted to her for that. Exhausted from the exertions of the last few days, I collapsed back into bed after the last bout of dry heaving ended.

I couldn't remember the last time I'd eaten something solid, but Dr. Sharp and the nurses told me I had to eat or they'd have to put a feeding tube in. Dr. Sharp had fat and nutrients added to my IV rotation the day before because he wanted to avoid surgery, even a minor one.

I thought it was because he didn't think I was strong enough to make it through surgery because I'd lost too much weight and fluids, as it would put excess stress on my organs, weakening me further. The last thing I wanted was to have another tube stuck in me, so I looked back at the forgotten dinner tray and grabbed the green Jell-O. I managed to keep it down and pulled the bowl of soup into

Promise

my hands and started to eat that as well. Lisa smiled at me and left the room to tend to another patient.

Just before I fell asleep, Ami came in to check on me and make sure I had everything I needed before I fell asleep for the night. I remembered the way she and Ben had looked at one another the other day and thought about how cute a couple they'd be. I let the matchmaking idea lull me into a peaceful sleep.

The next day was day five, and I knew what that meant and dreaded it. My mind was plagued with thoughts of Ethan and what I was about to endure again. Pain. Searing-hot pain.

It started when a pain in my lower back woke me in the middle of the night. It wasn't bad at first, but it was incessant and uncomfortable. I tried to breathe through it and prepared for it to worsen. What started as a dull throb transformed to sharp knives down my spine until finally it felt like someone twisted my muscles and bones together, like wringing out a wet towel.

I tried to hide my whimpers from the ears of the doctors and nurses, but there was nothing I could do about my heart monitor. With every deep breath I took, my heart rate increased a little more. I didn't know if Ethan was still there, but I wished he was because it hurt so much more than before—but as much as I wanted him, I still couldn't let him see me like this.

Cassie Gregg

The doctors had warned that because my body was weak, the pain could be greater with each treatment I received. Another wave of pain pushed through my body, and I screamed. I didn't recognize the sound that came from me at first because it was the most pitiful, wailing sound I'd ever heard, and it wasn't until my heart monitor alarm went off that I realized it was me. I screamed for the pain to stop. I screamed for it all to stop, and I sobbed for mercy.

A commotion at the door caught my attention momentarily when I saw pink scrubs, white coats, and the flash of a familiar face. The next wave of pain took over, and I let out another soul-crushing scream through gritted teeth as I curled into myself as tightly as possible. The pain made my vision blur, but I saw him break through the bodies guarding the door. At just the sight of him, a small wave of relief chipped a piece of the pain away.

"Ethan!" I cried as I squeezed my arms to my sides in hope that it would stop some of the pain. He reached to gently touch my arm, but I slapped his hand away.

"Don't," I warned through sobs. "Don't touch me. It hurts too much. Please don't touch me," I wailed as a doctor and a nurse finally made it to my bed. I moaned from so much pain and made the mistake of looking up at Ethan's face as he looked down at me. He looked totally helpless, like a boy lost from his mother, as his eyes widened with fear.

"Ethan," I let out in a ragged whisper, and held my hand out for him to take. Gently, he cradled my hand like it was an injured bird, and I squeezed onto his as the pain shot down my spine and sent my muscles into tight spasms.

"Make it stop, please," I pleaded.

"I will, sweetheart. I will. Just calm down and breathe for me."

"Charlie, if you can't calm down, we'll have to give you a morphine injection," Dr. Sharp warned.

"Please," was all I said.

"Just give her the injection!" Ethan yelled at the doctor, who turned to Lisa, who had a needle of morphine in her hand.

"Relief is on its way, Charlie. Just hang in there," Lisa consoled. "It'll take a few minutes, but once it takes effect, she'll go to sleep. Keeping her sedated is the best thing for her right now," she said to Ethan, who cradled my head as he whispered calming words to me. I focused on his voice and my breathing as the medication settled in my veins.

"Ethan," was all I could say as I gripped his shirt with both of my hands.

"I'm here, sweetheart. I'm not going anywhere. I'm here." I pressed my head into his hand as the meds took over and the pain dissipated. My body slowly relaxed, muscle by muscle, into sedation as Ethan softly ran his knuckles back and forth across my cheek.

Chapter 25

ETHAN

"Cancer?" I repeated aloud, more for myself than anything. How could she have cancer? How did I not notice? Why didn't she tell me?

"I know you all must have a lot of questions, and I will try to answer what I can," the doctor announced to the room.

"Please just tell us what is going on, Dr. Sharp," Jack asked anxiously.

"Mr. Montgomery, your daughter came to the hospital a few months ago after suffering a terrible fall." Jack nodded, as did everyone else who remembered the day I'd found Charlie on the sidewalk, bleeding and unconscious. I was opening the door to take Reese for a walk when he took off running. When I caught up to him, he was barking frantically at Charlie's gate, and that was when I saw her lying on the ground. The terror that sliced through me was unlike anything I'd ever experienced. I would never forget it, but I never wanted to remember.

Cassie Gregg

"Well, sir, your daughter had fainted, which was what caused the fall. We ran some tests to determine if there was an underlying cause for her fainting spell, and a few days after her release, her extensive blood work came back, and we found abnormalities. Her white-blood-cell count was significantly off, and other markers indicated that your daughter has leukemia."

"Wait," I interrupted, "you said you ran these tests back when she fell, but that was months ago. I don't understand..." I trailed off as my mind started to reel.

"Well, Ethan, when we called Charlie to come back in, we assumed she would bring someone with her. But she didn't, and said she just wanted to know what was going on. When we gave her the diagnosis, she handled the news fairly well for someone in her position, but she refused to let us call anyone for her. She said she didn't want to, wouldn't, and couldn't put her family through this again. At the time, we didn't know her full medical history, but after being informed and spending more time with Charlie, we now understand that her mother battled cancer. I'm sorry for your loss, sir," he added, turning to Jack.

"Now, against my advisement, she chose to keep this to herself. The choice to go through this alone was her decision. After the bone-marrow biopsy, we were able to diagnose her type and determine her prognosis. Charlie has AML, acute myeloid leukemia. It's a type of cancer that affects her white blood cells. Her type of cancer is common and treatable."

"So that's good then?" Maddie spoke up.

"Yes and no, for AML is aggressive if not found early, and because Charlie had already been exhibiting symptoms—fainting spells, fatigue, bruising, loss of appetite, and a great deal of weight loss—before we diagnosed her, we believe that we were lucky we found it when we did. Had she gone a few more months without treatment, we would be having a very different conversation, if we'd been able to have this conversation at all."

Jessica and Maddie began to cry, while Louis wrapped an arm around Megan, who'd covered her face with her hands. I felt numb. All that time I'd spent avoiding her, she was sick, and she needed me.

"So what do we do?" I asked expectantly as her oncologist stepped forward again to address the room.

"When we had her diagnosis, we were able to make a plan for her. Charlie put us off for a few weeks, but we were able to finally get her in to her appointments and get started on her chemotherapy treatments. She was scheduled for six sessions, one appointment every two weeks. At this point we had assumed Charlie had informed her family, because chemo is an extremely difficult and painful process and she would more than likely have required help. I found out after her second session that she still had not told any of you when I saw her being escorted home by this gentleman here." He pointed to the large, older man dressed in an impressive suit who stood quietly off to the side of the conference room, observing.

He'd introduced himself to all of us as Joe, and he'd apparently driven Charlie to and from the hospital for her appointments. After only five minutes with the guy, I knew he cared for Charlie, just like all of us did. And how could he not? It was Charlie.

"She never told us," Jack said solemnly.

"Was she in pain?" Jessica asked through tears. I could see the hesitance on Dr. Sharp's face before he answered my sister.

"It's hard for me to know the answer to that, since she had refused to be admitted for treatments. She spent most of the process at home after she'd come in and sat for a three-hour drip. From her reports, and what I've experienced with other patients, yes, there were times when she was in great discomfort and pain. There are a lot of side effects when you have copious amounts of what boils down to poison pumped into your body to battle another poison.

"I don't know how much detail you want to hear, but I can say that it's a very unpleasant process that I wouldn't wish on anyone. I know that she rarely used her morphine pills, and when she did, she gave herself half doses. Before her third treatment, her iron levels had been too low to have the chemo administered, which indicated that her body had become too weak to handle the treatments in combination with the disease. We believe it was at this point that her nosebleeds began to increase, which brought her into the hospital last week. As far as we know, what Charlie went through today has happened before."

"*Jesus Christ!*" I exploded as I stood abruptly from my chair, sending it clattering to the floor. I couldn't handle listening to any more of it. I'd watched my Charlie go through the pain she had earlier, and it was heartbreaking, but to know that she'd been through it before while she was alone was like a knife had been plunged deep into my already broken heart.

"How could she do this alone? How could she think we wouldn't be there for her? That we wouldn't want to be there for her!" I yelled at no one in particular as I began to pace the large conference room.

"Ethan, son, calm down. We need to hear this," Jack calmly announced, and I saw the pain in his eyes, much like my own. It was killing him, too. Over the last few days, he'd come to accept that I loved Charlie and I wasn't going anywhere.

"Please continue, Dr. Sharp," he added.

Cassie Gregg

"As I was saying, because Charlie went through this before, her body suffered tremendously. On top of that, she wasn't eating, or when she did, she didn't keep it down because she was sick from the chemo. Her lack of nutrient intake and increased fluid expulsion severely malnourished and dehydrated her, which affected her strength.

"A few days ago, Charlie sustained what is called a nonepileptic seizure. Basically, that means that she had excessive blood loss that dangerously lowered her blood glucose levels. The drastic drop in BGL caused her brain to essentially short-circuit and brought on a seizure. The seizure stopped her heart and breathing, and that's why you had to perform CPR. Her heart, essentially, had to be jumpstarted back into a normal sinus rhythm.

"We've already informed Charlie that she is to remain in the hospital for the remainder of her treatment because her body is too weak to handle any kind of extra exertion, and here we can be more proactive in the care that she needs. After running more tests once she was stable, we discovered that the cancer has spread to her spleen, despite the treatments. We've scheduled surgery for early next week so that Charlie can regain more of her strength before we go in and remove her spleen.

"This should give her more of a fighting chance, since the treatments will only have to fight the cancer cells in her bone marrow and not in her spleen as well. We'll need

Promise

to keep her closely monitored to be sure that it doesn't continue to spread to her liver and possibly her skin. We also started her on a more aggressive chemotherapy plan. We explained this to Charlie and luckily, she has chosen to go through the new treatment plan.

"When this last chemo round went through her system, the fever, chills, vomiting, and pain took more out of her than she had to give. We've postponed the surgery until we know that it will be safe to operate, but we really can't put it off for too long. We'll monitor her prognosis and make the best decisions we can for Charlie. For now, we've sedated her to keep her as comfortable as possible while the chemo works through her system."

I couldn't listen to any more. I turned and walked out of the room, ignoring the calls from my family as I practically ran to the nearest exit in search of some much-needed air.

Charlie. My sunshine was so sick and hurt, and she did it alone. She thought she had to do it alone. How could I let her do that? Why didn't I notice? Why didn't I push harder when I saw all those changes in her? I knew something wasn't right, but I never would have guessed this. Was I so wrapped up in my own happiness to not see her struggle?

"Please, God. Please don't take her from me. I need her. I need her more than life itself. Please save her, please." I threw my desperate prayer into the night sky, hoping beyond hope that God answered. I pulled out my phone and saw I had a multiple missed calls. I'd been dodging calls from Dan and Perry since Charlie had been admitted last week. I'd called Perry when all this had started to clear my schedule and refer all client calls to Dan. I'd called Dan after that and told him I was taking some personal days. At the time, Charlie wouldn't allow me to see her, and I hadn't seen that changing anytime soon, so I thought I'd only be out a few days and figured if something happened the nurses knew to call me.

Then today happened. There was no way in hell I was leaving now. I couldn't possibly leave her. She needed me whether I had to sit outside her door every day or I got to sit next to her bed. I wasn't going anywhere. How could I leave when my heart was in that room? I pulled my phone back out and called Dan.

"Shaw," he answered curtly.

"It's me. I need you to do me a favor."

"Where the hell have you been? I've been calling you for two days. We have important client meetings that you've missed, and they aren't happy about it, and frankly neither am I. I signed up to be your business partner. I don't know shit about architecture design. You'd better have a really good excuse."

"I'm at the hospital." I felt him go into alert mode.

"What happened?" he demanded.

"It's not me. Relax. It's Charlie."

"Again? Dude, what is up with that girl? She's turning into a klutz," he laughed tightly. I told myself to breathe, he didn't know. He didn't mean anything by it. He loved Charlie.

"She has cancer, Dan." Silence. "You there?"

"Yeah, I'm here. Jesus, Ethan, is she okay? Is she going to be okay?"

"I don't know. It's bad, D, really bad. They've admitted her indefinitely for the rest of her treatment. She's been getting treatment for weeks and didn't tell anyone. The doctors just told us everything, and I swear I feel like I just got shot in the chest."

"Jesus," he said again. "Can I do anything?"

"Not with this. I just need to be here with her. I have to make sure she's okay." I paused for a few beats. "I don't know what I'll do if I lose her, man. I can't lose her. She's my whole world."

"I know, E-Man, I know. That's what Debra is to me, so I get it. I'm sorry I gave you a hard time earlier. Had I known Charlie was so sick I never would have said anything, but I am glad you finally pulled your head out of your ass long enough to realize she's the one for you. That girl is the best thing that has ever happened to you. If the guys were here, I know they'd kick your ass for ever hurting her. You know they were all in love with her."

"Yeah, yeah, I remember how much y'all loved her, but trust me: I love her more. And you're right—she is the best thing that has ever happened to me." I paused, trying to stay ahead of the memories that threatened to overtake me. "Anyway, I've got to get going. I've been away from her for a while, and she should be waking up soon. I just need you to cover for me for a while. Send me over the files and particulars on the new deals, and I'll try and read through it when I get a chance."

"Don't worry about it, E-Man. I've got it covered."

"I know, but once things settle down here, I'll be back. I know you can handle it without me for a few days, but I don't want to leave you hanging for too long."

"All right, man, go see your girl. Give her a kiss for me and tell her I hope to see her in the office with a basket of muffins real soon."

"Will do," I laughed. "Hey, Dan?" I asked seriously.

"Yeah?"

"Thanks, man."

"Hey, no worries, E-Man. I know you'd do the same for me."

"In a heartbeat. Talk to you later."

"Later," he said before he hung up. I made my way back inside and up to Charlie's private room. I pulled a chair up to her bedside so I could watch over her and be there when she woke up.

Promise

"Lee?" I asked quietly. She continued to sleep, still in her bed. "Why, Lee? Why wouldn't you tell me? All this time you suffered alone, and I let you. I'm so sorry, sweetheart. I'm sorry you thought you needed to hide from me. I'm sorry you thought you had to protect me. I'm sorry you are in so much pain." I barely got the last part out as silent sobs wracked my body. I held her delicate hand in mine as the tears I'd been holding in for hours fell freely down my face.

Chapter 26

CHARLIE

I WOKE SOMETIME LATER AND felt the soothing touch of someone holding my hand. I opened my eyes and found Ethan sat beside my bed, next to my head.

"Gray."

"Hey, Lee," he said softly as he pushed a wayward strand of hair from my face. I looked into his pain-filled eyes, and I knew he knew. Tears fell unbidden from my eyes.

"I'm so sorry, Ethan. I'm so sorry," I said over and over.

"Shh, shh, it's okay. I'm here. You're okay."

"I'm sorry," I repeated again.

"No, Charlie. I'm sorry. I'm sorry I wasn't there. I'm sorry you thought you had to do this alone. I'm the one who's sorry, sweetheart, not you," he cooed as he placed soft kisses to my forehead, nose, and cheeks.

His touch and sincerity were my undoing. Everything I'd been holding together seemed to come loose all at once. All the plans I'd had for us, for myself. All the things I thought I'd do, but wouldn't be able to. The sadness and pain I'd been trying not to show broke open from just the touch of his lips to my skin. I cried harder and harder, sobs choking out of me as I shook with each ragged breath.

"Sweetheart, you have to calm down. You've been through a lot and you need to rest."

"Ethan," I sobbed, "I love you. I love you so much I don't know what to do. I didn't want this for you. I wanted you to find happiness and love and forever. I can't do that for you anymore. I don't want you to hurt because of me. And Daddy! He is going to break without me here, and Maddie has a baby coming, and the café. I had all these plans and dreams, and they're all gone now. I don't know what to do. I'm so scared, and I don't know what I'm going to do!" I stumbled through my rambling words as sob after sob escaped from my chest.

"I know, Lee. I know. And I get it, I do, but, honey, I love you, stubborn and beautiful Charlotte Elizabeth Grace Montgomery. I am happy with you. I love you. My forever is you," he implored earnestly as he wrapped me in his arms. "I swear to God, Lee, sometimes I think your heart is bigger than your brain."

"Thank you," I whisper-sobbed into his neck as I held him as tightly to me as I could manage.

"Just don't leave me, Lee. I can handle you being sick and standing by your side, or even if you didn't love me anymore and I had to let you go, I'd handle it. But if you leave for good, I can't handle that."

"Tell me a story."

"What kind of story do you want?"

"I love that you call me sweetheart, but why do you sometimes call me sunshine?" I asked softly.

He smiled down at me, caressing my cheek with his fingertips. "Now that is a great story."

"Tell me," I asked again.

"I will, sunshine, but you have to answer what I said earlier."

"I'm not going anywhere, Ethan."

"Promise?" he asked me.

"Pinky...swear," I choked out between gasps for air. I'd calmed down more, but I'd gotten so worked up earlier that I could feel blood drip from my nose.

"Ethan something doesn't feel right," I tried to say as calmly as I could but failed as panic laced my words when dizziness swarmed my head as I fumbled to push my call button. Ethan rushed to the bathroom and then swiftly returned to my side with a towel for my bleeding nose.

"It's okay. I'm here. I've got you," he soothed.

It was getting harder to focus as I heard the rhythm of my heart monitor ramp up. Then suddenly, like before, my body went into a full spasm as another seizure took hold of me. The pain was excruciating, but the fear of not having control was unbearable. I didn't know how long the seizure lasted, because I blacked out, but when I came to, doctors and nurses, all with concern in their eyes, surrounded me. I looked past them for Ethan, reaching my hand out for him.

"I"—gasp—"can't"—gasp. Fear filled Ethan's eyes at the realization that I couldn't breathe.

"Help her!" he yelled frantically. I stilled as blackness oozed into my vision. "Hang on, Lee. Hang on for me, sunshine. You're going to be all right. Stay with me, I have to tell you about my sunshine."

I heard the fear and pleading in his voice as he brushed the hair from my face. I was about to break the promise I'd just made to him. I could feel it. It was different this time. I was about to break him. I was about to leave. I had to tell Ethan. He had to know that I didn't mean to break my promise. He had to know that he meant the world to me.

"I'm sorry," I whispered to him as the pain in my chest subsided, and everything around me faded as the most peaceful calm descended.

Chapter 27

ETHAN

PANIC OVERCAME ME, AND ALL my years of training escaped me. I stared as Charlie's gasps for air gradually became shallower and shallower. She grew paler by the second as the blood continued to flow from her nose.

"Hang on, Lee. Hang on for me, sunshine. You're going to be all right. Stay with me. I have to tell you about my sunshine," I pleaded with her. Then she shattered my world with two of the most heartbreaking words I'd ever heard.

"I'm sorry," she whispered before her eyes closed, and her heart monitor rang out a single tone. The alarms of all her machines went off, and the panic inside me turned into full-blown hysteria.

"No! No! Charlie! Charlie, wake up! Wake up, sweetheart!" I yelled feverishly when the team of doctors and nurses pushed me out of the way.

"She's coding!" the doctor yelled, spurring everyone into action.

Promise

"Step out of the way, son. We need room to work," one of the nurses said to me as a couple of orderlies grabbed on to my arms and moved me away from Charlie. I took one last look at her before I was escorted from the room. She lay there so still, so pale, and so fragile.

"Charlie!" I tried yelling to her again, hoping and praying she'd wake up.

"Sir, we need you to wait here," the man on my right said as he deposited me outside the door.

"We need you to try and calm down. Let them do their job, son," the older one on my left added.

"They have to save her. They have to!" I yelled as they took a step back and exchanged a look.

"They'll do everything they can, sir. Just wait here and someone will come get you when there is news." He smiled reassuringly at me, but I didn't return it.

The door slid closed, and I collapsed to my knees and rocked back and forth as I prayed to God, Jesus, and whoever else would listen to save my girl.

Jack, Grant, my sister, and my parents came running from the waiting room once they heard the code-blue call for Charlie's room.

"Please God, please!" I repeated over and over as I continued to rock myself back and forth. "She can't leave me. She can't, she promised. She's my best friend," I prayed, then thought, *She's the love of my life...my forever.*

Chapter 28

CHARLIE

THE FAMILIAR TUNE OF ELLA Fitzgerald's "Dream a Little Dream of Me" floated through my ears. It was Mom's favorite, and I could hear the familiar clang of pots and pans as she moved through the kitchen, but it was background to the soft, melodic sound of my mother's voice as she sang while she worked. How I missed that voice. It soothed me unlike anything else I'd ever known, and the last bit of pain dissipated completely. Everything inside me went numb. I felt so warm and light, like I was lying in the grass on a warm, sunny summer's day. I began to hum along to my mother's singing as a single high-pitched tone rang in the distance, but I felt myself float from the grass, higher and higher, away from the sound and into the sky. I floated toward the warm light of the sun, its rays blindingly bright, but soothing the closer I got. Just as quickly, the light faded, and an all-encompassing darkness took over. But the sound of my mother's voice kept the panic and fear at bay as peace and warmth settled over me like a warm blanket.

Chapter 29

ETHAN

"At this point, it's hard to tell when she'll regain consciousness."

"What does that mean?"

"She's had another seizure, and, in her condition, her body went into shock from the trauma and essentially shut down. She just can't handle any more, and, as a protective measure, we're keeping her in a medically induced coma. Her heart stopped completely and cut off her oxygen supply. When the brain is cut off from oxygen, it goes into a type of hibernation to recover. Since we were lucky to catch it early, we've decided it's best for her if we prolong the coma she's gone into to give her body the time it needs to heal without further harming her."

"And when she wakes up, will she be okay?"

"Like I said, Mr. Stone, we responded very quickly to her condition, but her brain and her body have sustained a lot of imbalance and trauma in a very short period of time. It's hard to know what her condition will be if she regains consciousness."

Cassie Gregg

"What do you mean *if*? She could never wake up?"

"There is a possibility that her coma becomes persistent, but again, we don't know. She's showing signs of brain activity, though diminished, but it is very encouraging that she's showing any activity at all. We just have to see how she does though the night, and from there, we take it a day at a time. We will have to wait and see what goes on before we can determine the best course of action for the remainder of her treatment."

"So all we can do is wait?"

"I'm sorry, sir, but that's the best I can give you right now. She's lucky to be here after all the upset her body has endured. She's a fighter, though. She's proved it time and again, especially now, since she is still here." With that, the doctor left the room, and I returned to my seat beside Charlie's bed.

"Did you hear that, Lee? You're a fighter, and I'll be here when you wake up. I pinky swear," I added on a whisper before I kissed the small tattoo on her pinky.

* * *

The first night she was in the coma, I sat by her bed and held her hand, listening to the slow beat of her heart monitor. The two times it slowed to a stop, I swore mine did too. Over the next few days, our families came for visits, and her father often stayed for long hours, but I saw the pain it caused him to see his little girl lying in a hospital bed.

Madeline had her baby around day four of Lee's coma, and when she was able, Max wheeled her down from the maternity ward with a beautiful pink bundle sleeping in her arms. It was sad to see Lee unable to hold her niece while meeting her for the first time, because I knew how much she loved children and how much she'd adore her little niece, Annabelle.

The rest of the family came that day to see Charlie and to meet Annabelle. After a few hours, they all left, but I refused to leave Lee's side. I was afraid that she'd wake up and I wouldn't be there. The nurses and doctors had insisted that I leave when visiting hours were over, but after profusely refusing and shamelessly throwing my name and hers around, we came to an understanding that I wasn't going to leave her no matter what. Days passed, and with each one that she didn't awaken, my heart grew heavier.

After six days in an induced coma, the doctors were pleased with Charlie's heart rate, and she was breathing on her own, so they removed the ventilator and stopped the medication to keep her sedated. What we hadn't expected was for her not to wake up. One day turned to two, and by week two, I wasn't sure I'd ever see the love of my life wake up. I'd visit her every day for as long as I could, but there were matters at work I had to take care of, so I made sure that if ever anything changed, Ami or Lisa would call me right away.

At the start of her third week, I sat alone in her room, looking down at the perfectly still angel who held my whole world in her frail hands.

"Hi, sunshine. How're you doing today?" I asked her, like I did every day. I waited just a beat, hoping she'd answer me today, but when she didn't I continued on. "Reese really misses you. I know you think it's just your home-cooked dog treats he misses, but it's you, sweetheart. That boy fell in love with you faster than I did," I laughed to myself. "He would do just about anything for you, as would I. I think he'd really like it if you woke up soon and baked for him." I smiled down at her, brushing a piece of her hair off her forehead.

"I went to the shelter last week. Jan had called and left a few messages on your machine at home, and when I went up there to see what she wanted, I was surprised to hear what you did for them. Well, not that surprised, really, you've always had such a big heart." I kissed her hand. "Anyway, I knew that they wouldn't appreciate my cooking like they do yours, so I had some meals taken over there on your Thursday. While I was there helping to hand it out, a man approached me about you. Gus, I think you know him. He was real worried about not seeing you these last few weeks. When I told him who I was, he about ripped me a new one for not taking better care of you.

"He said he'd watched you get sicker and sicker every week and swore he'd give a piece of his mind to your family if he ever came across them. Well, let me tell you, he gave me a piece of his mind, and if he'd been ten years younger, I swear he'd have tried to deck me," I laughed, but not hearing her answering giggle, I looked down at her still form in the bed.

She'd lost her perpetual summer tan, and her thin frame seemed to have more angles than curves now. Dark circles marred the beautiful skin under her eyes, and her rosy-pink lips had lost their color, now blending in with the pallor of the rest of her skin. Her hair was dull and lifeless, lying around her, unlike the bouncy waves that used to float around her when she walked. The woman who lay before me didn't look like the same woman I'd fallen in love with. The vibrant, warm, loving girl who'd stolen my heart now held it trapped in a lifeless body.

"I'm sitting here looking at you, and I want you to know that I love you, sweetheart. More than anything in this world, I love you. You look so different, but you're still the girl I fell in love with all those years ago. I was such an idiot to have wasted those years between us. I loved you since we were kids, but I was just too stupid to see what I had right in front of me. You're the best thing that ever happened to me, and I don't know what I'll do if you don't come back to me..." I whispered, tears clogging my tight throat.

"I think, just before all this happened, I'd promised to tell you about where my sunshine endearment came from. I think now is as good a time as any to tell you about it." I slid forward out of my chair and sat on her bed and cradled her hand between mine.

"You glowed like summertime sunshine. There was just something about you that made you seem effervescent," I told her, picturing her in my mind as she once was. "The first time I heard you sing in the fort, I was a goner. You were maybe seven at the time and lying on your stomach coloring, papers and crayons all around you, and you just started to sing. It stopped me in my tracks. I don't remember what I was doing, but I remember sitting there listening to you sing 'You Are My Sunshine' and thinking that was exactly what you were: sunshine. You were my sunshine." Pausing, I whispered, "You still are." Tears began to fill my eyes as I remembered the day. Clasping her hand tightly between mine, I got down on my knees beside her bed and prayed.

"Please God, I need my Charlie back. Please, *please* don't take my sunshine away."

Chapter 30

CHARLIE

Two weeks later

I OPENED MY EYES AND felt completely disoriented. I remembered being in the hospital and being in pain, but after that it all went black. I felt like I'd been gone, but I didn't know where I went or for how long. A blurry pink blob moved over me, and it said something, but all was muffled to me. Next a white blob, then another; then a blue blob moved around me. They made me dizzy with all their movements, and I closed my eyes to elude the dizziness, but it clung to me. It wasn't long before I fell back asleep, but it was just normal sleep, not the blackness I'd been stuck in before.

A while later, a warm hand rested on my arm as I stirred from sleep. My arm tingled where he touched me, and I knew who it was.

"Ethan," I whispered. My voice was hoarse as it passed my lips, and I coughed painfully.

"Easy. Sweetheart, easy. I'm right here," he soothed.

At the sound of his voice, I settled back into my pillow and opened my eyes, staring at the ceiling until I was able to see clearly. Once everything was in focus, I slowly turned my head until my eyes fell on his gorgeous face.

"Hey, you," he whispered softly as he smiled down at me with tears in his eyes. I looked into his deep-blue eyes, wet with tears, and reached up and cupped his face with my weak hand, and, as soon as it was there, he leaned in to my touch.

I wiped his tears with my thumb and whispered to him, "Please don't cry."

He grabbed on to my hand and held it reverently to the side of his face, kissing my palm and inside of my wrist.

"I'm just happy you're back, sunshine. So damn happy."

"I told you I wasn't going anywhere."

"But you did. You left me, and there was nothing I could do about it. I didn't know what to do," he whispered as more silent tears fell from his beautiful eyes.

"Shh...it's okay, Gray. It's okay. I made you a promise, and I wasn't about to break it. We don't break our promises, Ethan. I'm here and I'll never leave you again."

"Promise?"

"Pinky swear."

Epilogue

Three years later

I STEPPED INTO MY PRISTINE white shoes and straightened my dress for the hundredth time. Maddie and Jessica were flitting around behind the kids, trying to get them into their clothes. They'd look absolutely adorable, once we got them on them. I'd decided that since both kids could walk now, I wanted them to have a part in the big day.

Annabelle was our flower girl, and Luke the ring bearer. The little outfits we'd gotten them were just to die for, and I couldn't wait to see them on my niece and soon-to-be nephew. Everyone in the room was milling around, trying to get any last-minute things done, but it didn't bother me because today I got to marry my forever.

I fixed the veil in my hair one more time and smiled at the commotion around the room. Now that I had enough to style it, my hair looked beautiful all curled and pinned. I looked at my reflection in the mirror and saw the excitement in my eyes. My hair looked perfect, as did my makeup, and I smoothed my hands down my mother's wedding dress and smiled at the thought of her. One final check and I was ready to go.

Amelia stepped into the room just as my bridal party was lining up. "Charlie, darling, you look absolutely stunning, just like your mother."

"Don't you dare make me cry, Mrs. Stone, I just got my makeup all set."

"I won't be the only Mrs. Stone after today." She smiled brightly at me.

"And here I go!" I said with a watery smile as Amelia handed me her handkerchief.

"You will still look beautiful, Charlie. I just wanted to step in before the ceremony started to tell you that I am so incredibly happy, Mr. Stone and I both, that you are marrying our son. I had always hoped that one day you would be my daughter-in-law. All those years I watched my son love you and you love my son, I wanted to shake you both silly so many times, but I knew that God's plan for you both had yet to be revealed. Now that it has, I just wanted you to know that I could not have picked a better woman to marry my son. And I know your mother felt the same way." She hugged me to her, holding me tightly.

"Thank you, Amelia. That means the world to me to hear."

"It's heartfelt, darling. All right now, that's enough of the mushy stuff. Let's get you down the aisle." She smiled and patted my cheek before turning and leaving the room. The orchestra started to play, signaling it was finally time.

I peeked into the church pews and caught Ben's eyes. He held a beautiful towheaded baby boy in his arms; his stunning wife waited in the line before me. He smiled and waved with Wyatt's little arm at both Ami and me. I smiled back at their adorable family and sent a little prayer of thanks to God for bringing them both into my life. They were both invaluable friends.

I was glad Ben and I had worked everything out when we did, because he'd been an amazing friend to have through my recovery. It took a while for him and Ethan to be civil with one another, but when I told them to do it for me, they both grudgingly obliged. It wasn't long after the ceasefire that the two became friends, and not long after that that I convinced Ami to ask Ben out. And the rest, as they say, is history.

Beside Ben, Joe sat with his wife, Rose, talking with the people around them. Joe had continued to come to the hospital routinely throughout my recovery and had brought Rose by to meet me one afternoon. The two of them continued to visit from then on. She was a formidable woman who had the kindest heart, and she seemed like the perfect match for Joe. I loved to watch the two of them together.

Ethan and Joe had become really close while I was in the hospital. I think their military background strengthened their bond, and it was fun to listen to them talk about their experiences. Joe looked at Ethan as more of a son than a friend, but Ethan didn't seem to mind, for he respected Joe like he respected his father.

Dr. Sharp and Lisa sat in the same row with their spouses, and they all smiled back at the door in anticipation. The rest of my friends and family sat patiently as they waited in the pews for the procession to begin. But the one who mattered most to me today waited for me at the end of the aisle.

I stepped out of the hallway, and my father took my hand and looped it through his arm. "You look beautiful, baby girl," he whispered as he kissed my temple.

"Thank you, Daddy." I smiled at him.

As we took our first steps down the aisle, I looked up to the beautiful, ornate stained-glass window behind the altar. It was a beautiful day, and the sun shone perfectly through the glass, casting the chapel in a kaleidoscope of colors.

"Mamma's here," Daddy whispered to me.

I squeezed his arm tighter as I fought back tears. I knew that Mom would have been so happy to see Ethan and me get married, and it warmed my heart to think that she was there watching over us on this magical day. I pulled my eyes away from the window and down to the man who waited for me at the end of the aisle, where Ethan's eyes were fixated on me. He looked so impossibly handsome in his tuxedo.

A smile nearly split my face in two as I continued to look into his warm eyes. He returned my smile with an equally stunning one of his own, and I walked a little faster toward him. Daddy chuckled beside me as he too sped up his steps to get me down the aisle faster. I couldn't wait to make it to the end of the aisle where the man of my dreams waited to promise me forever. And when the pastor asked me to make those same promises, I'd undoubtedly reply with a *pinky swear*.

* * *

As we waved good-bye to all our friends and family at the reception, Ethan bent down and swept me into his arms and sat us in the back of the waiting limo.

"Hey! Just because I married you doesn't mean you get to manhandle me anytime you want."

"I think that's exactly what it means, wife." My heart melted at his new favorite endearment for me. He hadn't stopped saying it since the pastor had pronounced us husband and wife.

"Say it again," I whispered into his ear.

He cradled me tighter in his lap and whispered back, "Mrs. Stone, I do believe you are my wife."

"Mr. Stone, I do believe you are my husband."

"Forever and always, sweetheart."

"Forever and always, Gray." I kissed him passionately as the car pulled from the curb toward the airport.

Thirty minutes later, Ethan and I were settled on the private plane bound for our honeymoon. Ethan still hadn't told me where we were going. He'd had Maddie and Jess pack my bags for the next two weeks, and I was very eager to know what he'd planned for us.

"Now will you tell me where we're going?" I asked petulantly. The stewardess handed us each a flute of champagne with her congratulations before joining the pilot in the cockpit.

"I believe there was somewhere you wanted to go back in the hospital—"

"You're taking me to Bora-Bora?" I interrupted excitedly.

"Was that not where I promised to take you when you got better? I'm sorry it took me so long to plan." He smiled wickedly at me. He knew how much it meant to me that he'd remembered and made this dream come true. I launched myself out of my seat and into his lap.

"You are the best husband in the whole world!"

"Say *that* again."

Promise

"Husband," I whispered huskily, twining my fingers through his short hair and pulling him down to me for a sweet kiss. I felt him respond and shifted myself on his lap, teasing him more. A deep growl rumbled from his chest. I untangled myself from his lap and grabbed his hands, pulling him with me backward toward the small bedroom at the back of the plane.

"I think I'll need some help getting out of this dress," I teased.

"I think I'm up to the task." He smiled back, his eyes darkening with lust.

"I hope so, because there is something under here I got just for you."

"Is that right? Anything else you've got for me?"

"You'll just have to come find out, but you're going to like it."

"Promise?"

"Pinky swear."

Made in the USA
San Bernardino, CA
09 March 2017